WICKED
APPETITE

Also by Janet Evanovich

Sizzling Sixteen
Finger Lickin' Fifteen
Fearless Fourteen
Lean Mean Thirteen
Twelve Sharp
Eleven on Top
Ten Big Ones
To the Nines
Hard Eight
Seven Up
Hot Six
High Five
Four to Score
Three to Get Deadly
Two for the Dough
One for the Money

Plum Spooky
Plum Lucky
Plum Lovin'
Visions of Sugar Plums

Troublemaker
Motor Mouth
Metro Girl

How I Write

WICKED APPETITE

JANET EVANOVICH

**Doubleday Large Print
Home Library Edition**

ST. MARTIN'S PRESS   NEW YORK

WICKED APPETITE. Copyright © 2010 by Evanovich, Inc. All rights reserved. Printed in the United States of America. For information, address St. Martin's Press, 175 Fifth Avenue, New York, N.Y. 10010.

ISBN 978-1-61664-655-4

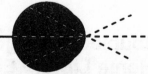

This Large Print Book carries the Seal of Approval of N.A.V.H.

WICKED
APPETITE

CHAPTER ONE

My name is Elizabeth Tucker. I'm Elizabeth to my mother, but for as long as I can remember, I've been Lizzy to everyone else. And for as long as I can remember, I've baked cupcakes. I enrolled in the culinary arts program at Johnson & Wales in Rhode Island right out of high school, hoping to someday get a job as a pastry chef. I graduated J&W in the top ninety-three percent of my class, and I would have graduated higher, but I flunked gravy. My gravy had lumps in it, and that pretty much sums up my life so far. Not that it's been all bad; more that it hasn't been entirely smooth.

I grew up in Virginia and when I was in third grade, Billy Kruger gave me the nickname Buzzard Beak, and I carried it with me all through grade school. I got my brown eyes and distinctive nose from Grandpa Harry, and while the nose wasn't great, I told myself it could have been worse, because Billy Kruger's nickname was Poop Pants.

And then when I was in eighth grade, during a moment of misguided curiosity, I made out with Ryan Lukach, and the jerk told everyone I wore a padded bra. I mean, give me a break here. I was a late bloomer. Anyway, the truth is, my bra was so padded I didn't know I was getting felt up.

I got engaged to fellow classmate Anthony Muggin while I was at Johnson & Wales. Two weeks after graduation and a week before the wedding, Anthony and his Uncle Gordo were caught hijacking a refrigerator truck loaded with sides of beef. It turned out to be a lucky thing, because after I visited Anthony in jail and returned the ring, I sobbed myself through a couple tumblers of vodka, fell off the toilet in a drunken stupor, crashed into a sink, and broke my nose. When they patched me up, I was no longer Buzzard Beak.

So here I am with the cutest nose in town, and I've finally grown breasts. They're not huge, but they're better than a poke in the eye, and I've been told they're perky. Perky is good, right?

In January, three days after my twenty-eighth birthday, I inherited a house from my eccentric Great Aunt Ophelia. The house is in Marblehead, just north of Boston and southeast of Salem. I emptied my bank account to pay taxes on the house, quit my job at a downtown New York City restaurant, and I moved into Ophelia's money pit. Probably, the smart thing would have been to sell the house, but no one could accuse me of always doing the smart thing. Truth is, New York wasn't working for me anyway. The restaurant hours were horrible, the kitchen politics were toxic, and the executive chef hated cupcakes.

For the past five months, I've been living in my new Marblehead house and working as a pastry chef at Dazzle's Bakery in Salem. The bakery has been owned and operated by a Dazzle since Puritan times, and is now managed by Clarinda Dazzle. She has an apartment above the bakery, she's twice divorced, approaching forty, and looks like Cher on Cher's day off. At 5'5", she's the same height as I am, but Clara looks taller. I think it's the hair. Clara's hair is black and shot with gray. If it were straight, it would be shoulder length. As is, Clara's hair is a huge mass of out-of-control energy coming to just below her ears, sometimes pulled back into a half-assed knot. She has piercing blue eyes and a nose and mouth said to have come from Wampanoag Indian blood on her mother's side. I'm not nearly so exotic, having Austrian and Danish ancestors who left me with wimpy blond hair and a body that looks more athletic than it actually is.

It was Tuesday morning, the June sun was shining bright over Salem, and Clara and I had been baking since five A.M. I was in my usual outfit of running shoes, jeans, T-shirt, and white chef coat. I had my hair pulled back into a ponytail, and I was dusted with flour and powdered sugar. Everything was good with the world, except Clara was in a state. It was eight o'clock, time to open for business, and we were missing the counter girl, Gloria Binkly.

"For crying out loud," Clara said. "It's not like I'm a factory. It's just you and me and Glo. How are we supposed to finish baking when we have to keep running out to the front to sell a muffin? Where the heck is she?"

We were standing in the large front room that constituted the retail part of the bakery. The floors were wide plank pine and the plaster walls were uneven. It was in decent shape, considering it pre-dated the witch trials. The display cases were old-fashioned glass and dark wood trim, and they were at the moment home to a batch of cinnamon rolls, four different kinds of muffins, almond tarts, and apple strudels. The breads were against the wall in wire baskets. The remaining space behind glass was about to be filled with my cupcakes. The cash register was from 1920. The credit card swiper was state-of-the-art.

A sexy, low-slung black car pulled to the curb in front of us and a man got out. He was maybe six foot tall, with glossy shoulder-length black hair swept back from his face in a wave. His skin was unearthly pale. His eyes were as black as his hair. He was dressed in a perfectly tailored black suit and black dress shirt.

He approached the bakery, and my skin prickled and a hot flash ran through my chest. "Holy moly," I said to Clara.

"There's nothing holy about him," Clara said.

The man stopped inches from the front door and stared in at me. His mouth was sensuous and unsmiling. He looked to be my age, and he was eerily handsome. He crooked his finger at me in a *come here* gesture.

"Do you suppose he wants a muffin?" I asked Clara.

"Either that or your soul."

I stepped up, opened the door, and peeked out at him. "Can I help you?"

"That remains to be seen," he said. "I'll return for you when I need you. Until then, you'll remember me."

He touched his fingertip to the back of my hand, and when he removed it, there was a burn mark beginning to blister. I stumbled away and slammed the door closed between us. The guy in black turned on his heel, got into his flashy car, the engine growled, and he drove off.

"What the heck?" I said to Clara, staring at my hand.

"I'm freaked," Clara said. "And when you live in Salem all your life, it takes a lot to freak you."

Personally, I hate being freaked. I avoid it whenever possible. "I'm going to convince myself this is a bug bite," I said to Clara. "Probably a very small spider with a lot of venom."

"Yeah," Clara said. "That's probably it. You just didn't see it."

At ten minutes after nine, the front door banged open and Glo rushed in all breathless.

"I know I'm late, but you'll never believe what I've got!" she said, plunking her black canvas tote bag down on the glass countertop. "I was passing by that creepy store on Essex Street, the one that sells enchanted fry pans and jars of newt eyeballs, and this weird feeling came over me. It was like something was calling me into the store."

Glo is single, like me, four years younger than I am, and she's an inch shorter. She has curly red hair chopped into a short bob, freckled skin, a trim, perfectly average body, and her wardrobe runs heavy to black-and-olive drab. Today, she was dressed in black ankle boots, black tights, a short, twirly black skirt, an olive T-shirt, and a denim jacket.

Clara cut her eyes to Glo. "Last time you were late, you said you got mugged by a bridge troll."

"Okay, so it was actually Mr. Greber, and he fell into me in a drunken blackout, but this is different. I swear! It's *destiny*. You know how I've always thought I might be special? Like, you know, magical?"

"No," Clara said.

"Well, for one thing, I have a scar on my forehead that looks like a lightning bolt. Just like Harry Potter."

Clara and I examined Glo's forehead.

"I guess it could look a little like a lightning bolt," Clara said. "How did you get it?"

"I crashed into the coffee table when I was six years old."

"I don't know if that qualifies," Clara said.

Glo ran her finger along the scar. "An evil spirit could have pushed me."

Clara and I rolled our eyes.

"And then there was that time I told you I saw a green aura around Mrs. Norbert," Glo said. "And a week later, she hit the jackpot at Foxwoods."

"That's true," Clara said. "I remember."

"Anyway, this is *big*," Glo said, pulling a weather-beaten, leather-bound book out of her tote bag. "This book called me into the shop. I was meant to have this book."

Clara and I looked over Glo's shoulder at the book. The leather was cracked with age; hard to tell if the aging was man-made or natural. The front cover was hand-tooled, with scrollwork that bloomed into flowers and leaves and tiny dragons. The book was secured with a hammered-metal clasp.

Glo slipped the clasp and opened the book to an elaborately inked frontispiece. On the page facing the frontispiece someone had written in perfect old world penmanship R*ipple's Book of Spells*.

"Who's Ripple?" Clara wanted to know.

"No one in the store knew," Glo said. "But the book is dated June 1692. That was right in the middle of the Salem witch trials."

"Turn it over and see if it says 'Made in China' on the back cover," Clara said.

Glo looked at Clara. "You, of all people, shouldn't be so cynical about this book. Everyone knows the Dazzles aren't normal."

I was new to this. I'd moved to Marblehead five months ago and wasn't up to speed in the rumor department.

"How so?" I asked.

Glo dropped her voice to a whisper. "The Dazzles have always had special abilities. I heard some of them could fly."

I cut my eyes to Clara. "Can you fly?"

"Not without a plane."

Glo thumbed through a couple pages in the book. "I bet I can find a flying spell in here."

"How about finding a *working* spell," Clara said. "There are six trays of cookies that need to be transferred to the display case."

I turned to go back to the kitchen and slammed into over six feet of hard muscle and bad attitude. He reached out to steady me, and I sucked in some air.

"Jeez Louise," I said. "Where the heck did you come from?"

"Bangkok. Not that it matters." He looked around. "I'm in Dazzle's, right?"

We all nodded, taking him in. His hair was thick and dark blond, somewhere between wind-blown, just woke up, and untamable. His skin was beach bum tan. His eyebrows were fierce and darker than his hair. His eyes were brown and assessing. His posture was confident. His body language was intimidating. His boots were dusty. His jeans were on their last legs but molded nicely to all the good parts. His navy T-shirt was splashed with flour from my chef coat.

He glanced down at his shirt and brushed at the flour. "I'm looking for Elizabeth Tucker."

It was my second encounter of the day with a big, sort of scary man, and I was on guard.

"That's me," I told him, taking a protective step back.

He gave me the once-over. "Figures."

I didn't think *figures* sounded entirely complimentary. "What's that supposed to mean?"

He blew out a sigh. "It means you're going to be trouble." He looked around. "Is there somewhere we can talk?"

"We can talk here."

"I don't think so."

I folded my arms across my chest and narrowed my eyes.

"Lady, I haven't got a lot of patience right now," he said. "Mostly, I just want to get on with it. Cut me a break and come outside where we can talk in private."

"No way."

He grabbed my wrist, yanked me to the door, and Glo and Clara rushed at him.

"I'm dialing 911," Glo said, cell phone in hand.

"As if that would help," he said to Glo. "Put the phone down and *stay*. This'll only take a minute."

He whisked me out of the shop, and we stood on the sidewalk, blinking in the sun's glare.

"What?" I asked.

"I'm looking for a guy. His name is Gerwulf Grimoire. Wulf, for short. My height, shoulder-length black hair, pale skin, evil."

"Evil?"

"Yeah. Have you seen him?"

"Maybe. He didn't give his name."

I inadvertently looked down at the fingertip burn on my hand. The scruffy guy's eyes followed mine and he gave his head a small shake.

"Wulf's work," he said.

He reached under my coat, unclipped my cell phone from my jeans waistband, and punched some numbers in.

"Hey!" I said. "What are you doing?"

"I'm giving you my number. Call me if you see Wulf."

"Who are you?"

He smiled down at me, and when he smiled, his teeth were white and perfect, crinkle lines appeared at the corners of his eyes, and my heart did a little flip in my chest. "I'm Diesel," he said. "I'll catch up with you later."

He crossed the street and disappeared behind a van stopped at a light. When the traffic moved, he was gone.

"Whoa," Glo said when I returned to the shop. "That's the most amazing hunk of raw testosterone I've ever seen. What was that about?"

"He's looking for a guy named Gerwulf Grimoire. He thought I might have run across him."

"And?" Glo asked.

"I have."

"It sounds like a warlock name," Glo said.

"You've got to stop watching *Bewitched* reruns," Clara told her. "The only warlocks in Salem are paid actors in the Salem Witch Museum."

CHAPTER TWO

As the chief cupcake and assorted pastries maker at the bakery, I'm early in and early out. I left Dazzle's at twelve-thirty and pointed my car south on Lafayette Street. I was driving a tan Chevy sedan. The age and model escape me, but needless to say it wasn't new, it wasn't expensive, and it was no longer pretty. There was a dent in the left rear quarter panel and a scrape running almost the length of the car on the right side. Aside from that, it was almost perfect. I crossed the bridge taking me into Marblehead, Lafayette turned into Pleasant

Street, and from Pleasant I wound around until I came to Weatherby Street.

Great Aunt Ophelia's house is a little salt-box dating back to 1740. It sits on a high rise of ground chockablock with other historic houses, and the back windows look down the hill at the flotilla of pleasure boats moored in Marblehead Harbor. The clapboards are gray, the trim is white, and there are two onion lamps on either side of the red front door. Somewhere in the late 1800s, a couple rooms were added. There were several more renovations and patch-up jobs after that, more or less bringing the house into the twentieth century. The ceilings are low, and the floors are wide plank pine and a little lopsided. Probably, I should have the foundation shored up, but it was going to have to wait for an infusion of money.

I parked at the curb and let myself into the house. I gave a squeak of surprise at seeing Diesel, boots off, sprawled on my living room couch.

"I've got a gun," I said to him. "And I'm not afraid to use it."

"Honey, you haven't got a gun. And if you did have a gun, you probably wouldn't know how to make it go *bang*."

"Well, okay, but I have a chef's knife, and I could carve you up like a Thanksgiving turkey."

"*That* I believe."

I was standing with one hand on the doorknob, ready to bolt and run for help. "How did you get in here?"

"There's this thing I can do with locks," Diesel said.

"Thing?"

"Yeah, I can open them."

He stood and stretched and headed for the kitchen.

"Wait," I said. "Where are you going?"

"I'm hungry."

"No, no, no. You have to leave."

"There's good news, and there's bad news, and it's both the same news. I'm here to stay."

Don't panic, I told myself. He's obviously a crazy person. Just quietly leave the house and call the police. They'll come get him and take him somewhere to get his meds adjusted.

"I'm not crazy," Diesel said from the kitchen.

"Of course not. Did I say you were crazy?"

"You were thinking it."

Oh great. The crazy guy can read minds. I inched away from the front door and cautiously peeked into the kitchen, where Diesel was going through the cabinets.

"Are you looking for money?" I asked him. "Jewelry?"

"I'm looking for food." Diesel opened the refrigerator, looked inside, and settled on leftover lasagna. "So what's going on with you? Do you have a boyfriend?"

"Excuse me?"

"I'll take that as a no. You have 'no boyfriend' written all over you. Sort of a surprise, since you make decent lasagna," Diesel said.

"My lasagna is better than decent. I happen to make *great* lasagna."

Diesel grinned at me. "You're kind of cute when you're all indignant like that."

I spun on my heel, huffed out of the kitchen, and headed for the front door and a call to 911. I reached the middle of my small living room and realized the door was open and the flesh-burning guy was standing in the doorway, looking in at me. I instinctively took a step back and came up against Diesel. Okay, so I know he might be crazy, but Jeez Louise, Diesel smelled great when you got close to him. Warm and spicy, like Christmas. And he felt good plastered against me, a protective hand resting on my hip.

"Hello, cousin," Diesel said to the man in black.

There was a flash of light, and a lot of smoke, and when the smoke cleared, the man was gone.

"That was Wulf," Diesel said. "But then, you've already met."

"How did he do that? He vanished into thin air."

"Smoke and mirrors," Diesel said. "He's read *Magic Tricks for Dummies*."

"Why did he leave?"

Diesel went to the door, closed it, and threw the dead bolt. "He left because I was here."

"Are you really his cousin?"

"Yeah. We grew up together."

"And now?"

"Now we're playing for different teams."

He handed me the lasagna dish and his fork and laced up his boots.

"I need to follow Wulf," he said. "Stay here and keep your doors locked."

"So Wulf can't get in?"

"No, so the weird guy across the street can't get in."

I looked out the front window. "That's Mr. Bennet. He's ninety-two and he thinks he's General Eisenhower. He lives in the house with the red geraniums in the window boxes."

I turned back to Diesel, but Diesel was gone. No smoke. No flash of light. Nothing. Just gone. I went to my small second-floor office and did a computer search for Gerwulf Grimoire. Nothing. Clean slate. No Facebook page. No matches found.

I called the bakery and got Glo.

"When I came home just now, Diesel was inside my house, waiting for me," I told her.

"Who's Diesel?"

"The big rude guy from the bakery."

"His name is Diesel? Like a powerful engine pulling a freight train?" Glo said. "That is so sexy."

I thought his *personality* was freight train engine, but his appearance was more unkempt ruler of the pride male lion.

"Is he still there?" Glo asked. "Are you okay?"

"I'm fine, and he's gone. I thought I should tell you in case I turn up missing or dead or something."

"Did he threaten you?"

"No. He ate some lasagna. And then Wulf walked in. And then they both disappeared."

"What did Wulf look like?"

"Scary in a sexy vampire sort of way."

"Wow."

"Am I being punked? Is this going to show up on *Funniest Home Videos*?"

"Not on my dime," Glo said.

I looked out my back office window. No sign of anyone lurking in my bushes or hiding behind the maple tree. Beyond the maple tree, the boats peacefully bobbed in the harbor. Marblehead was business as usual. And that meant not much business at all. It was originally a fishing village with narrow, crooked streets moving inland from the water. The nineteenth-century cod boats have been replaced with dories and fancy sailboats, and Marblehead is mostly a bedroom community for Boston and the North Shore now, but the low-key character of the colonial town hasn't been entirely lost.

"I'll be over as soon as I'm done here," Glo said. "I'll bring my book, and we can put a spell on your house to ward off vampires."

"I said he *looked* like a vampire. I didn't say he *was* one."

"I'll bring garlic, too."

"Put it on a pizza, and it's a deal."

CHAPTER THREE

Glo showed up a little after six. She had her book of spells, a pizza box, and a short-haired tiger-striped cat.

"What's with the cat?" I asked her.

"It's yours. It's a watch cat. It'll help protect your house. I got it at the shelter."

"I don't think I'm ready to commit to a cat."

"But this is a special cat," Glo said, setting the cat on the floor.

"How do you know it's special?"

"It was like the book of spells. You know how the book called me into the store? Well, this cat called me into the shelter. I was driving by the shelter on my way here, and the car just turned into the parking lot all by itself. I swear I didn't have anything to do with it. And then before I knew it, I was inside and there was the cat."

"Waiting for you?"

"Actually, he was waiting to get . . . you know."

Glo pantomimed throat-slashing.

"Euthanized?" I asked.

"Yep," Glo said. "They were gonna snuff him."

"How horrible!"

"Okay, so they weren't really going to snuff him. I just said that so you'd keep him. I think they were going to give him a bath."

The cat looked up at me.

"There's something odd about his eyes," I said. "And isn't his tail kind of short?"

"Word at the shelter is that he was sort of a brawler. Lost one of his eyes and part of his tail somehow."

I looked more closely. "He's got a glass eye?"

"Yeah. Cool, right?"

"Does he have a name?" I asked Glo.

"It says on the paper I got when I adopted him that he's Cat #7143."

"Maybe *you* should keep him."

"I'm not allowed. I rent from a guy who's allergic to cats."

This is how it happens, I thought. A series of unexpected events and *wham,* nothing will ever be the same again. Yesterday, everything was comfortable and going along as planned, and now I've got two scary men and a cat in my life. The cat I was pretty sure I could manage. The men had me worried.

Glo put the book of spells on my red Formica countertop and set the pizza box on my secondhand cherrywood kitchen table. She flipped the lid on the box and helped herself to a slice.

"I have a couple awesome spells for your house," she said. "We might not have all the ingredients for the potions, but I figure we can improvise."

"I don't want to put a spell on my house. I like it the way it is."

"Are you kidding? The vampire just walked right in."

"He wasn't a vampire. He was a weird guy with perfect skin and an expensive suit."

"How can you be sure?"

I took a slice of pizza. "I don't believe in vampires."

"Do you believe in the Tooth Fairy? The Easter Bunny?" Glo asked.

"*Yes* to the Tooth Fairy. *No* to the Easter Bunny."

I could deal with a fairy, but I wasn't buying into a giant rabbit hopping around in my house while I was asleep.

I heard the front door open and close, and a moment later, Diesel strolled into the kitchen.

"Holy crap," Glo said, admiring the view.

Diesel extended his hand to her. "Diesel."

"Gloria Binkly. Everyone calls me Glo."

Diesel took a slice of pizza and looked down at the cat. "Didn't know you had a cat," he said to me.

"He's new."

"What's his name?"

"Cat #7143."

Diesel fed a chunk of his pizza to the cat and turned his attention to the book of spells, sitting on the countertop. "I'm guessing this came with the pizza and the cat."

"It's mine," Glo said. "I just got it. I brought it over so I could put a spell on Lizzy's house."

"What kind of spell?"

"One that would keep you out," I told him.

Diesel gave a bark of laughter. "Honey, you'd need something a lot more powerful than anything in that book."

"There are some really good spells in here," Glo said, flipping the book open. "I could turn you into a frog."

"Been there, done that," Diesel said. "What else have you got?"

"Here's one for levitating a dragon."

Diesel took a second piece of pizza. "Not impressed. Everyone knows the hard part is finding the dragon."

Glo thumbed through a bunch more pages. "Warts, boils, impotency, insomnia, stuttering, hives. And here's a whole section on enchanted mirrors and cats."

We all glanced down at Cat 7143. He was sitting patiently, waiting for more pizza. I didn't think he looked especially enchanted.

"According to this, I could make Cat 7143 talk," Glo said, "but the potion involves a human tongue and toenails from a Romanian troll."

"Tough break," I said to Glo. "I've got toenails from Bulgarian trolls and Irish trolls, but unfortunately none from Romanian trolls."

"Okay, I know some of these ingredients are a little exotic," Glo said, "but these potions could be ancient. Probably, when the recipe was figured out, there were lots of Romanian trolls around."

"I hate to break up this pizza party, but we need to hit the road," Diesel said to me. "I need your help."

Hit the road? As in, get in a car? "No way. I don't know you. I'm not helping you. I'm not going anywhere with you."

"I'll go with you," Glo said to Diesel.

"Jeez Louise," I said to Glo. "He could be a serial killer, or a terrorist, or a kidnapper."

"I have a narrow window of opportunity here," Diesel said to me. "What's it going to take to get you on board?"

"A miracle," I told him.

Truth is, I'm not a risk taker. Not with men. Not with money. Not with shoes. I take a multivitamin every day. I lock my doors. I wear a seat belt. I don't eat raw meat. And I don't go off on wild goose chases with people I don't know.

Diesel watched me for a moment and

grinned. "Does mind reading count as a miracle?"

"Sure."

"You like me," he said.

"No I don't."

"That's a big fib. You think I'm hot."

"That's not mind reading," I told him. "That's wishful thinking."

"Do you have any more miracles?" Glo wanted to know. "Can you read *my* mind?"

Diesel shook his head. "I can read Lizzy's mind because we're cosmically connected."

"Cosmically connected!" Glo said. "That's so Salem."

At the risk of sounding cynical, I thought it was pure baloney. "Can you read my mind now?" I asked Diesel.

"Yeah," he said. "Good thing your mother can't hear your thoughts. Did they teach you those words in chef school?"

My attention swung from Diesel to Cat 7143. He was investigating the kitchen, walking the perimeter on high alert, snooping in corners, his ears erect in full listen mode.

"I read somewhere that cats can see ghosts and sense energy fields," Glo said. "Do you suppose he's looking for ghosts?"

I took a second slice of pizza. "My guess would be he's hoping to find food or kitty litter."

"I'm such a dunce," Glo said. "I almost forgot. I have food and a kitty litter thing in the car. The shelter gave me a start-up kit."

Five minutes later, Cat 7143 was locked up in my house with his new kitty litter. I was on the road, sitting next to Diesel, and Glo was in the backseat.

"I can't believe I'm doing this," I said, more to myself than to Diesel or Glo.

"We made a deal," Diesel said. "You wanted a miracle, and you agreed that reading your mind was miraculous."

"That was not miraculous. You took a couple lucky guesses."

"This is part of the problem with the world today," Diesel said. "People don't be-lieve in the mystical. I happen to be able to read your mind sometimes. Why can't you just go with it?"

"It's creepy."

"It's petty cash," Diesel said. "You should walk in my shoes."

"I believe in the mystical," Glo said. "I actually think I might be supernatural."

Diesel's eyes focused on the rearview

mirror and Glo for a moment before returning to the road.

"Where are we going?" I asked him.

"We're going back to Salem. I have an opportunity to search an apartment, and I need you to help me find an object."

"Why me?"

"Do you know what an Unmentionable is?"

"Underwear?"

"I know about Unmentionables," Glo said. "I read about them. They date back about a thousand years. An Unmentionable is a human with special abilities. There's like a brotherhood or something and a governing body."

"I work for that governing body," Diesel said. "I'm commissioned to pull the plug on Unmentionables who abuse their power."

I saw this as registering high on my bull-crap-o-meter, but I was curious all the same.

"How do you pull the plug?" I asked.

"I'd tell you, but then I'd have to kill you," Diesel said.

I'd heard that line before and always knew it was a line. This time I wasn't sure.

"Why do you need my help?" I asked him.

"You're one of us. You're an Unmentionable, and you have a skill I lack. I can find people. You can find empowered objects."

I was speechless. He actually looked serious. "That's ridiculous," I finally said.

Diesel turned off Lafayette Street. "Yeah, and I'm stuck with it. Nothing personal, but you're not my first choice for a partner. This is a monster assignment, and I could use a professional working with me."

"An Unmentionable professional? What does that even mean?"

"It means I need someone who understands and respects their gift and the responsibilities that come with the gift."

"What about me?" Glo wanted to know. "Am I an Unmentionable?"

"Not that I can see," Diesel said. "You're more of a *Questionable*."

My honest opinion was that I was in the presence of a genuine whacko. If I counted Glo, it would be two whackos. Although I had to give Diesel something for being a whacko with a work ethic.

CHAPTER FOUR

We were riding in a shiny new black Porsche Cayenne. A brown leather backpack that looked like it had gotten kicked halfway across the country was on the seat beside Glo. A couple empty water bottles rolled around on the floor. Diesel stopped for a light, and I debated leaping from the car and running as fast as my feet could carry me. Unfortunately, that would leave Glo with the crazy man.

"I don't want to agitate you or anything," I said to Diesel, "but I'm having a hard time with the whole Unmentionable gift thing. It sort of dropped out of nowhere on me."

"Yeah, well until you're comfortable with it, maybe you should think of it like a movie. Pretend you're Julia Roberts and I'm . . ."

"Brad Pitt," I said.

"I always thought I was more Hugh Jackman."

"He played Wolverine, right? No way. You're definitely Brad Pitt."

"Okay, screw it, I'm Brad Pitt. Can you go with that?"

"Maybe." I cut my eyes to Diesel. "So you're taking me somewhere to help you search for something. This search isn't illegal, is it?"

"Not by my standards."

"Oh great. What the heck is that supposed to mean?"

"It means the ends justifies the means."

We were within walking distance of the bakery, but unlike the area around the bakery, this part of Salem was mostly newer brick buildings built for commercial use. The street was wide. The sidewalk was unadorned by trees. It was a patch of Salem that felt almost normal, untouched by ads for Frankenstein's Laboratory, the 40 Whacks Museum, The Witches Cottage, The Nightmare Factory.

Salem was founded in the early 1600s and at one time was the sixth-largest city in the country and a thriving seaport. The Salem witch trials took place in 1692, and when Salem lost its prominence as a shipping and manufacturing center centuries later, it remained famous for one of the more bizarre episodes in American history. American ingenuity and the New England spirit of use-what-you-have-on-hand have turned Salem's infamous history into a thriving tourist business. The resulting prosperity has also brought traffic, hordes of sidewalk-clogging pedestrians, and the largest collection of weirdos living in a small-town environment east of the Mississippi.

The light went green, Diesel motored down one block and parked across the street from a three-story brick apartment building. We left Glo in the car, and Diesel and I entered the building. We took the elevator to the second floor, and I followed Diesel down the hall to apartment 2C. Hard to tell why I was going along with this. Probably, it was in the vicinity of morbid curiosity, like stopping to see a train wreck.

Diesel put his hand to the doorknob and the door opened.

"How?" I asked.

"Don't know," Diesel said, pushing into the apartment, closing the door behind us. "It's just one of those things I can do."

I was about to ask what else he could do besides open locks and pull power plugs on Unmentionables, but the apartment had me speechless. It was wall-to-wall food. Cases of peanut butter, SpaghettiOs, Froot Loops, Twinkies, Kraft Mac and Cheese, water-packed tuna, Cheez Doodles, Snickers bars, and cans of mixed nuts lined the walls. Bags of M&M's, Reese's Pieces, Peppermint Patties, butterscotch hard candies, malted milk balls, and Hershey's Miniatures were piled on the coffee table. Plus, every available inch on the kitchen counter was filled with giant jars of mayo, pickles, ketchup, olives, marinara sauce, chocolate sauce, marshmallow goop, hot peppers, and cheese sauce. It was like someone had hijacked Costco. And neatly stacked in the center of the dining room table, like the crown jewels of the food horde, were six Dazzle's bakery boxes.

I opened one of the boxes. "These cup-cakes belong to Shirley More. She comes into the bakery every day precisely at ten o'clock and gets thirty-six cupcakes. Half are carrot cake with cream cheese icing and the other half are chocolate with pink butter cream icing and party sprinkles."

"Yeah. Shirley's a Glutton, and this is her apartment," Diesel said.

"Okay, so she's a little on the heavy side, but I don't know if I'd say she's a glutton."

"I wasn't referring to her eating habits. I was referring to her heritage. Shirley's family has most likely guarded the Glut-tony Stone for centuries. The way it's been told to me is that there are seven deadly sins known collectively as SALIGIA. Envy, Pride, Greed, Gluttony, Lusty, Grumpy, and Sneezy."

"I think some of those were dwarfs," I said to Diesel.

"Maybe, but I'm in the ballpark. SALIGIA represents the first initials for the Latin names for the sins. Superbia, Avaratia, Luxuria, Invidia, Gula, Ira, Acedia. Any-way, the legend goes that there are seven SALIGIA Stones, each one holding the power of a different sin. If you combine the Stones in a single vessel, it's possible to unleash their power and create hell on earth."

Good grief. Just when I'm starting to roll with the Julia Roberts and Brad Pitt fairy tale, he throws hell on earth at me.

"Hell on earth would be a bummer," I said to him.

"Yeah. Supposedly, for a thousand years the SALIGIA Stones were guarded by an arcane sect. Then something happened, there was dissention among the elders, and Grumpy took charge and distributed the SALIGIA to the far corners of the earth. Over the years, some were lost and some were bequeathed, and eventually no one knew who held the Stones. Now a rumor's surfaced that the Stones have all found their way to Salem. Personally, I think it sounds like a low-budget movie script, and I wouldn't give a rat's ass, but Wulf is on the hunt for the Stones. And Wulf is my problem. So as it turns out, it's now your problem, too, since you're my ticket to the Stones."

My eyebrows were up around my hairline. "Are you serious?"

Diesel shrugged. "I follow orders. And my orders are to stop Wulf from acquiring the Stones. Probably, no one cares if he collects the dwarfs."

"What happens if you only get some of the Stones but not all of the Stones?"

"I don't know. Maybe you just create hell in Connecticut."

He handed me a bunch of forks from the silverware drawer. "Does this do anything for you?"

"Forks?"

"It's been a long time. The Stones could have changed shape."

"Yes, but this is a *fork*." I turned it over and read the name on the back. "It's Oneida. I know this brand. They're made in New York, and this looks new. Wouldn't we be looking for something old?"

"Old can be hidden inside something new."

"And I'm supposed to know it when I see it?"

"That's what they tell me. Actually, you have to hold it."

"And then what happens?"

"Don't know," Diesel said.

"What *do* you know?"

"Peach Pie, I know stuff that would knock your socks off. I could make you sing the 'Hallelujah Chorus.'"

I looked at the intelligent brown eyes under fierce eyebrows and the sensuous mouth made slightly sinister in a two-day beard, and I suspected he was telling the truth.

"I heard that thought," Diesel said.

"You are such a jerk!"

He tugged at my ponytail. "Yeah, but I'm fun."

He took the forks, put them back into the drawer, and handed me knives and spoons.

I hefted the knives and spoons and passed them back to Diesel. "Why do you think Shirley More is a Glutton?"

"Wulf's been following her around." He gave me a teapot to hold. "And all the signs are here. Word on the street is, the keeper can take on some of the sin."

Diesel opened one of the cupcake boxes and looked inside. "These cupcakes are a work of art."

"Thank you. I make all the cupcakes for Dazzle's. They're my specialty."

He took a chocolate cupcake out of the box and ate half.

"That's stealing," I told him.

"I've seen Shirley. This is an act of charity. Shirley needs to cut back on the cupcakes." He finished off the remaining half, licked his lips, and sent me his killer smile. "That was the best cupcake of my life," he said. "I'm in love."

"I'm guessing it doesn't take much to make you fall in love."

"It takes a lot. You underestimate your cupcakes."

Forty minutes later, I'd handled everything in sight and lots of things that were hidden away. Nothing tingled, buzzed, burned, or sent me subliminal messages.

"Two possibilities," Diesel said. "Either the *thing* isn't here, or else you're a dud."

"Hey, I didn't ask for this job. You were the one who decided I had magical powers."

"Not my call," Diesel said. "The BUM picked you out of the gene pool."

"BUM?"

"Board of Unmentionable Marshalls. And you don't have magical powers. That would be Siegfried and Roy. You have an enhanced ability to detect a certain kind of energy. At least, that's the theory. You and some weird guy in Florida."

"That's it? Only the two of us?"

"Apparently. And the jury is still out on you."

"Maybe you should be dragging the weird guy around."

"The critical word in that sentence is *weird*. I passed him off to an associate."

"What about Wulf? He must be able to find this *thing*."

"Wulf is like me. He can find people. He needs help to find an empowered object. And there are only two ways he can get that help . . . from the keeper or from you. And he can't have you. You're mine."

"Excuse me?"

Diesel grinned. "Lucky you."

"What about the guy in Florida?"

"He's on ice."

I thought about pinching myself to make sure I was awake, but it was such a cliché I couldn't bring myself to do it. And what if I was awake? How awful was that? It meant Diesel was real.

"I'm having a nightmare, right?"

"Wrong. I'm real," Diesel said. "And it wouldn't kill you to think a good thought about me."

"Are *you* thinking good thoughts about *me*?"

His eyes dilated black and the corners of his mouth softened into the hint of a smile. "Would you like to know my thoughts?"

"No!"

My attention went to a framed photo on an end table. It was a picture of a woman resembling Shirley, a second woman, and two men. They didn't look like couples. For that matter, they didn't even look like they were friends. The picture had been taken outdoors, and from the flowers in the background, I was guessing it was summer. The two men and two women were smiling, but their smiles looked forced.

"Do you suppose this is Shirley?" I asked Diesel.

"If it's Shirley, she was younger and a lot thinner." He put his hand to my back and moved me toward the door. "We need to get out of here. Shirley is a creature of habit, and she's due home any minute."

Enough said. I was out of the apartment like I'd been shot from a cannon. I got ten feet down the hall before Diesel grabbed me from behind and yanked me to a halt.

"Don't run," Diesel said, his hand still holding fast to my T-shirt. "It attracts attention."

I immediately went still. The last thing I wanted to do was attract attention. I looked around. "Do you think anyone saw us leave her apartment?"

"Sweetie, it's just you and me in the hall."

"Yes, but all these doors have peepholes. Maybe someone's looking out a peephole."

"You need to chill."

"You're telling me to *chill*? I just broke into a woman's apartment! I never do that sort of thing. I was a law-abiding citizen before I met you. That was illegal entry, gross violation of privacy, and not a nice thing to do. Do you know what happens to people who do breaking and entering and searching and snooping? They go to prison."

"Not always," Diesel said.

"Not always? That's all the comfort you can give me? What kind of an alien are you anyway?"

Diesel steered me into the elevator. "I'm not an alien. I'm a human with Unmentionable abilities . . . like you."

"I am *not* an Unmentionable."

Diesel punched the first-floor button. "How do you explain your cupcakes?"

"I'm an excellent baker. I've always made great cupcakes."

"Honey, those are Unmentionable cupcakes."

"That's ridiculous. My parents never said anything to me about being Unmentionable. It's not on my birth certificate."

"Maybe your parents didn't know. Sometimes the gene is passed from one generation to the next. Sometimes the gene just suddenly appears with no apparent history." The elevator doors opened to the ground floor and Diesel pushed me out into the small lobby. "Some Unmentionables can throw lightning, some can levitate a dump truck," Diesel said. "You can make cupcakes. You were born with the Unmentionable cupcake gene."

I slid a squinty-eyed sidewise look at him. "Are you laughing at me?"

"Yeah, but that doesn't mean it isn't all true."

CHAPTER FIVE

We left the building and crossed the sidewalk to Glo. She was waiting in the car, head back, eyes closed, hooked up to her iPod, singing at full volume. Diesel rapped on the back side window, and Glo jumped in her seat.

"Make a mental note," Diesel said to me. "You don't want to get caught like that by Wulf. He'll be all over you in a heartbeat. Stay vigilant when I'm not with you."

It seemed to me I might be in more danger from Diesel than from Wulf. Wulf only popped up twice, and he left right away. I couldn't get rid of Diesel, and I really had no way of knowing if he was a good guy or a bad guy.

Diesel looked down at me, and I suspected he knew my thoughts. His eyes darkened ever so slightly, but aside from that, his expression was unreadable.

"What happens if we find this Stone?" I asked him.

"I hand it over to the BUM, and they put it someplace safe," Diesel said.

"Suppose Shirley doesn't want to give it to you?"

"I persuade her to change her mind."

"Would you steal it?"

"That wouldn't be my first choice."

"And Wulf?"

Diesel opened the car door for me. "Wulf will do whatever it takes to get what he wants."

We got into the SUV, Diesel plugged the key into the ignition, and we went silent at the sight of a woman walking toward us on the opposite side of the street.

"Is that Cupcake Shirley?" Glo asked, leaning forward from the backseat.

"Yep," I said. "It's Shirley."

Shirley was alone, carrying an oversize purse and a take-home bag from a local restaurant. She had short, curly brown hair and a pretty face. I placed her at late-thirties. She was average height, and her weight was average for a woman who could eat thirty-six cupcakes in a single sitting. She was wearing a flower-print tent dress and low heels.

A silver Camry pulled up next to Shirley, and the guy in the passenger seat rolled his window down and called out to her. We were too far away to hear his words, but Shirley looked annoyed and shook her head no. There was a brief conversation, then Shirley turned and resumed walking. The guy got out, ran after Shirley, and grabbed her by her arm. Shirley spun around, coldcocked him in the face with her purse, and kicked him square in the crotch. The guy stood stunned for a moment, dropped to his knees, and went fetal. Shirley continued on her way.

"Ow," Diesel said.

The Camry driver got out from behind the wheel, dragged his passenger back to the car, and they took off.

"I know this is weird, but I'm pretty sure those were the men in the photo," I said to Diesel.

"What photo?" Glo wanted to know.

"Diesel was looking for something in Shirley's apartment just now, and while we were there, I saw a photo of her and another woman and those two men."

"Get out!" Glo's voice shot into Minnie Mouse range. "You were in Cupcake Shirley's apartment? What were you looking for? Is she a thief? A spy? An Internet porn star?"

"She's a Glutton," I said.

"Yeah, but you can't hold that against her," Glo said. "Did you get what you were looking for?"

"No."

"You should go back and confront her and demand that she hand it over. And if she won't hand it over, I could put a spell on her. There's a whole chapter in my book on making people spill the beans."

I looked over at Diesel. "What do you think?"

"The spell might be fun."

"I wasn't talking about the spell. I was talking about confronting her."

Diesel pulled the key out of the ignition. "We could try that, too."

Three minutes later, we were all at Shirley's door.

"What's the plan?" Glo asked.

"This is going to be the Lizzy Show," Diesel said, back on his heels. "Lizzy is going to explain to Shirley how she shorted her a cupcake."

"Works for me," Glo said. "And what are we trying to get?"

"The Gluttonoid," Diesel said.

I did a giant eye roll. "Good grief."

Diesel grinned at me. "You don't like Gluttonoid?"

"You just made that up."

"Yeah," Diesel said. "You got something better?"

I turned to Glo. "You know how when you go out to buy new shoes and you don't exactly know what you want until you see it? The thing we're looking for is sort of like that."

Diesel rang the bell, and Shirley opened the door and peeked out at us.

"Hi," I said. "We're from Dazzle's. I'm the cupcake baker, and you probably know Glo."

Shirley smiled wide. "Sure. I know both

of you. I love Dazzle's. I'm thinking about increasing my cupcake order."

She looked beyond me to Diesel, and her eyes glazed over a little, like she'd just seen the mother of all cupcakes.

"This is Diesel," I told her.

"'Lo," Shirley said.

I pushed past Shirley and eased myself in. "I wanted to talk to you about the cupcakes."

That got Shirley's attention off Diesel. "What about them? You're not going to stop making them, are you? I couldn't get through the day without them. I save them for bedtime."

"I just wanted to tell you there's a cupcake missing. I dropped a cupcake on the floor while I was filling the boxes, and I didn't have any extras. I meant to put a note in with your order but forgot. So we stopped by to tell you."

"Was it chocolate or carrot cake?"

"Chocolate."

"I love the chocolate ones," she said.

Glo followed me in, and in my peripheral vision I could see her head swiveling around, scoping out Shirley's apartment.

"Yowza," Glo whispered.

"It looked like you had a scuffle with a man just as we were driving up," I said to Shirley. "Are you okay?"

"That was my idiot stepbrother, Mark. I haven't seen him in seven years, not since my Uncle Phil died, and now all of a sudden he's following me around, asking for stuff."

Holy cow. She coldcocked her stepbrother. I had the guy pegged for a mugger or random pervert. "What kind of stuff does he want? Is he, you know, dangerous?"

"I don't know. My parents divorced when I was four, and my mom and I moved to Seattle. I never saw my stepbrothers or my cousins until Uncle Phil died. I came back for the funeral and never left. How strange is that, right?"

"So you lived here in Salem for seven years, but you never saw your stepbrother after the funeral?"

"I guess everyone was mad because I was in the will. No one was real friendly to me."

"What did Uncle Phil leave you?" I asked her.

"It's a secret. All the inheritances were

secret, and we were told we'd have eternal bad luck if we revealed what we got."

"Wow," Glo said. "Eternal bad luck would be for a long time."

"Yeah. And now idiot Mark wants my inheritance. He says he's a collector. Fat chance he has of ever getting it. He couldn't pay me enough. Him and his brother, Lenny. Too bad I didn't get a chance to kick Lenny in the you-know-whats. Except Lenny would probably like it. From what I can see, Lenny is a real glutton for punishment."

"That's an odd choice of words," Diesel said.

"It's a figure of speech," Shirley said.

I was watching Glo from the corner of my eye. She was feverishly thumbing through her book, her teeth sunk into her lower lip in concentration.

"Eureka," Glo said. "Here it is. Ibis by honor. Tongue tie not. Freely speaketh. Truth told, I command magpie Shirley More." Glo snapped her fingers twice and clapped her hands once. She pointed at Shirley, closed her eyes, and chanted, "Shirley. Shirley. Shirley."

Diesel had eyebrows slightly raised. "Have you ever cast this spell?"

"No," Glo said. "But I'm pretty sure I did it right."

"Glamma bamma," Shirley said.

We all turned to her.

"I wiggum big dick do flammy stick," she said. "Eep! Lick stick rubba dubba." Her eyes got wide, and she clapped her hands over her mouth. She shook her head. That wasn't what she meant to say. "Gooky ball. Big gooky ball!"

Shirley was talking gibberish. My first thought was stroke. My second thought was psycho mushrooms. My third thought was so outlandish I didn't even want to articulate it. My third thought was that Glo had done it.

"Holy cow," Glo said. "What happened? She wasn't supposed to talk gibberish. It was supposed to be a truth spell."

"Are you *sure* you read the spell right?" Diesel asked Glo.

"I read it straight from the book. I was supposed to have powdered yak brain, but I couldn't see where that would make a difference. I mean, we were in a crunch situation here, and I didn't have any yak brain."

Shirley glared at Glo. "You fart foreskin!"

"Criminy," Glo said. "That's harsh."

"Okay," I said to Glo, "assuming Shirley isn't yanking our chain, and you actually cast some sort of spell . . . how about removing it."

Glo had her nose buried in her book. "There doesn't seem to be an anti-spell here."

I looked over at Diesel.

"I've got nothing," Diesel said. "I don't do spells."

Shirley looked panicky. "Scooby booby," she said.

"Maybe it'll wear off," Glo said. "Some of these spells are temporary. The book isn't always specific about length of time."

"Hear that?" I said to Shirley. "Good news. The spell might wear off."

Shirley flipped me the finger.

"More good news," Diesel said. "She knows sign language."

Shirley pulled her middle finger back and extended her index finger.

"One minute?" Glo guessed.

Shirley nodded. She whirled around and went into the bedroom.

"Maybe she's going to come out with the secret inheritance," Glo said.

I cut my eyes to Diesel. "This isn't going well, is it?"

Diesel blew out a sigh.

A moment later, Shirley marched out of her bedroom with the tent dress billowing around her. She raised her arm and pointed a gun at us.

"Eat poop and clock," Shirley said.

I spun around and ran for the door, shoving Glo in front of me. *Bang, bang, bang.* A bullet embedded itself in the wall and a chunk of plaster fell to the floor. We flew flat out, down the stairs, through the small lobby, and across the street with Diesel behind us. We jumped into the SUV, and Diesel wheeled away.

It had all happened so fast. My heart was pounding, and I was scramble-brained. This was the first time I'd ever had a gun aimed at me. And as if it wasn't awful enough, I'd been shot at by one of my cupcake customers.

Diesel didn't seem to be overly bothered. He'd been the prime target, bringing up the rear, but he was looking calm behind the wheel.

"Are you okay?" I asked him.

"Yeah. She's not much of a marksman. And even if she'd tagged me, I'm not easy to kill."

Okay, I guess that explained his composure. He wasn't easy to kill. Unlike me. I was a wimpy human held together by skin and dumb luck.

We got halfway down the block, and Glo leaned forward. "Now what?" Glo wanted to know. "Is it still happy hour?"

I stared at Glo. "Happy hour? Are you serious? How could you think about happy hour? We were just shot at. We could have been killed. And we left a woman talking nonsense. And happy hour ended hours ago."

"I guess that was my bad," Glo said, "but honestly, I didn't think yak brain would make a difference."

CHAPTER SIX

It was way long past happy hour when we left the Golden Dungeon Pub. As a town, Salem is a mixed bag. There are new hotels and office buildings side-by-side with two-hundred-year-old houses, museums reflecting the town's nautical and heretic history, and shops catering to the weird and the curious.

The Golden Dungeon Pub was four steps down from the sidewalk in a converted basement that had nothing golden but was reminiscent of a dungeon, in a cozy sort of way. Dark wood booths, dark wood floors, dim light, a ghoulish waiter, sixteen taps, and theme-based food.

I'd had a couple Davey Jones crab cake sliders, a lot of bar nuts, and two sips of beer. I'd limited myself to two sips, because it seemed like it wasn't a good idea to have more than two mouthfuls of alcohol sloshing around in my brain when I was sitting next to a man who smelled like fresh-baked Christmas cookies, looked good enough to eat and bad enough to ruin my life. And it was very possible he wasn't entirely normal.

Glo hadn't felt the need for caution, so we dropped her off at her house, and Diesel motored out of Salem and into Marblehead. He parked in front of my house and walked me to my front door.

"Knowing what's going on in your head isn't doing much for my ego," Diesel said. "Most women want me to come in and get friendly. You're panicked you won't be able to keep me out."

"I have to go to work early tomorrow."

"That's it?"

"And, you're scary."

Diesel pushed my door open and nudged me in. "You'll get used to it."

"I don't want to get used to it!"

Diesel went still for a moment. "Wulf's been here," he said.

"Here? You mean in my house? How do you know?"

"I just know."

I looked around. "Is he still here?"

Diesel slouched into the couch and reached for the television remote. "No. Just you, me, and Cat."

Cat 7143 was at the edge of the room, watching us. He was back on his haunches with his half-tail curled around himself, seeming not overly upset that Wulf had come and gone.

"I kind of like having a cat," I said, more to myself than to Diesel.

"He suits the house," Diesel said. "Is this your furniture or was it part of your inheritance?"

"The furniture's mostly mine. I had a few pieces in New York, and I picked some things up at garage sales when I first got here. The big rag rug in the dining room was Clara's. She didn't want it anymore. The curtains were left with the house."

"I'll make a deal with you," Diesel said. "If you get me another piece of lasagna, I'll let you choose which side of the bed you want."

"Excuse me?"

"You have a television in your bedroom, right?"

"Wrong. Not that it matters to you. You won't be spending time there."

"We'll see."

I tried not to roll my eyes but wasn't successful.

"You've got to stop with the eye-rolling," he said. "You're going to strain something."

"It's you! You're . . ."

"Charming?"

Yes. And terrifying.

"I know you think you have to protect me," I said to Diesel, "but you can't stay here."

"Sure I can," Diesel said.

"What about a motel? Your car? A park bench?"

"Don't think so."

My eyes inadvertently took in the couch.

"Honey, do I look like I'd fit on this couch?" Diesel asked.

"Do I look like I care?"

"Maybe a little. Mostly, you look like you'd kick me out and not look back."

A light flashed into my living room window, and there was the sound of people talking on the sidewalk in front of my house. The light swept up to my second floor, held for a moment, and blinked off. More talking.

I went to the door and looked out. It was a ghost tour. Most of the ghost tours were conducted in Salem, but twice a week, a guide walked around Marblehead with tourists in tow, pointing out houses that were supposedly haunted.

The guide was in his late fifties, dressed in period clothes, carrying a lantern and a flashlight. Six women and two men were clustered around him.

"Are you the owner of this house?" the guide asked me.

"Yes."

"Congratulations," he said. "Your house has been added to our route. We had an amazing sighting earlier in the evening."

Diesel came up behind me. "What kind of a sighting?"

"It was an evil apparition," the guide said. "He appeared in the upstairs window. He was ghostly white and dressed in black, and when he saw me watching him, he vanished in a swirl of ectoplasmic vapor."

"Wulf," Diesel said.

"That was a visitor from out of town," I told the guide. "He always dresses in black. And he . . . smokes."

"I could feel the disturbance in the air," the guide said.

I looked back at Diesel. "Can Wulf disturb the air?"

Diesel did a palms-up. "Hard to say what Wulf can do."

I retreated into my house with Diesel, closed the door, and threw the bolt. "I'm resigning. I'm turning in my special ability that we're not even sure I possess."

Diesel stretched and scratched his stomach. "I'm hungry," he said. "I don't suppose you have any of those cupcakes laying around."

"Are you listening to me?"

"You can't resign," Diesel said, ambling off to the kitchen. "It would be irresponsible. Wulf could do really bad things with the Stones."

"Not my problem."

Diesel pulled the tray of lasagna out of the refrigerator. "Unfortunately, it *is* your problem. Wulf knows you have the ability to recognize a Stone. You won't be safe until all the Stones are turned over to the BUM."

"*All* the Stones? I have to find *all* the Stones?"

"That's the plan."

"What about my life?"

"We'll work around it." He tugged at my ponytail. "It'll be fun. You can make the cupcakes, and I'll eat the cupcakes. Play your cards right, and I might even be able to get you a date."

"I don't want you to get me a date. I can get my own dates."

Diesel got a fork from the silverware drawer. "When was the last time you went out on a date?"

"None of your business."

"Hah!" Diesel said, forking a noodle off the lasagna.

I took the lasagna from Diesel and sliced off a piece. I spooned some red sauce onto a plate, placed the lasagna on top of the red sauce, and nuked it. When it was done, I added fresh grated cheese and a sprig of fresh basil, and handed it to him.

"I could get used to this," Diesel said, digging in.

Oh jeez.

That got a smile from Diesel. "It was meant as a compliment, not a marriage proposal."

"How do I know you're not worse than Wulf?"

"Listen to your instincts."

I raised an eyebrow. My instincts weren't comfy with any of this.

"Okay," Diesel said. "Then listen to the cat's instincts. He likes me."

"How can you tell?"

"He hasn't bitten me or peed on my shoe." Diesel finished his lasagna, rinsed his plate, put it in the dishwasher, and headed for the living room. "We should be able to catch the end of the Red Sox game."

"Pass. I'm going to bed. I have to be at the bakery at five A.M."

Diesel remoted the television on. "Too bad. The Sox are playing the Yankees."

I was making an effort to be a Red Sox fan, but I hadn't yet achieved total rapture. So far, baseball for me was all about the hot dogs and peanuts at the ballpark.

"I don't suppose I could convince you to leave?" I said to Diesel.

"I don't suppose you could."

CHAPTER SEVEN

I woke up in a panic. The room was black as pitch, and I was having difficulty breathing. My eyes adjusted to the minimal light, and I realized a cat was sleeping on my chest . . . *my* cat.

I rolled Cat to one side, and I bumped into Diesel. He was tucked in next to me, warming the bed, his breathing even, his expression softened by sleep. My first reaction should have been more panic, but the truth is, Diesel felt comfortable next to me. Go figure that. This big, handsome, probably insane, wiseass guy was in bed with me, and not only wasn't I screaming in terror, I was actually hugely attracted to him. Not a healthy situation.

I looked at my bedside clock. It was 4:10, and my alarm was set for 4:15.

"Hey!" I said to Diesel.

"Mmmm."

"You have a lot of nerve, sneaking into my bed like that."

He half opened his eyes. "I didn't sneak. I asked if you were awake, you didn't answer, so I took my clothes off and got into bed."

"You took your clothes off?"

"You didn't notice?"

"No! Jeez Louise, I don't even know you."

"If you look under the covers, you'll know me better."

"I don't want to know you better!"

"That's a big fib," Diesel said. The alarm buzzed, Diesel reached across me, and shut it off. "Do you get up this early every morning?"

"Five days out of seven."

"Bummer."

I scooted Cat away and crawled out of bed. When the weather turned colder, I'd sleep in flannel jammies. For now, I was wearing shorts and a T-shirt.

"Cute," Diesel said, taking in my outfit, "but they're not exactly sex goddess clothes."

"I could be a sex goddess if I wanted."

"Good to know," Diesel said. And he rolled onto his stomach and went back to sleep.

I showered, blasted my hair with the hair dryer, and put it up in a ponytail. I got dressed in jeans and a fresh T-shirt, laced up my sneakers, and went downstairs, with Cat trailing behind me.

"He's a big pain," I said to Cat.

Cat looked like he might not share my opinion, and I suspected Cat had been bought off right from the beginning by that piece of pizza.

I poured some kitty crunchies into Cat's bowl and gave him fresh water. I started coffee brewing, sliced a day-old bagel, and dropped it into the toaster.

This was my favorite time of the day. The sky was growing brighter by the minute with the promise of sunrise, and soon I'd be making cupcakes. Boats were clanking in the harbor below me. Seabirds were waking.

I slathered cream cheese onto my toasted bagel, poured coffee into my favorite mug, zipped myself into a heavy sweatshirt, and ate my breakfast on my back porch. Everything was good . . . if you didn't count Diesel and Wulf.

I parked in the small lot to the rear of the bakery and entered through the back door. The kitchen was glowing with all the lights on, and the air was heavy with the scent of yeast dough rising in the oven.

Clara was already at work when I walked in.

I buttoned myself into my white chef coat, rolled the sleeves to my elbows, and wrapped an apron around my waist.

"How was your night?" Clara asked. "Glo was determined to protect you from evildoers."

"Glo arrived with a pizza, a guard cat, and her book of spells. Diesel showed up, we ate the pizza, I kept the cat, and I'd rather not talk about the spells."

"She didn't turn anyone into a mushroom, did she?"

"No."

"Then how bad can it be?"

Pretty bad, I thought, but with any luck Shirley woke up all fine and dandy this morning, wondering if she'd hallucinated the whole hideous episode.

Two hours later, there was no sign of Glo. Clara turned the CLOSED sign to OPEN and unlocked the front door.

"I'll work the counter," Clara said. "You can finish frosting the cupcakes."

"Did you try calling Glo?"

"Yes. No answer."

"She left her car at my house last night. I offered to pick her up when I came to work, but she said it was too early, and she'd catch a ride with her landlord."

"It's a real pain when she comes in late," Clara said, "but at least it's usually entertaining."

Glo bustled into the bakery a little before nine o'clock and dropped her tote on the back counter.

"Sorry I'm late," she said. "I missed my ride with Stanley, so I thought no biggie, I'll just conjure up a spell and pop myself over to the bakery."

Clara and I stopped working and looked over at Glo.

"And?" Clara said.

Glo was wearing a black leather bomber jacket, a black, stretchy T-shirt, skinny black jeans, black Converse sneakers, and a long red scarf. She unwrapped her scarf and tossed it onto her tote.

"The spell seemed easy enough," Glo said. "It wasn't like I needed testicles of snarf or something. I mean, it was a simple spell. And I'm sure I repeated it perfectly. I don't know what went wrong."

"Something went wrong?" Clara asked, looking like she didn't want to hear the answer.

"I was supposed to fly, but I couldn't get up in the air and moving. I think at one point I might have gotten off the ground a little, but that was it. Honestly, it was so annoying. I finally had to come to work on my bicycle."

Clara and I did simultaneous eye rolls.

"Maybe you weren't using the right broom," Clara said.

Glo's eyes went big and round. "I wasn't using a broom at all. Do you think that could be it? The book didn't say anything about a broom."

Clara pulled on a disposable glove and rearranged a bread display. "Everyone knows a witch needs a broom to fly."

"Yes, but I might not be a witch. Do you think that would make a difference? Diesel said I was a Questionable. And he said Lizzy is an Unmentionable."

Clara looked over at me. "Is that true?"

"That's what he said."

"Did you know you were an Unmentionable?"

"No. I thought bras and panties were unmentionables."

Glo slipped her purple Dazzle's Bakery smock over her long-sleeved T-shirt and buttoned up. "I bet there are lots of Unmentionables in Salem. Some of the Dazzles might even have been Unmentionables."

"It's possible," Clara said.

"How about you?" Glo asked Clara. "Do you have a secret Unmentionable ability? Mrs. Morganthal said you used to be able to bake bread just by touching it."

Clara snapped her glove off. "Mrs. Morganthal has conversations with vegetables."

She removed her apron. "I'm going to run out to the store. I'll be back in a half hour."

Even in a white chef coat, Clara is startling, with her electric hair and sharp features, and it wouldn't be too much of a stretch to imagine her as a sorceress of some sort.

Glo manned the counter, and I returned to the kitchen. I filled the big pastry bag with vanilla butter cream and swirled the icing on three different batches of cupcakes. I decorated the tops with flowers, multicolored sprinkles, miniature edible gold stars, and chocolate jimmies. I pulled Clara's loaves of raisin bread out of the oven and set them on racks to cool.

At precisely ten o'clock, Glo rushed into the kitchen. "Shirley's here! She's standing in front of the bakery with her back to the window, waving her arms and talking to herself."

"What's she saying?"

"I don't know. The door's closed. I can't hear her. What should I do?"

"Has she got a gun?"

"Not that I can see, but she has her purse. She could have the gun in her purse."

The bell tinkled when the bakery door opened, and Glo and I froze.

"Eeek," Glo whispered.

"Stay here," I told her. "I'll bring the cupcakes out."

I wrapped my arms around Shirley's cupcake boxes, plastered a smile onto my face as if nothing unusual was going on, and I walked out of the kitchen and up to the counter.

"Hi!" I said.

Shirley pressed her lips together and passed me a piece of paper with crayon drawings of two cupcakes. One was obviously my Sunflower Lemon and the other looked like my Dazzling Red Velvet.

"Do you want these cupcakes?" I asked her.

She nodded.

I reached into the display case for a cupcake and she shook her head. "Go go," she said.

"More than one?"

She nodded.

"A dozen?"

She nodded again.

"Of each? Are you sure you want to do that?" I asked her. "It's a lot of cupcakes."

Shirley nodded her head.

I ran to the kitchen and shoveled a dozen Sunflower cupcakes into a box. "Shirley's getting an extra two dozen cupcakes," I told Glo.

"The spell's broken? She can talk?"

"No. She gave me a note."

I filled a second box with the red velvets and carried them to the counter just as Clara walked in.

"Hello," Clara said to Shirley. "How are you today?"

Shirley bit her lip. "Hmmp," she said.

Clara leaned forward. "Excuse me?"

Shirley swiveled her head in my direction. Her eyes were approaching frantic. "Mmmph."

"Shirley isn't talking today," I told Clara. "It's hard to explain."

Shirley vigorously nodded her head.

"That's a lot of cupcakes," Clara said, eyeballing the two extra boxes. "You must be having a party."

More head nodding.

Glo peeked out from the kitchen, and Shirley spied her.

Shirley sucked in air, her eyes narrowed, and her lips squinched tight together.

"Oops," Glo said.

Shirley pointed her finger at Glo. "Butter turd blaster."

"Tell you what," I said to Shirley. "The extra cupcakes are on the house."

Shirley snatched her boxes up. "Briggum."

"You're welcome," I told her.

Clara put her hand on Shirley's arm. "Are you all right?"

"Squiggy wiggy," Shirley said. "Spooner fig rot iggam jeepers." She turned and pointed at Glo. "Bad bird beak. Booger bad."

Clara fixed her eyes on Glo.

"I sort of messed up a spell," Glo said to Clara. "I didn't have any yak brain."

"Well, for goodness sakes, reverse the spell!"

"That's the sticky part," Glo said. "I haven't been able to find a reverse spell. I was hoping it would wear off all by itself."

Shirley set the cupcake boxes on the counter, opened the box of Sunflower cupcakes, and ate one. "Shum," she said. And she ate another.

"Are you sure it's a spell?" Clara said. "Have you ruled out a medical problem?"

"It was an instantaneous coincidence," Glo said. "I'm pretty sure it was the spell."

Twenty-four hours ago, I wouldn't have considered such a thing. Even now, after seeing it happen, I wasn't entirely convinced. I mean, what do I really know about Shirley? It could all be a hoax. Or it could be a form of hysteria from seeing Diesel in her apartment.

"Did you look through the whole book for reverse spells?" Clara asked Glo. "How about the store where you bought the book? Maybe the shopkeeper can help you."

Shirley shoved a third cupcake into her mouth and looked from me to Clara to Glo. Hopeful.

"Worth a try," Glo said.

"I can manage on my own," Clara said. "You guys go back to the store and see if you can get the spell reversed."

CHAPTER EIGHT

We walked two blocks south and stopped in front of Glo's spellbook store. *Ye Olde Exotica Shoppe* was written in gold script above the weather-beaten wood door. The sign in the grimy window said COME IN IF YOU DARE.

"Unh," Shirley said.

My feelings exactly, but we went inside anyway. The store was small. The inventory was extensive. Every nook and cranny was crammed with who-the-heck-knows-what. Floor-to-ceiling shelves held jars labeled blue eyeballs, brown eyeballs, bullock nose hairs, rabbit gonads, milkweed pods, rotted monkey brain, pickled toes, gummy bears, Irish pixie dust, screech owl beaks, kosher salt, rat tails, beetle legs, pig ears, troll phlegm, candied earthworm.

Shirley stopped in front of the gummy bears. "Chewy snot gobbers!"

"Not now," Glo told her, snagging her by the elbow, moving her to the back counter. "You can have all the snot gobbers you want after we talk to Nina. She owns the store, and she sold me the book of spells."

Nina was in her early sixties. She had frizzed white hair that hung halfway down her back, her face looked like it had been dusted with cake flour, and her fingers were long and boney and loaded with rings. She was wearing a frothy white gown that I was sure was previously owned by Glinda the Good Witch from *The Wizard of Oz.* The gown had been accessorized with brown Birkenstock clogs and wool socks. In my mind, not a good fashion mix.

"So nice to see you again," Nina said to Glo. "How are you getting along with Ripple's spell book?"

"Actually I've been having some issues," Glo said.

"It's to be expected with a brand-new

owner," Nina said, "but practice makes perfect. You haven't turned anyone into a roach, have you? I've been told the transformation spell on page 37 can sometimes go awry."

"You're kidding, right?" I said to Nina. "I mean, this is just a fun shop filled with tourist trinkets."

Nina looked around her store. "Some of my merchandise is tourist-directed. They love the Harry Potter sorcerer's wands and the pickled troll balls. But then, I stock other things that are historically important to Salem and necessary for brewing potions and stews. It used to be potions had fallen out of favor, what with needing an iron cauldron and all, but it turns out a slow cooker works just fine. Just plug it in, and seven hours later, you're in business. Of course, you need a good book of spells like Ripple's."

I cut my eyes to Nina. "I'm having a hard time believing the whole book of spells concept."

"Well, a book of spells is nothing more than a cookbook. Over the years, recipes have evolved for sponge cake, lobster bisque, spontaneous combustion, cheese soufflé, levitation, enchantment. It's really not rocket science. Needless to say, some recipes work better than others. Personally, I have a preference for *Cooking Light*."

"I had a small mishap with a truth spell," Glo said. "I did it perfectly, except for the powdered yak brain."

Nina looked alarmed. "Oh dear. Don't tell me you omitted the powdered yak brain!"

"It didn't seem like a big deal," Glo said. "The thing is, the spell partly worked, but not entirely. And now I'd like to reverse it, but I can't find a reverse spell."

"It isn't that easy. If you left an ingredient out, you have an entirely different spell," Nina said. "You have to find the appropriate spell before you can reverse it. What sort of spell did you cast?"

"Beggar ass diddle piddle pot," Shirley said. "Icky bickham red cracker."

"That's a scramble spell," Nina said. "There are many different kinds, and some are very powerful."

"Prac," Shirley said. "Rub a dub me."

Glo bit into her lower lip. "I was hoping it would wear off all by itself."

"Most temporary spells expire at twenty-four hours," Nina said. "If the spell lasts beyond twenty-four hours, it's likely to be permanent."

"Maybe there's a one-size-fits-all reverse spell," I said. "Something generic."

"I could look through *The Big Book of Oaths and Potions*," Nina said. "It's the definitive work. In the meantime, you can try to find the spell in *Ripple's*."

"One more thing," Glo said. "I couldn't fly."

"Flying is tricky," Nina told her. "You might want to add pixie dust to the base spell. I have some on sale."

Diesel was lounging in front of the bakery when we returned.

"Hey," he said to Shirley. "How's it going?"

"Yellow apple crap," Shirley said.

Diesel nodded. "I hear you."

"We're still working on finding the reverse spell," I said to Diesel. "And Glo got some discounted pixie dust to help her fly."

"To infinity and beyond," Diesel said to Glo.

We pushed into the bakery and Shirley retrieved her boxes of cupcakes.

"Don't worry," Clara said to her. "We'll get this straightened out."

"Yeah, and be careful on your way home," I told her.

Shirley gave a curt nod. "Hockey puck."

Diesel followed me into the kitchen and swiped a cupcake. "Did you get a chance to talk to Shirley?"

"Shirley talks gobbledegook. The Exotica lady said if the spell was temporary, it would wear off in twenty-four hours. That means if we're lucky, Shirley will be coherent at seven-thirty tonight. We can talk to her then. Unless it's not really a spell at all, and she's just yanking our chain. Or maybe she's had a stroke. Do you think we should have taken her to the emergency room?"

"I think we should have signed her up for Cupcake Eaters Anonymous."

I put my chef coat back on and re-wrapped my apron around myself. I still had several dozen chocolate chip cupcakes to decorate before I could leave for the day. I filled the pastry bag with icing and went to work, with Diesel watching me.

"Don't you have something important to do?" I asked him.

"I'm doing it. I'm protecting you."

"You didn't feel the need to protect me at five o'clock this morning."

"I can't see Wulf getting up at five. Wulf mostly goes to bed at five."

I finished topping the cupcakes, sprinkled chocolate jimmies on them, and transferred them to the rolling rack, so Glo could box them for a party pickup.

"Now what?" Diesel asked.

"Now I clean up after myself, and then I can go home to work on my cookbook."

"I didn't know you were writing a cookbook."

"I need money so I can fix my foundation. I had a good idea for a cookbook, but now I have to write it and sell it."

"Is it a cupcake book?"

"Not entirely."

I turned my back on Diesel and loaded the industrial-size sink with dirty mixing bowls and pastry bags. I didn't want to get into cookbook details with him. The title of the book was *Hot Guys Cooking for Hungry Women*, and all the recipes would be presented by a hot guy. I thought it was a good marketing ploy, but I was worried about the message it might send to a man who was already way too comfy sleeping in my bed.

Glo came back with her book of spells and a packet of pixie dust. She placed the book on the work island, opened it to a marked page, and followed along with her finger.

"Uppity uppity rise thyself," Glo read from the book. "Wings of magic, heart of believer, eyes open, spirit soar. Uppity uppity rise thyself."

Nothing. She didn't rise.

"Darn," Glo said.

Diesel was watching, thumbs tucked into the pockets of his jeans, smiling. "Personally, I think you need more uppities."

"No," she said. "I read it perfectly."

"Maybe you don't have wings of magic," I told her. "Or the heart of a believer." Or how about this . . . how about the book is fiction.

"I'm pretty sure I have the heart of a believer. It has to be the wings of magic, but I might be able to compensate with the pixie dust."

She took a pinch from the packet, repeated the spell, and sprinkled the pixie dust onto the top of her head.

Nothing happened.

"Pixie dust is supposed to sparkle," Diesel said. "Your dust doesn't have any sparkle."

"It was on sale," Glo said. "Maybe I didn't use enough."

She chanted the spell one more time and threw a handful of dust at herself. Some of the dust flew past her onto the gas range and ignited like a July 4th sparkler. *Pop, pop, pop, pop*. The pops turned into *swoosh* and a ribbon of flame raced along the top of the stove and set fire to a roll of paper towels. Diesel calmly grabbed the flaming towels and pitched them into the sink.

Glo looked dejected. "I suppose there's no substitute for wings of magic."

"Flying is overrated anyway," Diesel said.

I removed the soaked towels from the sink and finished scrubbing my bowls.

"How do you know so much about sparkling pixie dust?" I asked Diesel.

"Tinker Bell."

CHAPTER NINE

It was almost one when I cruised down Weatherby Street. The street was narrow and slightly winding, as befitting a road originally designed for horse traffic. Houses were close together. Windows were thrown open to catch the fresh air. Flowerpots had been crammed onto small front stoops. Paint schemes dated back to colonial days. Some houses were freshly painted and some had paint peeling. This was no Stepford neighborhood.

Diesel had driven Glo's car to the bakery, so he was riding shotgun. I stopped at the entrance to my driveway, and we swiveled our heads toward the two vans parked in front of my house. Six men stood on the sidewalk beside the vans. Two of the men had Handycams. A third guy had a rolling hard-side suitcase. I parked, and we walked over to the men.

"What's going on?" Diesel asked.

"Spook Patrol," one of the guys said. "We're here to investigate a sighting. Are you the home owner?"

"Nope," Diesel said. "The ticked-off-looking blonde is the home owner."

The guy plastered a smile onto his face and stuck his hand out to me. "Mel Mensher. We'd like to take a daytime and a nighttime reading."

Mel Mensher was in his late twenties. He was slim, dressed in jeans and layers of shirts—T-shirt, flannel shirt, sweatshirt. His brown hair was receding at a good clip.

"There's been a huge mistake," I said. "There was no sighting. Just a nicotine addict dressed in black looking out my bedroom window."

"That's not what our ghost-o-meter says. We ran it across your front door, and it went off the chart."

"That's ridiculous," I told him. "That's impossible."

"Not entirely," Diesel said.

I looked up at him. "Anything you want to tell me?"

"It's possible that Wulf and I have an unusual energy field."

"There you have it," I said to Mel Mensher. "The big guy here has an unusual energy field."

"Lady, I'm talking full-blown spectral phenomenon."

"Well?" I asked Diesel.

"I'm not spectral, but I've been told I can be pretty damn phenomenal."

Of all the outrageous statements made today, this one I feared might be true.

One of the men approached Diesel with a handheld instrument. The machine clicked and hummed, and colored lights blinked. The guy reached out and touched Diesel.

"Sonovagun," he said. "He feels real."

"Is that a ghost-o-meter?" I asked.

"The best money can buy," the Spook Patroller said. "It measures three different kinds of energy, plus humidity."

He pointed the gizmo in my direction, and it gave off a couple wimpy beeps.

Diesel grinned. "I guess we know who wears the pants in this partnership."

I rolled my eyes, unlocked my front door, and the Spook Patrol rushed up to it.

"Hey," I said, hand to the ghost-o-meter guy's chest. "Back off. I'm not interested in ghost readings."

"But what about the phenomenon?" he asked.

"He isn't interested, either."

I closed and locked the door behind us. I waited a couple minutes and looked out the front window. The Spook Patrol was hunkered in, huddled in a clump by their vans.

"Do something," I said to Diesel.

"Like what?"

"I don't know. Use your phenomenal powers to get rid of them. Vaporize them, or something."

"I'd need special permission to vaporize."

"Really?"

Diesel grinned wider and slung an arm around my shoulders. "I like a woman who's gullible. It makes everything so much easier."

Cat 7143 swaggered into the living room

and sat his rump on Diesel's shoe. "Rhowl," Cat said.

"I can't be all bad," Diesel said. "Cat likes me."

"This cat has one eye and half a tail. I'm guessing in the past he hasn't made good character assessments."

"I'm guessing he was a brave defender of a defenseless lady cat," Diesel said.

I bent to pet the defender. "I'm afraid your Romeo days are over, but I see a lot of whipped cream and rotisserie chicken in your future."

Cat looked like he was willing to consider the trade-off, and he and Diesel followed me into the kitchen.

My kitchen wasn't large, but it was thoughtfully planned out. The inexpensive refrigerator and stove worked just fine. The floor was wide plank yellow pine. The over-the-counter cabinets were painted Wedgewood blue, with glass-paned doors. The sink was porcelain, with only a couple chips in it. The countertops were red Formica. I'd added a small butcher-block work island and two wooden bar stools. My pots and pans hung over my workstation on hooks screwed into the low ceiling.

Diesel hit his head on a fry pan and put out a couple good cuss words. So much for the superior sensory perception.

"I need to work on a muffin recipe today," I told Diesel. "You and Cat can watch television."

"Nothing on."

"How about you read a book."

"Not in the mood."

I set a couple bowls, measuring cups, and measuring spoons on the counter next to the sink.

"Here's the thing," I told Diesel. "You need to get out of my kitchen. You're big. You take up too much space."

Plus, he made it hard for me to keep my mind on my cupcakes. When he got close, his heat was contagious, warming my skin, seeping into my chest and, against my best efforts, working its way south.

"I like watching you," Diesel said, sliding onto a stool.

"Yes, but you're distracting, and I really need to fix my muffin recipe, so *go away*."

"No."

"No? That's it? *No?* Criminy, you are *so aggravating*. I can't make you do anything. I have no control over you."

Diesel sat with one foot on the floor and one on the lower rung of the stool. "You have more control than you realize."

"What does that mean?"

"It means, the more I like you, the more vulnerable I become."

Whoa. That caught me by surprise. I put my hands flat on the island to steady myself and looked at him. "You don't seem like you would ever be vulnerable to anything."

"The list is short."

I didn't know what to say. Under normal circumstances, this would lead to romance, but there was nothing normal about any of this.

"No need to panic," Diesel said. "There are limits to how far I can go with you."

I should have asked about the limits, but I was too distracted by the possibility that he couldn't read my mind after all. If he'd been reading my mind, he would have known I was mush inside. I wasn't feeling panic. I was feeling gut-twisting attraction. The knowledge that Diesel liked me enough to be vulnerable had me in a knot.

"Probably, I should get on with my muffins," I said.

All right, I know it was lame, but it was all I could manage. For my entire life, I've eased myself over crisis situations and disastrous, embarrassing moments by making muffins and cupcakes.

I hauled a bag of flour out of the cabinet and opened my notebook to the recipe for gingerbread muffins.

"What's wrong with the recipe you already have?" Diesel asked.

"It's okay, but I think I can make it better. I'd like to punch up the flavor and improve the texture."

I lined my muffin pan with three different-colored wrappers and whipped up the base batter. I fiddled with three variations, poured them into the muffin tin, and slid the tin into the oven. I changed the recipe on the base batter and repeated the process. By the time the first batch of muffins was ready to come out of the oven, the entire house smelled like cloves and ginger.

I slid the second batch into the oven and set the first on a wire rack to cool.

"You can be my guinea pig," I said to Diesel. "Tell me which muffin you like the best."

By the time Diesel was done, he'd eaten six muffins, and Cat had eaten one. Cat sat back and groomed himself. Diesel stood and scratched his stomach. "Ahhhhh," he said.

"Well?"

"Well what?"

"Which muffin was best?"

"They were all great. What happens when you get all your recipes together?"

"I hope by then I'll have sold the book, and the publisher will take over."

"Have you sent it out to anyone yet?"

"I've been sending a query letter with a sample chapter. So far, there haven't been any takers, but some of the rejection letters have been encouraging." I pulled a shoe box from under the counter and opened it. It was crammed with responses from editors and agents.

Diesel picked a letter off the top and read aloud. "This is a great idea, but it won't fit into our publishing program at this time." He chose another. "This is not for us, but we wish you the best of luck placing it elsewhere." He pawed through the rest of the box. "Here's one written in crayon on a cocktail napkin."

I knew that one by heart. All it said was *NO!* I closed the box up and put it away.

"The important thing is that I stay positive," I told Diesel. "I read a book about getting published, and it said persistence would pay off."

Diesel grabbed me and kissed me on the top of my head. "Works for me." His phone buzzed, and he opened the connection. "Yeah?" He stood and listened for a couple minutes, staring down at his shoe. He glanced over at me, not looking happy. He nodded in silent confirmation to whatever the caller was telling him. "I'm on it," Diesel said. And he disconnected.

"Bad news?" I asked him.

"When Wulf feels the need to kill, he uses an ancient Chinese technique called Dragon Claw. To my knowledge, he's the only human alive who kills like this. We can both channel energy to our hands, but Wulf can channel enough to burn flesh. You already know this. His signature move is to break his victim's neck and simultaneously brand him with his handprint. The man assigned to guard Steven Hatchet, your crazy counterpart in Florida, was just found stuffed into a trash can. His neck was broken, and he was branded with a handprint. And Hatchet is missing."

I felt myself sway, and I reached for Diesel. The blood had all rushed out of my head and settled in my feet, and there were a lot of cobwebs and clanging noises in my brain.

"Good night," I whispered.

Diesel sat me down on a bar stool and forced me to bend at the waist. "Head lower than your heart. Keep breathing," he said. After a minute, he pulled me up by the back of my shirt and looked at me. "I get this reaction a lot from women. Are you okay?"

I nodded. "The burning flesh thing got to me."

"You wouldn't mind if he used his skills on a pot roast," Diesel said. "Think pot roast."

"How about if I think *this is a nightmare*?"

"Think what you want, but we need to wrap it up here and get over to Shirley's. My source said it looked like Hatchet was snatched this morning. That means Wulf could be back in the area with him by now. We need to talk to Shirley before Wulf gets to her."

"Shirley can't talk."

Diesel had me by the hand, tugging me to the door. "We'll work around it."

I dug my heels in. "I need to put my muffins in a container."

Diesel yanked me forward. "Later."

The Spook Patrol was still on the sidewalk in front of my house when Diesel shoved me out the door. They were joined by the guide from the ghost tour and four senior citizens who I assumed were with the guide.

"It's the ghost man!" one of the old people said.

Everyone went cameras-up and took Diesel's picture.

CHAPTER TEN

It was almost four o'clock when Shirley opened her door to us.

"Frack," Shirley said, holding a three-pound roasted turkey leg.

I looked over her shoulder into her apartment. "Are you alone?"

Shirley nodded and gnawed on the leg.

"We'd like to talk to you."

"Hah!" Shirley said. "Grape lucky."

"Has a guy named Wulf been here?" I asked her.

Shirley looked confused.

"Gerwulf Grimoire," Diesel said. "My

height, long black hair, pale skin, smells like fire and brimstone."

Shirley shook her head no.

"You have something he wants," Diesel said. "And we need to get it before he does."

"Dog off," Shirley said. And she slammed the door closed and threw the bolt.

Diesel put his hand to the door, the bolt slid back, and he pushed the door open.

"Nice," I said.

"Yeah, it's good to be me," Diesel said.

Shirley stared at her dead bolt. "Quack?" she asked. "How stucky rag it?"

"I don't know," Diesel said. "It's a mystery."

Shirley turned to me. "Quack?"

"No clue," I told her.

"If you can't talk, you at least need to listen," Diesel said to Shirley. "This is important."

Shirley vigorously shook her head no. "Da, da, da," emphasizing the last *da* by poking Diesel in the chest with her turkey leg.

"I could be laying in the sun on a beach somewhere, but no, I have to save the world," Diesel said, snatching the leg.

Shirley reached for her turkey leg, and Diesel held it high over her head. "No talk, no turkey."

Shirley kicked him in the knee and ran to her refrigerator. Diesel beat her to the refrigerator and held the door shut.

Shirley narrowed her eyes at Diesel. "Duck pecker."

"Sticks and stones," Diesel told her.

I grabbed the turkey leg from Diesel and gave it back to Shirley. "Here's the thing," I told her. "Diesel thinks you have an object in your possession that has special power. This object represents gluttony, and it might be the reason you're hoarding food."

That got Shirley's attention. "Greely?"

"Problem is, we don't know what this thing looks like. Do you have any ideas?"

Shirley made a zero with her thumb and forefinger.

"Let's start with the secret inheritance," Diesel said. "Was it money? A car? A necklace?"

Shirley made a sign like she was locking her lips and throwing the key away.

Diesel was hands on hips. "You gotta be kidding." He looked at me. "She's kidding, right?"

"Guess she believes in the bad luck thing," I said.

Shirley nodded.

"So you have eternal bad luck if you reveal the inheritance," I said. "Suppose someone guessed it? That wouldn't exactly be revealing it."

Shirley shrugged.

I was sure I'd previously fondled everything in her apartment. The object, if it existed, had to be on her.

"Let me see your necklace, your ring, and your watch," I said.

Shirley took them off and put them in my hand. Nothing. I returned her jewelry, and I saw Shirley's eyes flick to her purse on the kitchen table.

"Your purse," I said.

Shirley handed it over, and I dumped everything onto the counter. Seven Snickers bars, lipstick, compact, wallet, pack of tissues, hairbrush, hand sanitizer, three Peppermint Patties, keys, notepad, pen, a handful of Hershey's Kisses, a crumpled Whopper wrapper.

I picked everything up and held it in my hand, one by one. The lipstick, compact, wallet, hairbrush, and pen said nothing to me. The instant the keys hit my palm, they radiated heat. I dropped them onto the table, and the heat went away. I picked them up, and they warmed my hand.

"Holy cow," I said.

"That's it?" Diesel asked. "The Stone is disguised as a key?"

"This is too weird," I said. "It's got to be a setup. How did you get the keys to radiate heat?"

Diesel took the keys from me and examined them. "Lizzy, you're the only one who can feel the heat."

Shirley had finished the turkey leg and was working her way through the Snickers bars.

"You inherited a key," I said to her.

Shirley vigorously shook her head.

I took another look at the key ring. There were three keys and a ladybug charm on the ring.

"It's the charm," I said.

Shirley nodded. "Clam bake."

I removed the ladybug from the ring and held it in my hand. It vibrated slightly and grew warm.

Shirley pointed to the photo on the end table. "Twinkies," she said. And she counted off on three fingers. "Huey, Dewey, Louie."

"I don't like what I think she's trying to tell us," I said to Diesel.

Diesel fixed his eyes on the photo. "Three people got inheritances?" he asked Shirley.

Shirley nodded. "Beeswax."

I looked over at Diesel. "Don't tell me we have to collect more charms. One is good enough, right?"

"I'm on a learning curve," Diesel said, "but I suppose to be safe we need all the charms."

"Maybe Wulf doesn't know about the other charms."

"Hard to believe. Shirley had no knowledge of the Stone. She thought she had a keepsake ladybug. So we know Shirley didn't leak information. Uncle Phil, on the other hand, probably knew. He divided the charms as a safety precaution and tried to scare everyone into silence with the threat of eternal bad luck. Wulf had to know about the uncle and the divided inheritance."

"Do you have addresses or phone numbers for the people in the photograph?" Diesel asked Shirley.

Shirley shook her head.

"Names?" he asked.

"Maggie, Booger Slammer, Ice Cream," Shirley said. She rolled her eyes and thunked herself in the forehead with the heel of her hand. "Mix Master, Matches, Nail File." She squinched her eyes closed and tried again. "Candle, Piss Pot, Queen Elizabeth." She opened her eyes and grunted. "Fruck."

"They're stepbrothers," I said to Diesel. "Their last name is probably More."

Shirley nodded. I'd guessed right.

"We need to keep your charm," Diesel said to Shirley. "We need to put it someplace safe."

"Good riddleness," Shirley said, popping a Peppermint Pattie.

Diesel called a contact for information on Shirley More's stepbrothers, and by the time we reached the Cayenne, Diesel had his answer.

"Leonard More is the stepbrother with the silver Camry," Diesel said. "He lives in Salem. His brother, Mark, lives in Beverly. We'll visit Leonard first. He's a claims adjuster for an insurance company and should be home from work by five o'clock."

CHAPTER ELEVEN

Lenny lived in a medium-size colonial on a tree-lined street in north Salem. A plaque on the house proclaimed it to have been built in 1897. The Camry was parked at the curb when we arrived. A FOR SALE sign was stuck in a patch of sketchy grass in the front yard. Diesel found a space half a block away, parked the Cayenne, and we walked back to Lenny's house.

"According to my source, Lenny's recently married and recently divorced," Diesel said. "He was a junior exec in a bank, got fired six months ago, and picked up the claims adjuster job at the end of March."

Lenny answered the door in dress slacks and a rumpled dress shirt. He had a drink in his hand, his breath was hundred-proof, his eyes were bloodshot, his thinning, sandy blond hair was mussed, and he was wearing a thick, spiked dog collar around his neck.

"Had a hard day?" Diesel asked him.

"Not necessarily," Leonard said, "but things could pick up. What can I do you for?"

"I'd like to talk to you about your inheritance."

"You and everyone else."

"Who's everyone else?" Diesel asked.

"My brother, for starters. And some cool dude who looks like he has real pain potential." Lenny slurked down his drink and stared into the empty glass. "Uh-oh, all gone." He turned and walked into the kitchen, and we followed.

"Do you know the cool dude's name?" Diesel asked.

Lenny poured more whiskey into his glass. "Wolf. Is that a badass name, or what?" He blinked up at Diesel. "You want some hooch?" He squinted over at me. "You want some?"

"No," I said. "But thanks. This thing you inherited, it was a ladybug, right?"

"Wrong. And I'm not telling anybody anything, because then I'll have bad luck forever and ever."

"That's baloney," I said. "No one can put a whammy on you and give you bad luck forever."

"Hah!" Leonard said. "You didn't know Uncle Phil. He was a scary kookadoo. He could give you the stink eye." Leonard held one eye closed with his finger and looked at me with his other bloodshot eye. "And one time, I saw him turn a cat into a fry pan."

Two days ago, I wouldn't have believed that was possible, but now I didn't know what to believe.

Diesel was handing me things off the kitchen counter. Egg timer, key ring, Ping-Pong paddle. I held each of them for a moment and gave them back. Spatula, pot holder, saucepan.

"What's with the dog collar?" Diesel asked.

"It's an accessory," Lenny said. "Some men wear ties. I prefer a dog collar."

"Fondle it," Diesel said to me.

"No way!"

"It's an accessory," Diesel said. "Think of it like jewelry. He probably got it at Cartier."

"Wrong," Lenny said. "Petco."

I reached out and touched the collar. Nothing. I touched his watch. Nothing there, either.

"Suppose I guessed the inheritance?" I asked Lenny. "Would that be okay?"

"It's a free country," Lenny said. "I can't stop you from guessing. Anyway, you'll never guess it, and even if you do guess right, you'll never find it. It's hidden and booby-trapped."

Diesel opened an under-the-counter drawer and pulled out handcuffs attached to a heavy chain.

"Sometimes I'm a bad boy, and I need to be punished," Lenny said. "I have more stuff in my bedroom if you want to see."

"No!" I said. "Gee, look at the time. I have to go now."

Diesel wrapped an arm around me. "We can take a couple minutes to check out the dude's bedroom," Diesel said. "I bet he keeps his inheritance in there."

"Don't know. Don't care," I said.

"Has Shirley seen your inheritance?" Diesel asked Lenny.

"Nope. Nobody's seen it but me and good ol' deader-than-a-doorknob Uncle Phil. And nobody's gonna see it, either, because I can keep a secret. You can ask my wife. Oops, I mean ex-wife. She didn't know about lots of things. And then when she found out, she turned into a real party pooper."

"Did you tell her about your inheritance?" I asked.

"No. I told her about my paddle collection and my cyber slut. I thought she'd be excited, but she packed her bags and left."

"Gosh, go figure," I said, thinking I'd touched the Ping-Pong paddle, wondering if I had hand sanitizer in my purse.

"When did you start collecting paddles?" Diesel asked Lenny.

Lenny rocked back on his heels. "Five or six years ago. One day, it just came over me that I needed a good whacking. And now I can't get enough of it."

"Jeez," I said.

Diesel leaned close, his lips brushing my ear. "At least it's not fattening."

If I had to make a choice between getting disciplined by the cyber slut or gaining a hundred pounds, I'd probably go with the cupcake obsession.

"We need to talk to you about the inheritance," I said.

"Sure. What about it?"

"Where is it?"

"That's for you to know and me to find out," Lenny said.

Diesel and I exchanged glances. Lenny was snockered. Helpful for extracting information. Not helpful if he didn't make any more sense than Shirley.

"Is it in the bedroom?" I asked.

"Used to be." He looked into his glass. "Empty," he said. "So sad."

"He needs food," I said to Diesel.

Diesel opened the refrigerator and looked inside. "A half-empty bottle of Aquavit, a can of Crisco, and a rubber chicken. That's it."

"There's no food in here," I said to Lenny.

Lenny stuck his head in the fridge. "There's a chicken."

"It's rubber," Diesel said, looking like he was going to rupture something trying not to laugh out loud.

"Is that bad?" Leonard asked.

I looked around the kitchen. No bread. No fruit. No coffeemaker. No kitchen knives. No cookie jar. The lone metal spatula I'd tested was propped up in the dish drain. I now had new concerns about its use. I ransacked the cupboards and came up with a box of granola bars. I gave one to Diesel and one to Lenny.

"About the inheritance," I said to Lenny.

"Can't get it," Lenny said. "It's booby-trapped."

"Yes, but you know how to disarm it, right?"

Lenny shoved half a granola bar into his mouth. "Nuh. Didn't think of that. It was during the divorce, and the party pooper took the toaster, and so I got this idea that she was after my inheritance, so I hid it and booby-trapped it. I was doing recreational drinking at the time. Anyway, it doesn't matter. It's a piece of junk."

"Here's the thing," I said to Lenny. "It turns out your inheritance might be . . . enchanted."

"Don't care."

"Of course you care. It's a Gluttonoid."

Diesel grinned at me and rocked back

on his heels. "Gluttonoid. Boy, that's a great name. How'd you ever come up with that one?"

Lenny slumped against the counter. "What's a Gluttonoid?"

"It's an object that turns people into gluttons. In your case, you're a glutton for punishment. If we remove the object, there's a good chance you'll return to normal," I told him.

"No more hanky panky spanky?" Lenny asked. "What if I'm a bad boy?"

"Dude, you're freaking me out," Diesel said. "Get a grip."

"This is creepy. And I don't like the whole booby-trap thing," I said to Diesel. "Why don't we let Wulf get this one? With any luck, he'll blow himself up."

Diesel looked at Lenny. "Tell me about the booby trap. Are we talking major explosion?"

"Not atomic," Lenny said.

"Would it kill Superman?"

"You'd need kryptonite to do that."

"Okay, how about Batman?"

"I don't know. Batman is tricky."

"So the let-Wulf-get-the-charm plan won't

work," Diesel said to me. "Doesn't sound like we can count on it to kill him."

The house was around two thousand square feet. Living room, dining room, kitchen, powder room, mudroom leading to the back door. The bedrooms were obviously upstairs. Impossible to know if Lenny had gone to the dark side because of the charm, but going on the assumption that this was the case, I thought the charm most likely was in the house. Hard to believe any of this was real but even more difficult to believe the charm could leak onto someone without consistent exposure. And if I booby-trapped something in my house, it wouldn't be in a high-traffic area. I'd want it out of the way, hidden from sight.

"Do you have a cellar?" I asked Lenny.

"Yep."

"Did you hide your inheritance in your cellar?"

"I don't think so."

"You don't know for sure?"

"I'd had a lot to drink. A real lot. And I tried a bunch of different places before I settled. And it was a long time ago."

"Your wife's only been gone for three months," Diesel said.

"She was a party pooper," Lenny said. "Did I already tell you that? Anyway, you can look around the cellar if you want, but I'm not going. It's scary down there. And I might have booby-trapped it."

Diesel opened the cellar door and went down the steep, narrow stairwell. He got to the bottom and looked back at me.

"Well?" he asked.

"Well what?"

"Are you coming down?"

"No."

He was wearing jeans and a cream-colored cotton crew-neck sweater with the sleeves pushed to his elbows. His teeth were white against his beach bum tan. And he was looking very big in the small cellar.

"There are some things I'd like you to hold," he said.

"I bet."

"I meant potential charm things."

"I knew that. Are you sure it's safe down there?"

He did arms outstretched. "No bad guys or obvious booby traps."

"What about spiders?"

"Haven't seen any."

I cautiously crept down the stairs, stood next to Diesel, and looked around. The cellar floor was crudely poured cement. The walls were mortar and stone. A bare 60-watt bulb lit the space. The air was cool and damp and smelled musty, like rotting wood and mildew. The ceiling was riddled with pipes, and wires running along support beams. The water heater and furnace were to one side. The rest of the cellar was cluttered with plastic bins and cardboard boxes.

"You don't expect me to go through all these bins and boxes, do you?" I asked Diesel.

"Yeah."

"It'll take hours. And what about the hiding and the booby-trapping? This stuff's just sitting here."

"No stone unturned," Diesel said. "No pun intended."

Okay, let's get this out in the open. First, I'm a big coward. I don't like the idea of getting blown up, and I don't like spiders. I know at first glance we don't see any spiders, but they're sneaky. They hide in places and then jump out at you. And second, what about my muffins and my cookbook? I don't have time to save the world. I need cookbook money to fix my foundation, or my house is going to fall over. And third, this whole thing is weirding me out. It would make a good television show, but things like this aren't supposed to happen in real life.

"If we go back to my house, you can eat more muffins," I said to Diesel.

"If we stay here and go through these bins, I'll get out of your bed."

"Really?"

"Scout's honor," Diesel said, wrangling the lid off a plastic bin.

I looked inside the bin and found it was filled with sheet music for classical guitar. The second bin Diesel opened held CDs. Opera, guitar, symphonies. A lot of Haydn and Mozart and artists out of my scope of knowledge.

"Hey, Lenny!" I yelled up the stairs. "Do you play the guitar?"

"Used to," he said. "Traded it for a fraternity paddle used in the movie *Animal House*. It's a collector's item."

"That's so sad," I said to Diesel. "He

had a whole other life before his inheritance."

"Focus," Diesel said. "At the risk of seeming insensitive, I don't care about his life then or now. I care about the charm. Anyway, he's got the paddle used in *Animal House.* I'm jealous."

Fortunately, the rest of the bins contained neatly folded men's clothes, which was sad only in Lenny's sometimes unfortunate choices in ties. I ripped through the bins in record time, and Diesel opened the first of the boxes.

"Are you okay up there?" he called to Leonard.

"I want a pizza."

"We have three boxes to check out, and then it's pizza time," Diesel told him.

The boxes were filled with the sort of junk you acquire over a lifetime and can't discard but no longer need. A baseball mitt, a broken stapler, a bunch of photos, Hardy Boys books, a commemorative chunk of the Berlin Wall, a cassette player, a bicycle chain, his high school yearbook, a kitty litter scooper.

I was making my way through the last box when there was a *whoosh* of air, the cellar door slammed shut, and the light went out, throwing us into utter blackness. Diesel moved flat against my back, his arm tight around my waist. There was thirty seconds of wind screaming on the other side of the door, and then all was quiet and the light blinked back on.

"What was th-th-that?" I asked, my heart knocking around in my chest.

Diesel took my hand and tugged me up the stairs. "That was Wulf."

"Is he here?"

"Not anymore." Diesel opened the cellar door and stepped into the kitchen. "And neither is Lenny."

"Where'd they go? Are you sure Lenny isn't here?" I looked around the kitchen. Nothing was out of place. No sign of struggle. No damage from the howling wind. "It sounded like a tornado blew through here. Why aren't things tossed around?"

"I guess that wasn't part of the show," Diesel said.

"And you think it was Wulf?"

"I know it was Wulf. I can sense his presence."

"How?"

"I know his scent. The air pressure changes. I get a cramp in my ass."

I didn't notice a change in the air pressure, and my nose was still stuffed with cellar smells. Fine by me. I didn't want to add any more special skills to my Unmentionableness. I already had one too many. I could deal with baking Unmentionable cupcakes. I'd like to lose the empowered objects thing.

"Where did Wulf take Lenny?" I asked Diesel.

Diesel shrugged. "Someplace to talk."

I had a really icky feeling in my stomach. Lenny was creepy, but he didn't seem like a bad person, and I wasn't happy about him being whisked away.

"Wulf won't do the death claw on him, will he?"

"Not as long as he needs him," Diesel said. "A dead man can't tell you where the treasure is hidden. If we weren't here, I'm sure Wulf would have stayed and had Steven Hatchet sweep the house."

"So now what? Do we chase Wulf down and duke it out with him?"

"That would be the movie version. In

the real-life version, we go through the rest of the house and look for the inheritance."

I wasn't crazy about either of the versions. I wanted to get back to my muffins.

"The muffins will wait," Diesel said. "Let's start upstairs."

CHAPTER TWELVE

There were three bedrooms upstairs. I stepped into the master first, immediately turned to leave, and bumped into Diesel.

"Out of my way," I said to him. "You can't make me go in there."

"Of course I can," he said. "Look how big and strong I am. And I'm insensitive, too."

The bed was a tangled mess of twisted sheets and lumpy pillows without pillow-cases. Empty liquor and beer bottles were everywhere. Drawers were open with clothes spilling out, and dirty clothes were scattered across the floor, interspersed with crumpled fast-food wrappers, half-eaten bags of chips, two roaches the size of lab mice taking a feet-up permanent siesta, and another rubber chicken.

"I'm not touching any of this," I said to Diesel. "And I'm especially not touching whatever is hanging on the doorknob."

Diesel checked out the doorknob. "It's underwear."

"Ick!"

"He's a single guy," Diesel said. "This is the way we live."

I looked at him, and I think my eyes went blank for a moment and my mouth dropped open.

"Not me," Diesel said, smiling. "But *some* guys."

I did serious mental eye-rolling. "Where do we begin?"

"Look for something that might contain a charm, and be careful not to explode yourself."

I cautiously picked through the mess, testing out watches, shoes, beer bottles, belt buckles, and the rubber chicken. Nothing glowed or felt warm.

"This is stupid," I said to Diesel. "It's none of these things. We should be looking for a booby trap."

"Problem is, most of the time you don't recognize a good booby trap until it's too late," Diesel said.

"Have you ever been booby-trapped?"

"Yeah, and it's usually not pleasant."

It took a while to get through the master, but things went faster with bedrooms two and three. The furniture had been removed from these rooms, leaving only a few dents in the carpet as evidence of habitation.

"Looks to me like the Missus backed the truck up to this house before Lenny even knew she was leaving," Diesel said. "He got picked clean."

We went downstairs and searched the living room. Not hard to do, since the furniture consisted of a matching brown leather couch and chair that had seen better days. Probably picked up at a yard sale after his ex-wife took the good stuff. No furniture in the dining room. That left the kitchen, and I'd already handled everything that wasn't nailed down in the kitchen.

"Let's think about this for a minute," Diesel said. "We've done the object-touching routine, and I've had my eyes open for anything remotely resembling a booby trap or secret hiding place. What have we missed?"

"Maybe it's not in the house. Maybe it's in his car or his office."

"If we're to believe him, he was drunk when he hid the inheritance, so it had to be something fairly easy to do. I think that leaves out his office, and probably his car. Most likely, he set the device when he was relatively sober and then walked around the house with a bottle of liquor in his hand, trying to decide on a hiding place."

"We didn't check appliances," I said, peering into the microwave, flipping the door down on the dishwasher. I opened the oven and burst out laughing. There was a rubber chicken in the oven.

"What's with these chickens?" I asked Diesel. "He's got a rubber chicken fixation."

I took the chicken out of the oven, held it by its long skinny neck, and a metal-and-glass cylinder fell out of its butt.

"Uh-oh," Diesel said.

An instant later, he had his hand clamped onto my wrist, pulling and shoving me out the kitchen door, half carrying me in a sprint across the small backyard. We were maybe thirty feet from the house when there was an explosion, followed by a second mega-explosion. The second explosion blew the back of the house apart and sent us sprawling. I felt Diesel roll on top of me, and all around us, debris was falling out of the sky. Bits of paper and wood and flaming chunks of mystery material. Diesel got to his feet, dragged me up beside him, and we moved into the adjoining backyard.

"Looks like you found the booby trap," Diesel said.

I had my fingers curled into his shirt in a death grip, and I was babbling. "What the? How? Who?"

Diesel pried my fingers open. "Honey, I love that you've got ahold of me, but I think you've got some chest hairs in there."

Flames raced up the side of what was left of Lenny's house and black smoke billowed into the sky. Sirens screamed a couple blocks away and people were stepping out of their houses and gathering in the street.

"There isn't going to be anything left of Lenny's house," I said, barely able to hear myself over the ringing in my ears.

"Yeah," Diesel said. "The historical society's going to be pissed."

"It's so horrible. Everything's gone. All

his treasures from high school. All his sheet music. All his clothes."

Diesel had an arm wrapped around me. "Don't forget his paddle collection, and his inheritance."

"Omigosh. His inheritance! It must have gotten blown up into smithereens. We'll never find it."

"No, but Wulf won't find it, either. And that's what we really care about."

We walked around to the front of the house and watched the spectacle for a while. A police car was the first on the scene. A fire truck arrived seconds later. More cop cars and fire trucks. Two EMT trucks. They'd responded fast, but the house had burned even faster. By the time the hoses were working, there wasn't much left to save.

I stood with arms slack at my side, pretty much dumbfounded by the whole incomprehensible event.

"The booby-trap gizmo was so small," I said. "How did it make such a disaster?"

"I suspect it ignited a gas line. I don't know what else would account for the second explosion and fire."

We left the scene, buckled ourselves

into Diesel's Porsche, and motored off, giving one last look at the smoldering rubble that used to be Lenny's house. The FOR SALE sign was still standing, and behind it, the brick skeleton of the fireplace was blackened but intact.

I choked back emotion, overwhelmed by Lenny's loss and the destruction of a house that had survived for over a hundred years.

Diesel reached over and tugged at my ponytail. "It's okay," he said. "No one was hurt. And everything will eventually recycle."

"Recycling sucks."

Diesel nodded. "Sometimes it definitely does suck."

It was a little after seven o'clock, and now that I was away from the action, I was hungry. I'd had some bites of muffin around three but nothing since, and I'd expended a lot of energy being terrified.

"I'm starving," I said to Diesel. "And you're going in the wrong direction. Marblehead is south."

"I'm not going to Marblehead. I'm going to Beverly. When Wulf finds out Lenny's inheritance isn't available, he's going to go after the remaining piece to the puzzle."

"Mark More."

"Yeah. We need to get to him first."

"What about dinner?"

"Keep your eyes peeled for fast food."

"There!" I said. "On the left. It's a cluster fast-food stop. Burgers, doughnuts, chicken, subs."

"Which do you want?"

"I want them all."

"Pick one," Diesel said.

"Burgers. No wait. Chicken. No, no. Burgers. Definitely burgers. With extra cheese. And fries. A large size. And a chocolate shake. And doughnuts."

Ten minutes later, we were back on the road with bags of burgers and fries and a dozen doughnuts. I ate my double cheeseburger, finished off my fries, and eyed Diesel's fries.

"Are you going to eat all those fries?" I asked him.

"Yeah," Diesel said. "Do you have a problem with that?"

"Just asking."

I opened the box of doughnuts and almost passed out. Boston cream, maple glazed, jelly, strawberry with sprinkles, chocolate, lemon pudding. I grabbed the

Boston cream and devoured it. "Oh man," I said. "Oh jeez, this is good." My second doughnut was the maple glazed. "I bet I could eat all these. I bet I could eat them in record time."

Diesel reached for the chocolate, and I sucked in some air.

"What?" Diesel asked.

"You took the chocolate."

"There are two of them. We got two of everything."

"I didn't realize there were two. It's fine. I'm good." I finished the maple glazed and snatched the second chocolate out of the box.

"Ordinarily, I like a woman with strong appetites," Diesel said, "but you're down-right scary. I'm afraid when you finish the doughnuts, you're going to start gnawing on my arm."

"Sorry. I panicked over the chocolate."

Diesel handed me his phone. "I have the GPS working. Copilot me to Mark's business address."

I had the phone in one hand and my strawberry doughnut in the other.

"Turn left at the next street," I told him. "And then go one block and turn left again."

Marblehead is quaint. Salem is weird. And Beverly is a normal, hardworking town. Mark More lived and worked in a part of Beverly that was devoted to commercial real estate. Warehouses, light industry, a seafood processing plant. I followed the directions to a two-story redbrick cube of a building with a two-bay loading dock on one side. The sign on the front said MORE IS BETTER.

The sun was low in the sky and lights were on in what I assumed was the office. One car was parked in the lot. The bay doors were closed. Diesel parked next to the car in the lot, and we walked around to the street entrance.

"After seeing what the inheritance did to Shirley and Lenny, I'm almost afraid to go inside," I said to Diesel.

"According to my assistant, Mark is the local distributor for Momma Jane's Green Mints. So I guess we'll find a lot of mints."

"You have an assistant?"

"Yeah."

"What's his name? Where is he? Do you have an office?"

"Her name is Gwen. And I'm not sure

where she is. And no, I don't have an office."

Diesel opened the glass-paned door, and we stepped into a small room with a desk at one end and a couple utilitarian plastic waiting room chairs at the other. A hallway led to the innards of the building. Somewhere down the hallway, we could hear machinery at work.

We followed the sound of machinery, stopped in front of an open door, and looked into the large warehouse. The floor was polished cement, the ceilings were high, and the walls were cinder block. The area was well lit. Cartons of mints, shrink-wrapped on pallets, were stacked along one wall. A forklift had been parked in front of them. A pile of what looked like assorted junk filled a corner on the opposite wall. The junk was one-and-a-half stories high and extended about a third of the way into the warehouse. Mark More was rearranging the pile of junk with the help of a backhoe. I recognized him from the street encounter with Shirley. He was average height, with light brown hair cut too short on the sides for his Dumbo ears. I guessed his age at late thirties. He wasn't fat, but he wasn't fit, either. He was wearing jeans and a white shirt, and he looked like he was concentrating hard on his job.

Diesel and I walked halfway into the room, and Mark spotted us and cut his engine.

"Can I help you?" he called out.

"We need to talk," Diesel said.

Mark swung down from the backhoe and crossed to us.

"I hope this is about mints," he said. "Because I've got a lot of them."

"I've never heard of Momma Jane's Green Mints," I told him.

"They go to hotels and restaurants, mostly," Mark said. "They're the crummy little things they put on your pillow or have out in a bowl."

"I'm interested in your inheritance," Diesel said to Mark.

"From Uncle Phil? What about it?"

"I'd like to see it," Diesel said.

"No can do," Mark said. "Uncle Phil wanted it kept secret."

"The object you inherited might be putting you in danger," I said. "Has anyone else approached you about it?"

"Nope. Just you. And there's no way it

could put me in danger, except from Uncle Phil."

If I looked over Mark's shoulder, I could see the mountain of junk glittering under the overhead lights. It appeared that most of the pieces were silver or brass, with an occasional small splash of color. I left Diesel to talk to Mark, and I wandered closer, skirting the backhoe to get a better look at whatever was filling an entire corner of the warehouse. It took me a moment, but then I got it. I was looking at a mammoth collection of padlocks. Some were large, some were small, some were real, and some looked like trinkets.

I returned to Diesel and Mark, and from both men's body language I assumed things weren't going well.

"So," I said. "What's happening?"

"Your friend is a nutcase," Mark said to me. "He thinks my inheritance is possessed."

"I didn't say it was possessed," Diesel said. "Possessed implies that demons or other disincarnate entities have temporarily taken control of a body. I said the inheritance was possibly infused with a dangerous energy."

"How about I infuse you with a bullet up your butt if you don't leave," Mark said. "I have a gun."

"I'm curious," I said to Mark. "This was the only address we could find for you. Do you live here?"

"Just about. My wife got the house and the dog in the divorce settlement, so I found a little apartment not far from here."

"Is the divorce recent?"

"It's been a couple years. She said I liked my collections more than I liked her . . . and that probably was true. I get a lot of satisfaction from my lock collection here. Lately, I pretty much eat, sleep, and dream locks."

"Boy, that's really interesting," I said.

"Yeah," Diesel said, cutting his eyes to the junk corner. "Interesting."

"Well, I guess we should be moving on," I said to Mark. "Sorry if Diesel was an annoyance. I'll take him home and give him a pill."

"I know Uncle Phil was weird," Mark said, "but he wasn't some voodoo guy."

"Of course not," I said. "Did you ever see him change a cat into a fry pan?"

"No, but I saw him change an opossum

into a flowerpot. I could never figure out how he did it. It was Uncle Phil's best trick. It was like one of those Vegas magicians making a school bus disappear."

We said adios to Mark, let ourselves out, and climbed into Diesel's SUV. Diesel drove half a block down the street, made a U-turn, and parked.

"Waiting for Mark to leave?" I asked.

"Yep."

"Do you know what he inherited?"

"No, but I know where to start looking. If it's a charm in the shape of a lock, it's probably going to be at the bottom of the pile, since it would have been his first lock."

"This could be fun," I said. "I always wanted to run a backhoe." I looked at my watch. "It's going to be a long night. We should get some snacks to tide us over. Maybe a bucket of chicken."

"Honey, you just ate ten doughnuts."

"But what if we get stuck here and there's no food?"

Diesel grinned at me. "Maybe you should let me hold Shirley's ladybug."

"You don't suppose I'm turning into a glutton, do you?"

Even as I asked the question, I was

thinking I should stock up on pork chops and graham crackers.

"A couple more days of carrying Shirley's inheritance, and you're going to have a snout and a tail," Diesel said.

I fished in my pocket, found the charm, and handed it over. "No one said anything about Uncle Phil having any of these obsessions. Is it possible it's all mental with Lenny, Shirley, Mark, and me? The SALIGIA Stone story is pretty far out there."

"Personally, I'm a lazy kind of guy, and leaving the door open on the mystical saves me work. I don't have to stress my brain trying to explain the unexplainable. It's magic. End of discussion."

"So you're buying into the SALIGIA Stone fairy tale?"

"Yeah. I'm believing the whole enchilada."

CHAPTER THIRTEEN

The light blinked off in Mark More's office, and Mark exited via the front door and walked to his car. The engine caught, and he drove out of the lot and down the street.

"Showtime," Diesel said.

"What if he set an alarm?"

"Not a concern. I didn't see a security system keypad anywhere in the building."

We covered the short distance to the warehouse, Diesel opened the door, and we walked in. No alarm sounded. No little red diode flashed from anywhere in the room.

I heard Diesel move toward the hall in

the pitch-black building and I followed him, immediately smashing into the desk.

"I suppose you can see in the dark," I said on a sigh.

"Yeah, and obviously you can't, so stick close to me."

I put my hand to his back.

"Closer would be better," he said.

"How close did you have in mind?"

"Really, really close."

I kicked him in the back of the leg, and he grunted.

Okay, so maybe I wouldn't mind getting close, but holy cow, not when I'm doing B&E on a chocolate mint warehouse.

"I hear you," Diesel said, "but I'm only human . . . sort of."

"What about the limit on how far we can go?"

"I'll let you know when we reach it."

He led me to the warehouse, and once we were inside and the door was closed behind us, he switched the lights on.

"Do you want first crack at the back-hoe?" he asked.

"Yes!"

I climbed on board and studied the controls. I turned the key, stepped on the gas, and rolled to the pile of locks. I lowered the shovel and dug in. I backed up and carried the locks to the other side of the room and dumped them next to the cartons of mints. I did this ten times, motored over to Diesel, and parked it.

"It's all yours," I said, jumping off. "I don't want to be a backhoe hog."

"It's boring, right?"

"Yes."

Diesel hauled himself up behind the wheel and went to work shoveling locks. I watched him for a while, wondering who on earth he was. When I found myself fantasizing him naked, I gave myself a mental slap and looked for something else to do. If I'd had my computer, I'd have googled SALIGIA Stones. In the absence of the computer, I called my mom.

"So, how's it going?" I asked her.

"It's going just fine. How's it going with you? Do you like your new job?"

"Yes. My job is terrific."

I grew up in Fairfax, Virginia, just outside the Beltway. My parents still live there, in the same redbrick ranch with a dogwood tree in the front yard and picnic table and swing set in the back. My dad's old

Bonneville and my mom's new Camry are tucked away in a two-car attached garage, and at this time of the year, the azaleas are beginning to bloom.

My mom teaches fifth grade, and my dad drives a public transport bus, like Ralph Cramden on *The Honeymooners*. My sister, Sara, is a year older than me and already has two kids. My brother, Tommy, is a year younger, is still single, and works in an auto body shop, customizing motorcycles. We're the typical all-American family . . . except at least one of us might be an Unmentionable.

"Is there anything weird about our family?" I asked my mother.

"Weird?"

"Maybe *special* is a better word. Like, do we have any special abilities?"

"Your Uncle Fred can touch his tongue to his nose."

"How about turning cats into fry pans?"

"Fred can't do that. And besides, it would be mean."

"I've always been able to make cupcakes better than anyone else."

"That's true," my mother said. "You make

wonderful cupcakes. You got that from your Great Grandmother Fanny."

"I never knew her. Was she an Unmentionable?"

"Unmentionable? Heavens, no. We talked about her all the time. She was a hoot."

"What about Ophelia? I only remember her from photographs."

"Ophelia was Fanny's little sister. She married a man named Wilbur Snell. He owned a shoe factory in Salem, and two weeks after the wedding, he disappeared and never was seen again. Ophelia stayed in Snell's house in Marblehead until the day she died. The shoe factory closed long ago, but I guess it left Ophelia with enough to keep going. The family drifted apart, and the last time we saw Ophelia, you were five years old. She thought you were very special. She said you had a complicated destiny. I've remembered her words all these years. Ophelia was a little New Age in her old age."

"Do you know why she left me her house?"

"She stated in the will that you were a

kindred spirit. And of course, she didn't have any children of her own. Only a one-eyed cat. And she could hardly leave her house to him."

My heart skipped a couple beats. "What happened to the one-eyed cat?"

"I don't know. I imagine he went to the animal shelter."

"Do you know any more about him?"

"No. Your grandmother spoke to Ophelia from time to time, and she would mention the cat."

I made a little more small talk, then disconnected and watched Diesel some more. I offered to take another shift, but he declined.

"More to the left," I yelled out to him after a couple hours. "The pile is uneven."

He looked back to me. "You want to take over, Miss Picky?"

"Just trying to be helpful."

"You can be helpful by looking through all the locks that are left."

My eyebrows went up an inch into my forehead. "Are you serious? There are still hundreds of locks. Maybe thousands."

Diesel cut the engine and swung down off the backhoe. "I've reduced the pile by ninety percent. I can't cut it down any more than that. These locks have been pushed around for years. The lock charm isn't going to be exactly where it was originally placed."

He was right. Problem was, I'd been going since four this morning, and I was running on empty. I walked to the edge of the remaining lock pile and began working my way through it, picking locks up, tossing them to Diesel, who pitched them across the room to the new heap of locks. After an hour, there were no more locks, I hadn't come across a charm, and nothing had glowed or buzzed in my hand.

"Now what?" I asked Diesel.

"Now we go home. And tomorrow we have another conversation with Mark More."

It was a little past midnight when we parked in front of my house. The Spook Patrol was absent, and the street was dark and blissfully quiet. Diesel let us in and flipped the lights on. Cat 7143 was sprawled in the middle of the floor, feet in the air.

"Omigosh," I said. "He's dead!"

Cat's good eye opened, his tail twitched, and the eye closed.

"Sleeping," Diesel said.

I looked more closely at Cat. He had muffin crumbs stuck to his face fur. "Looks like he helped himself to dinner."

Diesel sauntered into the kitchen and stood hands on hips, surveying the carnage. "If Uncle Phil were here, he'd turn Cat into a waffle iron."

Every muffin had been sampled. Some more than others. And some were completely destroyed.

"He prefers the muffins in the pink wrappers," Diesel said.

They were my favorites, too. Good to have my opinion verified, even if it was by a cat. I cleaned the kitchen, and when Diesel wasn't looking, I ate the untouched muffin bottoms, since Cat had mostly eaten the muffin tops. I struggled up the stairs and collapsed onto my bed.

"Are you going to sleep like that?" Diesel asked. "Don't you want to get undressed? Do you need help?"

"If I sleep like this, I don't have to get dressed in the morning . . . which is only three hours away."

"It would be more fun if you put those little shorts back on."

"I'm not interested in fun. I'm interested in sleep. And you promised you weren't sleeping here."

Diesel crawled onto the bed. "I lied."

I fluffed my pillow and pulled the quilt over myself. "If you touch me, I'll hurt you."

"I'm hard to hurt."

"I'll find a way. I'm motivated."

CHAPTER FOURTEEN

We both groaned out loud when the alarm went off.

"I need to get you a new job," Diesel said. "One that starts at noon."

"I had that job. I like this one better. And *my* job would be fine if it wasn't for *your* job."

I dragged myself to the bathroom, stumbled down the stairs, and started coffee brewing. I fed Cat and ate half a loaf of bread while I waited for the coffee. I scrambled four eggs and ate them with two more slices of bread. I had a second cup of coffee and caught myself pawing through the trash, looking for muffin bottoms. I yelled for Diesel, but there was no response.

I ran up the stairs and looked at the man in my bed. He was sound asleep, and from what I could see from the clothes on the floor and the half of him that wasn't covered by quilt, he was naked. I enjoyed the view for a couple minutes, thinking it would be nice to kiss the back of his neck, his bare shoulder, the small of his back . . . Good grief! Get a grip, Lizzy.

"Hey!" I yelled at him. "Wake up."

"I'm awake."

"I'm hungry," I told him.

"And?"

"And I'm not supposed to be. I'm not carrying the ladybug. Why am I still hungry?"

"Can we discuss this in five or six hours?"

"I'll weigh two hundred pounds by then. I just caught myself looking for muffin leavings."

"Honey, anyone would be tempted to do that. They were really good muffins."

"The cat ate them! They were in the *garbage*!"

"Yeah, that's a little extreme," he said. "If you come back to bed, I'll take your mind off it."

I mentally ticked off reasons to crawl back into bed. Number one: He was hot and mouth-wateringly handsome. Number two: I was almost certain he was a good person. Number three: He was already naked, so that awkward undressing moment would be cut in half. And here was the big, scary number four: I was possibly enamored. Diesel was fascinating, and hard as I tried to keep things in proper perspective, I found myself increasingly attracted to him. Of course, this morning I'd also felt that way about the muffins in the garbage.

"Returning to bed has some appeal," I told him, "but I have to go to work. Don't you want to get up and protect me?"

"No."

"What if Wulf gets me?"

"Wulf has crazy Steven Hatchet. He doesn't need you."

"Yes, but suppose he thinks I've got the charm and maybe even the rest of the inherited whatevers?"

"It's no big deal. He'll do a strip search,

and when he finds out you're clean, he'll turn you loose."

A strangled sound emerged from the back of my throat and my stomach got sick. "Ulk."

"You're right," Diesel said. "It would be more fun if I did the strip search."

"That's not what I was thinking!"

He swung his legs over the side of the bed. "I guess it was what *I* was thinking. Give me a minute and I'll drive you to the bakery."

I liked riding in Diesel's SUV. It still had new-car smell, the seats were leather, and everything worked.

"Is this a company car?" I asked him.

"I never thought of it that way, but I guess it is. Gwen had it waiting for me when I got here."

"Have you ever seen Gwen?"

"Yeah."

"Is she pretty?"

Diesel smiled. "Do you care?"

"I'm curious."

"She's pretty, but she's not my type," Diesel said.

"What's your type?"

"Easy."

"I guess that leaves me out, too."

"Yeah. And it's a real pain in the ass."

A light rain started to fall, and Diesel switched the wipers on. Even in bright sunlight, New England mostly looks practical. When it rains, it can be downright grim. The outside of the bakery is weathered gray clapboard, with nautical blue shutters, and the hand-painted sign over the door simply says DAZZLE'S. I like the way the building has aged, and that I have a sense of history when I walk through the front door. And I especially like that on a dark, rainy day, the inside light pours out through the two large display windows onto the sidewalk, like a beacon advertising cake and happiness.

Henley's Hardware is to one side in a structure almost as old as Dazzle's. The small, bedraggled saltbox on the other side of the bakery has changed hands twice in the short amount of time I've been here. The current occupants are trying to make a go of a vintage movie poster shop.

Diesel cruised past Vintage Posters, Dazzle's, and Henley's and turned at the corner. At this early hour, the bakery showroom was dark and the front door was locked. Diesel drove down the service alley running behind the bakery, and from half a block away, I could see light spilling out the open back door to the bakery kitchen.

"I guess if you have to go to work at this unholy hour, a bakery is about as good as it gets," Diesel said. "I wouldn't mind being surrounded by cakes and pies every morning."

I looked over at him. "You aren't gluttonously hungry, are you?"

"No. I'm *normally* hungry. How about you?"

"I'd eat your sneakers if they had barbecue sauce on them. It's not fair. You've got the charm, and I'm the one eating everything in sight."

"I guess you're the chosen one," Diesel said. "Too bad we aren't collecting the SALIGIA charms that control lust. You'd be thinner, and I'd be happier."

The thought sent a shudder through me. I already had a lot of lust for Diesel without help from an enchanted charm. I didn't want to contemplate enchanted lust. I mean, suppose I wanted Diesel with the same intensity I wanted a jelly doughnut or a Rice Krispies Treat! I might cripple him.

Diesel smiled.

"You didn't hear that, did you?" I asked him.

"No, but you were looking at me like I was a turkey dinner."

He parked in the small lot behind the bakery, cut the engine, and released his seat belt.

"You don't have to come in," I told him.

"Sure I do. I'm the big strong Unmentionable who's protecting you. I'm sticking to you like glue."

"I've changed my mind. I don't want you anywhere near me. I want you to go far, far away. I think it must be that the charm is too close to me. Maybe you should put it in a safe-deposit box or FedEx it to your boss."

"I can't give the charm to the BUM yet. I need to keep the charm until we get all the pieces and I'm sure we have the original Stone."

"I'm having a hard time thinking straight right now," I said. "I can't get my mind off bacon, but I'm sure I'll be fine without you. I have Clara and Glo to protect me."

I jumped out of the SUV, ran to the bakery door, and made shooing gestures at Diesel. Diesel watched me for a moment and took off.

"We have an order for sixty cupcakes for a lunchtime baby shower today," Clara said. "Yellow cake with pink icing."

A warm flush ran from my chest to my stomach. "I love yellow cake and pink icing."

"You look kind of goofy," Clara said. "Are you okay?"

"I'm fine. I was just thinking about the cakes."

Clara powered up the big bread mixer. "And don't forget Shirley increased her order."

I got butter and milk from the fridge and set it out on my workstation. "I'm on it."

Ten minutes later, I had a cauldron of cake batter in front of me.

"What are you doing?" Clara yelled from across the room.

"I'm making cake."

"No, you're not. You're eating cake. I've been watching you. You've eaten half the batter."

I stared into the bowl. Clara was right. There was a lot of batter missing.

"I've never seen you scarf down raw batter like that," Clara said. "What's going on?"

I told her about the SALIGIA Stones, Shirley's ladybug charm, and my food obsession.

"I'm on board with the Unmentionable thing," Clara said. "I understand that people have abilities in varying degrees and that sometimes those abilities are beyond normal. The SALIGIA Stones are different. They're a tough sell."

"Kind of Indiana Jones."

"Yeah. Maybe Diesel has doctored the story. I could see him trying to get his hands on something valuable. I'm having trouble buying the hell-on-earth bit."

I nodded in agreement. I was attracted to Diesel, but let's be honest, it wasn't much of a stretch to think he would fib if it suited his purposes.

"What do you think I should do?" I asked Clara. "I can't lock him out of my house. He just lets himself back in. And I feel better about him than Wulf. At least when Diesel's around, I don't have to worry about getting burned."

And he looks wonderful with or without

clothes, I thought, and I like the way he feels when he's next to me.

"Just be careful, and try to be smart," Clara said. "And if you feel really uncomfortable about it all, you're welcome to stay upstairs with me. And for goodness sakes, stop eating the cake batter."

"I'm hoping after Diesel and the charm are out of my space for a while I'll get back to normal."

"That would be good, because at the rate you're snacking on batter, we're not going to have anything to sell today."

CHAPTER FIFTEEN

At five minutes to eight, Clara stopped at my station to watch me tube pink icing onto the vanilla cupcakes.

"You haven't eaten anything for almost an hour now," she said.

I set my pastry bag aside and took up a shaker of red sugar sprinkles. "Yeah. And I have no desire to eat anything ever again."

The back door banged open and Glo charged in.

"Oops, sorry," she said. "Guess I pushed the door too hard. My mind was someplace else."

"Where was it?" Clara wanted to know.

"It wasn't in any place good. I have a big problem."

"Gosh, imagine that," Clara said.

Glo shrugged out of her black sweat-shirt and into her bakery smock. "A couple months ago, I was at a party and one of the guys worked for an animal rescue group. He was a really cute guy, and that's such a good cause. I mean, how could you not like a guy who rescues sad little baby animals? Anyway, I sort of signed up to give a home to one of the sad little abandoned babies."

"Sort of?" Clara asked.

"Okay, I totally signed. It was a moment of weakness, and this guy was such a hot-tie. And I didn't know back then that my landlord was allergic. And the bottom line is, I totally forgot all about it until the critter was delivered first thing this morning."

"I don't want it," Clara said.

"I know!" Glo wailed. "And Lizzy already has a kitty. I'm so screwed. I don't know what to do."

"Just give it back to the rescue people," Clara said.

Glo buttoned her smock. "I tried that. They said possession was nine-tenths of the law, and they wouldn't take it back. I guess some of these animals have behavioral problems."

"And you agreed to take on a pet with behavioral problems?"

"Did I mention how cute the guy was? And that he drove a Corvette?"

Clara and I exchanged glances.

"Where's the problem child now?" Clara asked.

"In my car," Glo said.

I had a vision of some poor, scared kitten locked up in Glo's car all day.

"You can't leave it in your car," I told her. "I suppose I could see if it gets along with Cat 7143."

Glo's eyes opened wide. "Omigosh, that would be so awesome. That would be amazing!"

Glo ran out the door, and a moment later, she returned with a monkey on a leash.

"That's a monkey," I said to her.

"Yeah."

"I thought you got something from animal rescue."

"Actually, it was Monkey Rescue."

"I don't want a monkey," I told her. "I'm not a monkey person."

The monkey did a gruesome monkey smile, its lips pulled back to reveal a mouthful of monkey teeth, his monkey eyes overly big and bright, as if he was trying hard to look happy but was completely insane.

"Look how cute he is," Glo said. "And he likes you. He's smiling."

I thought he looked like he was planning to chop me up into little pieces and stuff me into the blender.

"I have to open the bakery," Clara said. "You guys are going to have to work something out with the monkey. He can't stay here." Her attention moved to the back door and her mouth dropped open. "Holy cow," she said.

It was Wulf. He was standing in the doorway, his dark eyes fixed on me. He was wearing a black leather jacket, black slacks, black boots, and his glossy black hair was tied back at the nape of his neck. I felt a chill run through me, and I went breathless at the sight of him. He was terrifyingly compelling.

"I believe you have something that be-longs to me," Wulf said.

I opened my mouth to deny it, but it took a while for sound to come out. "N-n-no," I finally said.

Wulf moved toward me. "We'll see."

I scrambled to the other side of the workstation, putting the island between us. "I swear I haven't got *anything*."

"Stay away from her," Glo said. "Or else."

Wulf's focus never wavered. His eyes were fixed on me with an intensity that made my skin prickle.

"Come here," he said. "Trust me, you don't want to make me angry."

Glo was standing by the table we used for the meat pies. She snatched a garlic clove out of a bin and threw it at Wulf. It hit him in the side of the head and bounced off onto the floor.

"Death to vampires," Glo said.

Wulf flicked his eyes to the garlic. "If only it was that easy," he said.

"Lenny's inheritance got blown up with the chicken, and Diesel has Shirley's," I told Wulf.

There was a flash of fire and lots of

smoke, and when the smoke cleared, Wulf was gone.

The monkey peeked out from behind Glo. "Eep!"

That pretty much summed it up for all of us.

"I'm impressed," I said to Glo. "You were really gutsy to throw that garlic at him."

"Yeah, but now I might fall over," she said. "I've gotta sit down. I need a cupcake or something. Holy bejeezus, he's one scary guy."

Clara scooted a chair under Glo, and I gave her a cupcake. The monkey looked freaked, so I gave him a cupcake, too. Everyone took a moment to breathe.

"Okay, I feel better," Glo said. "I'm not going to throw up or anything."

"Someone's pounding on the front door," Clara said. "I'm ten minutes late to open."

Glo and I followed Clara into the shop and looked out at Shirley hammering on the door. She was bug-eyed, and her hair was Wild Woman. She was wearing a mis-buttoned white shirt, and her skirt was twisted off center.

"Eek! Eek, eek, eeeeek!" Shirley said, charging into the bakery, waving her arms.

"Boogie man ramma framma me. Icky poopy." Shirley gave a shiver and made spitting sounds. "Pthu, pthu."

"Something bad happened?" Clara asked.

Shirley nodded her head and gave herself a frantic pat down. "Grabby flabby big boys, bum, scooter pie." Her eyes narrowed. "Slippery fur forest and brown Betty!"

"We don't make scooter pies," Glo said.

Shirley pointed to her crotch. "Scooter pie!"

A wave of nausea slipped through my stomach. "You were strip-searched."

Shirley put her fingertip to her nose. "Beck."

"Was it Wulf?" I asked.

Shirley nodded. "And peepee Snatch Bagger."

"You should go to the police," Glo said.

Shirley rolled her eyes and pointed to her mouth. "Snot gobble."

"Yeah, that's a problem," Glo said, "but we could translate."

I gave Shirley a cupcake to calm her down. "Language isn't the biggest problem. I'm not sure the police can do anything with Wulf. Either he's a figment of our imaginations, or else he actually disappears in a puff of smoke."

Diesel strolled in from the kitchen. "The smoke is just theatrics. Wulf thinks it's fun. The problem would be with containment."

"What are you doing back at the bakery?" I asked him. "Did you know Wulf was here?"

"No. I knew food was here."

"Wulf was here, but Glo hit him with a clove of garlic and scared him away. Or maybe he left because I told him you had Shirley's inheritance."

Diesel looked over at Shirley. "Shirley looks like she had a rough night."

"More like a rough morning," I told him. "Wulf came looking for the charm."

"Was Wulf alone?" Diesel asked.

Shirley held up two fingers. "Nut sucker by Snatch Bagger." She jumped around making slashing motions like she had a sword.

"I'm not getting an exact translation on this," Diesel said.

Shirley stopped jumping and her eyes practically popped out of her head, spotting the monkey for the first time. "Jeepers!"

The monkey was sitting on a counter,

stuffing his face with cupcakes. He realized everyone was staring at him and his mouth opened and a chunk of cake fell out.

"If the board of health sees this, I'll be shut down," Clara said. "It'll be the first time in four hundred years the bakery was cited."

Diesel rocked back on his heels and grinned at the monkey. "Carl?"

"Eep!" The monkey stood, squinted at Diesel, and gave him the finger.

"Looks like you know each other," I said.

"Our paths crossed in Trenton," Diesel said. "How did he get here?"

"Monkey Rescue," Glo told him. "He was abandoned."

"Figures," Diesel said.

The monkey gave him the finger again.

"Does he do that all the time?" I asked Diesel.

"Not *all* the time."

"I got him by mistake," Glo said. "And now we don't know what to do with him."

"You could turn him loose and let him go play in traffic," Diesel said.

Glo, Clara, and I looked horrified.

Diesel helped himself to a red velvet cupcake. "I'll take him off your hands if

Lizzy only works until noon. After noon, she's mine."

"Deal," Clara said. "Just get him out of here."

Diesel left with the monkey and a dozen mini cupcakes.

"I'm afraid your cupcakes aren't ready yet," I told Shirley.

Shirley shrugged. She didn't care. She dusted off her hands.

"You're done with cupcakes?" I asked her.

She nodded.

"Completely?"

She nodded again, rebuttoned her blouse, smoothed her hair down, and left.

"I know I should be happy for her, but she was my best customer," Clara said. "I need twenty new customers to make up for the loss of all those cupcakes."

Diesel strolled through the front door of the bakery precisely at noon. I was transferring the last of the lunch pies into the refrigerated display case, and Glo was waiting on two women. The women turned and stared at Diesel, and one gave the other a nudge with her elbow.

Diesel looked like he was used to the stares and nudges. He stood just inside the door, thumbs stuck into his jeans pockets, not smiling, not frowning. Waiting.

"Be with you in a minute," I told him.

I changed out of my chef jacket, grabbed my sweatshirt, tote bag, a couple bottles of water, and a box of meat pies, and I returned to the front of the shop. I smiled at the ladies and waved at Glo.

Diesel put his hand to the small of my back and ushered me out the door. "That box smells like lunch."

"We had some meat pies that weren't pretty enough to sell, but were still okay to eat."

"How's your appetite?"

"Back to normal. And Shirley canceled her cupcake order. Apparently, everything gets back to normal pretty quickly once the charm is removed."

Diesel was parked at the curb in front of the bakery. We both got into the Cayenne, and I noticed Carl was buckled into the backseat. Carl gave me a little finger wave and the scary-monkey smile.

"What's going on with the find-a-home-for-Carl program?" Diesel asked.

I gave a meat pie to Diesel and one to Carl, and I took one for myself. "Glo's trying, but it doesn't look hopeful."

"No surprise," Diesel said.

"Eep!" from the backseat.

"I hate hearing *Eep*," Diesel said, checking Carl out in the rearview mirror. "*Eep* is never good."

I looked over my shoulder and saw that Carl had meat pie all down the front of him and was carefully picking it out of his monkey fur with his little monkey fingers.

"No problem," I said to Diesel. "He's grooming."

Twenty minutes later, we were in Beverly looking for Mark More's apartment. We were close to the warehouse, in an area that was a mix of commercial and residential properties. There were small businesses at the sidewalk level on More's street and apartments above. According to Gwen, More lived in one of those second-floor apartments.

"There," I said to Diesel. "Number 29. He's in the apartment above the dry cleaner."

Diesel parked half a block away and

locked Carl in the car. We took four steps, and Carl banged on the window.

"I think he wants to go with us," I told Diesel.

Diesel turned and looked at Carl, and Carl shrunk back into his seat, hands in lap. We took four more steps, and Carl blasted us with the horn.

Beep, beep, beep!

"Jeez Louise," I said to Diesel. "He's going to have the entire neighborhood out on the sidewalk, and we'll get charged with animal cruelty."

Diesel walked back to the car, opened the door, and Carl bounced out.

"Behave yourself," Diesel said to Carl.

Carl nodded his head and did the monkey smile. When Diesel turned his back to walk away, Carl gave him the finger.

"This isn't a normal monkey," I said to Diesel.

"Tell me about it."

CHAPTER SIXTEEN

Diesel opened the downstairs door to Mark's apartment, and we all trooped upstairs into the living room. Mark had only the bare essentials for furniture. A couch with a quilt draped over the back, a side table with a table lamp, a flat screen television set into a shelf system. Every other space was taken up with gnomes crammed into an eclectic assortment of glass-fronted display cases. China gnomes, plaster gnomes, wooden gnomes, bejeweled gnomes, paper gnomes, books dedicated to gnomes, intricately carved marble gnomes.

Carl rushed up to one of the cases and stared at the gnomes. "Eee?"

"Gnomes," I told him.

He tapped on the glass, but the gnomes didn't do anything. He frowned and tapped harder. He looked up at Diesel.

"That's as interesting as it gets," Diesel said to Carl.

Carl moved on to the open shelves around the TV and stopped in front of a bobblehead gnome. He carefully touched the head with his fingertip, and the head bounced and jiggled. He looked at it more closely and touched it again. More vigorous bouncing. He grabbed the head, and it came off in his hand.

"Eep!"

He set the head back on the spring, but the head fell off and rolled onto the floor. Carl looked up at Diesel.

"Broken," Diesel said.

Carl thought about it a beat, gave the headless gnome the finger, and kicked the head across the floor.

The gnome collection extended into the dining room and then gave way to stuffed rabbits. Big rabbits, little rabbits, pink rabbits, fluffy rabbits. Every kind of imaginable bunny. They were all stacked up in a jumble in the two far corners of the room.

Carl carefully skirted the two piles and moved into the short hall that led to the bedroom, on his best behavior after the gnome beheading.

"Mark has some strange collections," I said to Diesel. "Locks, gnomes, and stuffed rabbits. It's like he indiscriminately decides to collect something."

We started to follow Carl, and we both stopped at the same time.

"What the heck is that smell?" I asked, hand over my nose.

"Animal," Diesel said.

"Dead?"

"No. Alive."

"It must be Bigfoot."

There was a single bedroom at the end of the hall. I let Diesel go first, since he was the indestructible half of the team, and I hung back.

"Oh man," Diesel said. "You have to come see this."

I crept up behind him and peeked into a room filled floor to ceiling with cages housing slinky, sleek-coated, beady-eyed ferrets.

"This is a strange man," Diesel said. "He

could have chosen stamps or coins or bottle glass, but he decided to collect ferrets."

Carl looked mesmerized. He was in the middle of the room, his arms at his sides, knuckles resting on the floor, eyes wide as they went cage to cage.

"I think it's safe to assume Mark didn't inherit a ferret," I said to Diesel.

"I can't see him inheriting a gnome or a bunny, either. My money is still on the lock collection. Let's see what's in the kitchen."

At first glance, the kitchen looked cluttered but normal. At closer inspection, it became obvious all the bottles and tins were filled with olive oil. Virgin olive oil, slut olive oil, olive oil infused with herbs.

"At least this is healthy," I said to Diesel.

"Only if you eat it. I don't think collecting it does much for you."

From the corner of my eye, I caught something streak across the floor.

"Did you see that?" I asked Diesel.

"What?"

"Something ran through the kitchen."

There was a scratchy, scurrying sound, and a ferret popped up on the counter behind all the bottles of oil.

"Maybe he kept one as a pet," I said.

"Maybe he . . . yow!" A ferret was climbing up my pants leg and another ran over my shoe. "The cages in the bedroom were closed, weren't they?" I asked.

"They were, but I'm guessing they aren't now."

We got to the bedroom just as Carl was releasing the last ferret.

"Bad monkey," Diesel said, pointing his finger at Carl.

"Eee?"

Diesel scooped up a small black ferret. "I can't believe I'm saying this, but we're going to have to get the ferrets back in their cages."

They were running between our legs, and rolling around like balls. "They're having a good time," I said.

Diesel snagged another one and stuffed it into a cage. "Yeah, I wish the same was true for me. Help me out here. Mark isn't going to be in a cooperative frame of mind if he comes home and finds out we did the *Born Free* thing with his ferrets."

I caught one, but it squished out of my hands. Something crashed in the kitchen, and Diesel and I froze for a moment before I took off at a run. "I'm on it."

The kitchen was alive with ferrets. They were chasing one another up cupboards and over countertops, knocking over bottles of olive oil. A large tin had tipped, and olive oil was spilling down the side of the counter and pooling on the floor. The ferrets were lapping it up and skating through it, tracking olive oil everywhere. The entire kitchen floor was slick with it.

There was a giant crash in the living room. I stepped out to investigate and went flat on my back in the oil. It took a couple beats to catch my breath, and then I crawled hands and knees through the dining room toward the living room. Bunny stuffing was scattered across the dining room, mixed with the oil. And I suspect a ferret or two might have relieved itself in the excitement, because the dining room wasn't smelling great and there were a lot of raisins on the floor. One of the large display cases had been tipped over in the living room, and I was looking at a lot of dead gnomes.

Carl was flattened against a wall, his hands over his eyes.

I was still on all fours, and I saw Diesel's boots come into my line of vision. His hand hooked into my jeans' waistband, he hoisted me to my feet, and he looked me over. His first reaction was a grimace and then a smile.

"You're a mess," he said. "And you smell like a bad zoo."

"Have you seen the kitchen?"

"No, and I don't want to. The disaster in the dining room was enough for me. From the amount of oil you've got in your hair and soaked into your clothes, I'm guessing there was some spillage in the kitchen."

"Do you remember when the tanker *Exxon Valdez* broke apart in Alaska? It was like that."

"Here's the new plan," Diesel said. "There's no way we're going to round up the ferrets. We're going to sneak out like thieves in the night and never tell a soul what happened here."

"Works for me."

Five minutes later, we were in the Porsche and on our way to Marblehead. Diesel had the window rolled down, and Carl was holding his nose in the backseat.

"As soon as we get you out of this car, I'm turning it back to Gwen," Diesel said. "My advice to her will be to push it off a bridge."

"I must have crawled in something going through the dining room. I think the ferrets were doing the nasty with some of the bunnies."

"Honey, you smell bad way beyond the nasty."

I closed my eyes and slumped back in my seat. "Can we review what's happened here? In the interest of saving the world from a hellish future, we've got some poor woman talking nonsense, we've blown a man's house to smithereens, and now we've totally trashed another man's apartment. And if that's not enough, we've acquired a cat with one eye, and a monkey."

Diesel looked at me. "Your point?"

I blew out a sigh. "I don't have a point. My life is out of control. Everything was looking so good a couple days ago, with my own house and a terrific job. And now everything's facaca."

"Your life isn't out of control," Diesel said. "It's expanded."

I rolled the concept of an expanded life around in my head for a couple miles, and by the time we parked in front of my house, I was almost buying it. The Spook Patrol was back on the sidewalk, cameras and

Spook-detection gadgets at the ready. I stepped out of the car, everyone rushed up to me, and everyone gasped and fell back.

"Smells like ecto-slime," one of the Patrollers said, holding his ghost gizmo at arm's reach, pointing it at me.

"It had to be a really nasty spirit," another guy said. "Like a level five."

Spookmaster Mel spotted Carl getting out of the SUV. "What's with the monkey?"

"We're babysitting," I told him.

The gizmo guy wanded Carl with his ghost-o-meter. "No demonic possession registering."

"Maybe you need new batteries in that thing," Diesel said, opening my front door, shoving Carl into the house.

"So what does he do?" I asked Diesel. "Does he use a kitty litter? Do we need monkey diapers?"

Carl looked at me and gave me the finger.

"He uses the bathroom," Diesel said.

I didn't know if that was good or bad. I wasn't excited about sharing my bathroom with a monkey.

Cat 7143 strolled into the living room and went into killer cat mode when he spotted Carl. Arched back, bushy tail, hair on end, bloodcurdling growl.

Carl went rigid, eyes wide. "Eeeep!"

"Be nice," I said to Cat. "This is Carl. He's a houseguest." I turned to Carl. "This is Cat 7143."

Carl took a cautious step forward and smiled his insane, scary-monkey smile at Cat. Cat hissed and slashed at Carl, and Carl scampered up Diesel's leg and hunkered down on his shoulder, digging his boney monkey fingers into Diesel's shirt.

"You're going to have to deal with this," I said to Diesel. "I have to take a shower."

Diesel swung Carl down off his shoulder. "No problemo. Let me know if you need help. I've been told I'm good with soap."

I thought about rolling my eyes, but I'd been doing a lot of that lately. I also refrained from sighing, grunting, or doing what I really wanted to do, which was take him up on his offer. I ran upstairs, stripped, and decided the clothes were unsalvageable. I found a garbage bag under the sink, stuffed the clothes into the bag, and tossed the bag out the second-floor window. The bathroom instantly smelled better. Huge relief. The smell wasn't originating with me.

I stepped into the shower and let the water beat down on me. It took every drop of hot water in the house and a lot of shampoo to get the oil out of my hair. I did a fast blow-dry, got dressed in clean jeans and a long-sleeved T-shirt, and I went in search of Diesel.

I found him talking on his cell phone in the kitchen. Cat was hiding somewhere, and Carl was sitting on one of the bar stools. Somewhere toward the end of the shower, I was overwhelmed with a craving for chocolate. Now that I was in the kitchen, the quest for chocolate occupied my entire brain. I snatched three bars of baker's chocolate from the cupboard and cracked one open.

"As much as I would like more muffins, we don't have time for baking," Diesel said, eyeing the chocolate.

I shoved some chocolate into my mouth and put the other two bars in my jeans pocket. "I'm not baking. I'm eating." I looked around. "I need fudge and marshmallow. Make a list. We need to go to the store.

Costco. We can buy cases there, so I won't run out." I broke more off the chocolate bar and nibbled at it. "And I really need some Snickers bars. A couple cases of those. Are you writing this down?"

"You've got gluttonitis again," Diesel said. "I've got the charm on me, and it looks like it's leaking out to you."

"I do not have gluttonitis. That's ridiculous. I'm just making a food list. Suppose there was a hurricane, and I didn't have any Snickers, and the stores ran out? What then?" I opened a jar of peanut butter and ate it with my finger between munches of chocolate.

"Stop eating," Diesel said.

I swooped a big glob of peanut butter onto my finger. "Mind your own beeswax."

I had the finger with the peanut butter almost to my mouth, and Diesel grabbed my wrist.

"I'm asking you to stop," he said. "If you don't listen to me, I'll *make* you stop."

My eyes were narrowed, fixed on the peanut butter stuck to the end of my finger. I *wanted* the peanut butter *bad*. "Let go," I said to Diesel.

Diesel put his mouth to my finger and sucked the peanut butter off.

"Hey, Mister Jerk," I said, "that was *my* peanut butter."

And then it hit me. Heat. And a rush so strong it almost knocked me to my knees. His mouth had been warm and wet, and there was some tongue involved.

"Jeez," I said on a whisper.

He was inches from me, our bodies barely touching. His eyes were dark and serious, and his hand was still wrapped around my wrist. For a long moment, I was sure he was going to kiss me, but the emotion changed in his eyes, and he pulled back.

"We need to talk to Mark," he said.

"Un-hunh."

The corners of his mouth tipped into a small smile. "Are you hungry?"

I nodded.

"For chocolate?"

I gave him my squinty-eyed eat-dirt-and-die look. He knew perfectly well what I wanted. "I'm hungry for *everything*," I said.

Diesel grinned wide. "I like the sound of that."

"Can you read my mind now?"

"Honey, it doesn't take magic to read your mind on this one." He gave me a kiss on the forehead and released me. "Let's roll. Wulf is out there on the hunt. I can feel his energy polluting my air space."

The Spook Patrol jumped to attention when we exited the house. One of the guys shoved his gizmo at Diesel, and Diesel snatched it from him and threw it across the street.

"This is getting old," Diesel said. "I'm about done with the Spook Patrol."

CHAPTER SEVENTEEN

The More Is Better front office was manned by a tastefully dressed older woman. She was at her desk, hard at work painting her nails dark blue, when we walked in.

"We're looking for Mark," Diesel said.

"In the back," she told him, smiling, waving us through without so much as an eyebrow raise that one of us was a monkey. I guess nothing surprises you when you work for a man who owns forty ferrets.

Mark was in the warehouse rearranging his locks, returning them to the original pile. So far as I could see, no one else was in the building. The mint business didn't seem to be booming.

"How's it going?" Diesel said as an opener.

"Someone broke in last night and moved my locks."

Chump change, I thought. Wait until you see your apartment.

Mark shut the backhoe down and glared at Diesel. "I don't suppose you know anything about this."

"Has it happened before?"

"Never," Mark said.

"It looks like Wulf's work," Diesel told him.

"Wulf?"

"Gerwulf Grimoire. My age and height. Dresses in black. Looks like he's down a quart of blood. He's a really bad guy, and he wants your inheritance."

"He was here this morning!" Mark said. "Caught me in the office, fixing coffee. Scared the crap out of me. I told him I wasn't talking about the inheritance, and he put his hand to the coffee machine, and it caught fire. *Whoosh.* Went up in a fireball, and nothing was left but black glass and melted plastic. He said he could do the same to me. Is that true?"

Diesel shrugged. "Hard to say if he could actually melt you."

"I can't figure if I'm more scared of Uncle Phil coming at me from his grave or this Gerwulf guy roasting me like the coffee machine."

"So you didn't tell him about the inheritance?"

"No."

Diesel smiled. Friendly. "Would you like to tell me about it?"

"No."

So much for the smile.

"Call me when you're ready to talk about the inheritance," Diesel said, handing Mark a business card. "You haven't seen the last of Wulf."

Mark focused on Carl. "What's with the monkey?"

"We're not sure," I told him. "It's complicated."

The woman was gone from the front office when we left. Probably, she had no reason to stay after she finished her nails. We loaded ourselves into the Cayenne, and Diesel drove out of the lot.

"Where now?" I asked him.

"Salem."

"And?"

"He's at Lenny's house."

"Wulf? How do you know?"

"I just know."

The black Ferrari was at the curb, just as Diesel had predicted. Wulf was standing on the sidewalk by the front of the car. He was wearing a black duster, and his hair was still tied back in a low ponytail. He was watching a guy poking around in the rubble that used to be Lenny's house. The guy was dressed up like he was straight out of a low-budget Renaissance fair. He was wearing a mustard yellow long-sleeved hoodie under a tunic sort of thing with a coat of arms painted onto the front. A sword was stuck into a leather belt and scabbard, his scrawny legs were encased in green tights, and he was kicking through the ash in what might have been running shoes but were now unrecognizable. He was in his late twenties, with scraggly orange hair and a body that looked as soft and plump as a fresh-baked dinner roll.

"Steven Hatchet," Diesel said. "Hard at work for his lord and master."

"Does Wulf always make his captives dress like that?"

"No. Hatchet's a Medieval nut. If you take his tunic and tights away, he'll sit and sulk."

We parked behind the Ferrari, but Wulf never turned to look.

"Does he know we're here?" I asked Diesel.

"Yep."

"Is he happy?"

"Nope."

We got out of the car and ambled over to Wulf. Carl stayed in the Porsche, his monkey eyes huge and black as he peeped out the window.

"So how's it going?" Diesel said to Wulf. "How's Aunt Sophie?"

Wulf turned his head toward Diesel and looked amused but didn't go so far as a smile. His features were sharper than Diesel's. Diesel's eyebrows were fierce, and Wulf's eyebrows were raven wings. Wulf's nose was straight, his mouth was not as wide as Diesel's but oddly sensuous, his skin was ghostly pale.

Hatchet was sifting through ashes in what used to be Lenny's kitchen. He looked our way and unsheathed his sword. "Sire," he said, "dost thou need my protection? Are these crude and lowly persons bothersome?"

"Continue your search," Wulf said, his voice soft, his face devoid of expression. Only the barest whisper of a sigh hinted at his foul mood.

"It would be awkward if he found it while we were both here," Diesel said to Wulf. "We'd have to wrestle for it."

"I always won when we were kids," Wulf said. "I doubt much has changed."

"*Everything* has changed," Diesel said.

Wulf considered that and looked away, keeping his focus on Hatchet.

"Where's Lenny More?" Diesel asked.

"He told me what I needed to know, and I released him."

"Unharmed?"

"More or less."

Diesel followed Wulf's eyes to Hatchet. "Nice minion you've got there. What do they call that thing he's wearing? Is that a tunic?"

"Is there a point to this?" Wulf asked.

"Just hangin' out," Diesel said.

Wulf glanced at my hand. "You're hanging out with a woman wearing my brand."

"Cows get branded," Diesel said. "Women, no. And she's with me."

"For now, cousin."

"Forever."

"We'll see," Wulf said.

His eyes locked onto mine, and for a long moment, I was held captive with no clue to his thoughts. What I knew for certain was that I saw power and passion. I stepped back into Diesel, relieved when I felt him pressed into my back, his hand at my waist.

"I should be moving along," I said, making an effort not to gasp for air, praying my voice wasn't shaking. "The monkey is waiting."

Omigod, I thought. Did I just say *the monkey is waiting* to the liege lord of evil? I'm such a dork!

"Methinks a dastardly event occurred here, sire," Hatchet said, standing in a cloud of soot in the vicinity of Lenny's dining room. "I fear infidels have sacked the keep."

"I suppose that would be us," Diesel said. "We sacked the keep."

I waved at Hatchet. "Farewell, good knight. Fear not for the infidels."

"Safe journey, fair lady," he called back.

"Considerate of you to think of Carl," Diesel said to me, grinning, his arm draped across my shoulders, moving me toward the Porsche.

"I panicked."

"It's okay. The party was over."

"Do you know what I'd really like? A funnel cake. I went to a Renaissance fair once, and they had funnel cakes. An apple fritter would be good, too."

"Later."

"No. Now. I need it now! I feel weak. I need fried dough."

"This would be funny if it wasn't so awful," Diesel said, opening the car door for me. "You can't have fried dough. You'll get fat."

"I don't care if I get fat."

"I have to find a safe place other than my pocket to put the charm," Diesel said. "Keeping you away from food is turning into a full-time job. And I have no idea where to go to find fried dough."

"I could find some," I told him. "Give me your keys. I'll drive."

"Not gonna happen."

I tried to grab the keys out of his hand, but he held them high over my head.

"Give me the keys!"

"Nope."

I jumped for the keys, but I couldn't reach them.

"You need to control yourself," he said.

I clawed at his shirt, trying to get his arm lower. "I could control myself if I had a doughnut."

He shoved the keys into his jeans pocket. "No more doughnuts."

"That's mean. I need food. I can't think. I'm wasting away." I plunged my hand into his pocket and fumbled for the keys.

Diesel sucked air. "You keep fondling me like that, and I might have to marry you."

"I'm not fondling you. I'm looking for the keys!"

"Could you look a little more gently? You're scaring my boys."

"Sorry."

"No need to apologize. It's the most fun I've had since I met you."

I took a step back, and something crunched under my foot. I looked down and saw that it was a gold charm. I carefully picked it up, and it immediately buzzed in my hand and glowed.

"This is it," I whispered to Diesel. "It's another bug. It looks like a cockroach."

We looked back at Wulf and Hatchet. They weren't paying any attention to us. They didn't know we'd found the charm. Hatchet was still sifting through the debris.

"Better to be lucky than to be good," Diesel said. "Let's roll."

I buckled myself in and watched Diesel as he pulled the Porsche into traffic. "Is it enough to have two pieces of the inheritance?"

Diesel gave me Shirley's ladybug. "You tell me. Put the two pieces together in your hand and see if they do anything special."

I held the ladybug and the cockroach in my hand. They were warm, and they buzzed, but nothing else happened.

"What did you expect?" I asked Diesel. "Is there a black cloud forming over the SUV?"

"No black cloud. Also, no light beacon directing us to the missing piece."

"I'd rather see a beacon directing us to fried dough."

"Honey, I'd get you fried dough, but honest to God, I'm afraid you'd explode, and I'd have Lizzy guts all over the car."

I made a big effort not to groan or sigh or grind my teeth, and I gave the two charms back to him. "Now what?"

"Now we go home and regroup. I'm hoping Mark will leave work, freak out when he sees his apartment, and call me."

"I'm sort of afraid to go home. I'll want to eat everything."

"I won't let you eat everything."

"Promise?"

"Yes."

Okay, I could relax. Diesel was in control. It would all be okeydokey. No worries. Just sit back and watch the world go by.

"Stop!" I yelled. "Go back. *Go back.*"

Diesel hit the brakes and pulled to the side of the road. "What?"

"You just passed a supermarket! I don't have enough butter. And I need cereal. I want to make sure I have enough Raisin Bran. I mean, what if I ran out of Raisin Bran in the middle of the night? What would I do?"

Diesel thunked his forehead on the steering wheel. "I thought there was someone dead on the side of the road. Don't yell out like that."

"It felt like an emergency."

Diesel eased back into traffic. "Raisin Bran is not an emergency."

"Easy for you to say."

The Spook Patrol was gone when we parked in front of my house. Probably off getting their gizmo fixed after Diesel pitched it into the road. I checked my mailbox and took out three bills and a letter from a publisher. I read the publisher letter immediately.

"Well?" Diesel asked.

"Another rejection," I said, returning the letter to its envelope.

"Persistence," Diesel said.

"Persistence," I repeated.

Cat 7143 gave Carl the evil eye when we walked through the door, but he didn't hiss or slash Carl's chest open, so I figured that was a good sign. Carl played it safe and wrapped himself around Diesel's leg until we made it to the kitchen, where he could scamper up a cabinet and sit on the top of the refrigerator.

I got my notebook out and turned to the tabbed section that held recipes in progress.

"As long as I have this opportunity at home, I'm going to work on my cookbook," I told Diesel.

"Are you sure that's a good idea, being that you're under the influence of Shirley's glutton charm?"

"I don't have a choice. My house is sagging."

I thumbed through a couple pages and settled on biscuits. I wanted a savory biscuit, and I was working at selecting cheese and herbs. I went to the fridge and got milk, plus a pound of butter, a chunk of Vermont cheddar, a chunk of Emmentaler, and a chunk of Gruyère. I hauled a sack of flour out of the pantry and looked at the butter. There was only half a pound.

"What happened to the butter?" I asked Diesel.

"You took it to the pantry with you."

"Yes, but now there's only half a pound."

Diesel's eyebrows raised a fraction of

an inch. "Your face is greasy. Looks to me like you scarfed down the butter."

"You said you wouldn't let me eat every-thing!"

"You were sneaky. You ate in the pantry."

I went back to the refrigerator for more butter, but there wasn't any more.

"I'm out of butter," I said to Diesel. "Now I can't make biscuits."

"Make half a batch," Diesel said. "Or make something else."

"We should have stopped at the store."

"Put the cheese down," Diesel said.

"Excuse me?"

"You were eating the cheese."

I looked at the wedge of cheese in my hand. Sure enough, someone had eaten some of it.

"It has my cooties," I said. "I might as well finish it."

Diesel snatched the cheese from me. "No."

I narrowed my eyes at him. "It's *mine*."

"Not anymore, it isn't."

I kicked at him, but he moved away.

"Behave yourself," Diesel said.

"And if I don't?" I asked him. "What then?

Would you have to punish me? Would you put me over your knee?"

"Uh-oh," Diesel said. "You're sounding like Lenny."

"Lizzy's been a bad girl," I said to him. "Lizzy needs a good spanking."

"Lizzy needs to think about something else," Diesel said.

"Like what? Handcuffs? Do you have handcuffs? How about this? How about you spank me while I eat an entire jar of peanut butter with my tongue while I'm handcuffed." Even as I said this, I was feeling ridiculous, but I couldn't stop the trash from coming out of my mouth. "I'm possessed," I said to Diesel. "Lenny's charm's got me."

"Yeah," Diesel said. "This is so pathetic. This is the opportunity of a lifetime. Fantasy number seven and number eight on my bucket list. I've got a woman asking me to handcuff her and spank her . . . and I can't bring myself to do it."

"Maybe you should just lock me in a closet."

Diesel wrapped an arm around me and kissed me on the top of my head. "I'd be afraid you'd eat your socks. I'm going to take you to the bakery so Clara and Glo can keep an eye on you while I find a safe place to stash the two charms."

"I thought you didn't want to do that."

"I prefer keeping them on me, but obviously, that's not working for us."

CHAPTER EIGHTEEN

Clara had me sitting on a stool in the middle of the bakery kitchen. There was food all around but nothing I could reach. If I got off the stool, Clara and Glo yelled at me to get back. Clara was washing down work spaces, and Glo was tending the shop. Without warning, several of the machines turned themselves on. Excess frosting in the big mixer spewed across the room, the top popped off the blender Clara was using and rasberry puree exploded out at her, and the food processor danced across the counter.

Glo rushed into the kitchen. "Omigosh,

did I do this? I was trying to memorize a translation spell, but I might have accidentally read something from the mechanical transportation spell on the next page."

Personally, I was going with power surge. I didn't want to think Glo could turn appliances on by mumbling a few words.

Clara pulled the plugs on the blender and the food processor, and the mixer shut itself off. Puree dripped off Clara's nose, and her hair was dotted with butter cream frosting.

Clara put two hands flat on the island and did a ten-count. She took a deep, cleansing breath and looked at Glo. "Isn't it time for you to go home?"

"Officially, I have ten minutes left on the time clock," Glo said.

"I'm excusing you early. If you don't leave in the next two minutes, I might strangle you."

"That's excellent," Glo said, "because I thought I'd visit Shirley as soon as I got off work. I'm pretty sure I found a translation spell. It won't reverse the spell I put on Shirley, but it will translate gobbledegook."

"You should leave bad enough alone,"

Clara said to Glo. "If the spell doesn't work, it could make things worse."

Glo tucked her book under her arm and hung her tote bag on her shoulder. "Yes, but if it *does* work, it'll get Shirley talking again."

"Take Lizzy with you," Clara said. "I can't watch her and clean up this mess at the same time."

Glo drove a slightly used Mini Cooper that had been painted to look like a yellow cab. We squeezed ourselves into the car, and Glo drove the short distance to Shirley's apartment.

"I hope she's home," Glo said, parking at the curb, looking over at Shirley's building. "I really think I've got it this time."

We took the stairs, and Glo led the way down the hall to Shirley's door. I knocked, and Shirley answered immediately.

"Beetle ears," Shirley said, all cheerful.

I looked past her and saw she was at work packing food into cardboard boxes and grocery bags. There were boxes loaded with Pop-Tarts, jars of jam, bags of cookies, canned corn, tomato sauce, and mayonnaise. It was a glutton dream come true, and I felt my heart quicken and my eyes glaze over.

"What are you doing with all this stuff?" Glo asked Shirley.

"Shoe horn for poor poopers."

"That's nice," Glo said. "They'll be happy to get all this."

"Anyone would be happy to get this," I said. "Poor poopers, rich poopers, and in-between poopers." I ran my hand lovingly over the grocery bag filled with candy bars. "I could help you deliver this," I said to Shirley. "I'd be happy to take it off your hands."

"Don't give it to her," Glo said. "She'll eat it. She caught your gluttony."

"Blek?" Shirley asked.

"Yes," I said. "But it wears off if I stay away from the ladybug."

"Booger bug," Shirley said.

Glo nodded in agreement. "Anyway, we came over today because I have a spell that'll fix the scramble spell I accidentally put on you."

Shirley looked skeptical. "Icky wiggle waggle," she said.

"Don't worry," Glo said. "It's foolproof. I don't need powdered yak brain or anything." She opened Ripple's book and found her page. "Turn around word and talk not tongue. Shirley More speaketh now not gobbledegook, gobbledegook, gobbledegook but only gobble, gobble, gobble."

Glo and I held our breath and watched Shirley.

"Say something," Glo told her.

"Gobble."

"That's not funny," Glo told her.

"Gobble, gobble, gobble." Shirley's face turned red. "Gobble, gobble, gobble, gobble, gobble!"

"I'm sure I read it perfectly," Glo said. "How many gobbles did I say?"

"I think there were three."

"And three gobbledegooks, right?"

"Yeah."

"Honestly," Glo said. "This is so annoying."

Shirley stamped her foot and balled her hands into fists. She whirled around and huffed off to her bedroom.

"Oh boy," Glo said. "We need to get out of here before she comes back with the gun."

We ran for the door, sprinted down the hall, and flew down the stairs. We jumped into the Mini and roared away from the curb and down the road.

"So how's it going with Mister Tall, Blond, and Ferociously Handsome?" Glo asked.

"I don't know. He gets close, and he smells good, and he feels good, and I think he's going to kiss me, and then he doesn't. And sometimes he just scares the heck out of me. I mean, he's not normal."

"Yeah, but he's not normal in a good way. I bet he's got an Unmentionable schvansticker."

"I don't want to think about his schvansticker. It's enough to give me a panic attack."

Glo nodded in agreement. "It could be formidable."

"That's not what panics me. It's *him*. He's so big and confident and good at flirting."

"And?"

"And I'm such a dope. I'm *not* good at flirting. And I'm *really not* good at being sexy. I'm out of practice."

"Really? How long has it been since . . . you know?"

"Years."

"Get out! Years?"

"I've been busy. I worked long hours at

the restaurant in New York. I was tired a lot. And I didn't like any of the men I met."

Glo nodded in agreement. "I know. It's hard to meet nice men. Either they're married, or else they've got nails driven into their heads."

"You know men with nails in their heads?"

"I'm a magnet for them. Go figure."

Glo stopped at Lafayette Street. "Will you be okay if I take you home? I'd offer to stay with you, but I have a date tonight."

"I'll be fine," I told her. "Does he have a nail in his head?"

"No. He's adorable. I met him at the car wash. He's the interior specialist."

The house was quiet when I got home. Diesel and Carl were still off hiding the charms. The Spook Patrol hadn't returned. Cat 7143 met me at the door, looking relieved to see that I was alone.

"Were you my Great Aunt Ophelia's cat?" I asked him.

Cat looked at me and blinked.

"I'm going to take that as a *yes*," I told Cat.

I wasn't hungry anymore, and I had no desire to be spanked. All good things. I found my notebook right where I left it, open on the kitchen counter. I selected a recipe that didn't require butter and went to work. An hour later, Diesel walked into the kitchen with Carl close on his heels.

"It smells good in here," Diesel said. "What are you making?"

"Corn muffins. They just came out of the oven."

"Doesn't look like you've eaten any."

"I don't ever want to eat again."

Diesel selected a muffin and ate half. "This is delicious."

"I added roasted corn and jalapeños to that batch."

"Eep?" Carl asked.

Diesel gave him the remaining half muffin. Carl crammed it all into his mouth, and crumbs fell out onto the floor.

"You need to learn table manners," Diesel said to Carl.

Carl thought about it a beat and gave Diesel the finger.

"I'm surprised you get along so well with Carl," I said to Diesel. "You don't strike me as being a monkey person."

"I can take 'em or leave 'em," Diesel

said. "I guess I've always been more of a dog person. Dogs eat shoes and burp and dig holes in the backyard. I can relate to all that."

Carl stuck his belly out, opened his mouth wide, and burped.

"Good one," Diesel said. "But you're going back to Monkey Rescue if you eat my shoes."

I cleaned the crumbs up. "I've been thinking about Mark and how he saves things and pushes them around with his backhoe. It reminds me of Uncle Scrooge."

Diesel was blank-face.

"Didn't you ever read Donald Duck comics when you were a kid?" I asked him.

"No. I read Spider-Man and Swamp Thing."

"Figures. Long story short is that Scrooge was Donald's rich uncle. Scrooge hoarded money and treasures in a big money bin, and he pushed it all around with a bulldozer. But here's the good part. The first dime he ever made he kept with him because it was his lucky dime."

Diesel selected another muffin. "So you're saying you think Mark keeps his inheritance close to him, like Scrooge's dime."

"Yes."

"It's as good a theory as any."

I checked the time. "When do you suppose Mark goes home?"

"Hard to say. If he leaves at the close of business, he should be home now. If he stays to rearrange his lock collection, he could be at work all night." Diesel's phone rang, and he looked at the readout. "Bingo," Diesel said.

He had a short conversation, paused, and the line of his mouth tightened. He listened for a beat and disconnected.

"What was that about?" I asked.

"Mark was home. Borderline hysterical. He asked if I thought it was Wulf who made the mess. I said it was possible. He said he was scared. Didn't know what to do. And then he said *oh no*! There was a sound like a gunshot or small explosion and the line went dead."

I felt my heart constrict, and I bit into my lower lip. Before I met Diesel, the only danger I'd experienced was exposure to carving knives and horny line cooks. Now I was involved in explosions and abductions and who-knows-what-else. My stomach got sick just thinking about it.

Diesel dialed Mark's number and let it ring. No answer.

"We need to go over there," Diesel said.

"I don't want to go over there. I wasn't cut out for this. I never wanted to be G.I. Joe or Wonder Woman. I wanted to be Julia Child."

Diesel took one last muffin, turned to leave, and spotted Cat sitting in the doorway. "Cat looks hungry."

I put half a muffin in Cat's food dish and plastic-bagged the rest. Carl climbed down from the top of the refrigerator, gave wide berth to Cat, and followed us out the door to Diesel's SUV.

"I'm having an identity crisis," Diesel said, pulling away from the house. "I'm used to flying solo. Now, every time I look in my rearview mirror, I see a monkey. It's like having a hairy little kid back there. I'm starting to feel like a family man with a mutated gene pool."

"Do you like it?"

"No."

"Maybe you could think of him as a partner."

"No."

"Pet?"

Diesel flicked a glance at Carl. "There's no place in my life for a pet."

No place for a woman, either, I thought.

CHAPTER NINETEEN

There were fire trucks and cop cars angled to the curb in front of Mark's apartment building when we drove up. The downstairs door was open and hoses snaked out from the fire trucks, but the hoses didn't look like they were in use. Firemen and cops milled around, and after a couple beats, I realized what I was seeing. They were chasing ferrets.

Diesel parked halfway down the block, we locked Carl in the car, and we made our way to a fireman holding an extinguisher.

"What's going on?" Diesel asked.

"There was a small fire on the second

floor. We put it out, and then we realized there were about forty ferrets running loose in the apartment. It took them two minutes to figure out we left the door open. We're trying to catch them, but I think it's hopeless. Those suckers are off on the great adventure."

A ferret ran up the fireman's leg, jumped from him to Diesel, catapulted itself off Diesel to the ground, and disappeared into the night.

"Tricky little devils," the fireman said.

"Were any people in the apartment?" I asked him.

"No. Just the ferrets."

We got back into the SUV and drove to More Is Better. No lights shining from the office. No cars in the lot.

"Stay here with Carl," Diesel said to me. "I'm going to do a fast walk-through." Five minutes later, Diesel jogged to the SUV and slid behind the wheel. "Nobody home."

"Where do we go from here?"

"We go to Lenny."

"It's after work hours. Do you know where Lenny is living?"

"I had Gwen find him. He's living with his cousin Melody."

Melody lived in a small, lopsided, worn-out house in north Salem. The house didn't have a historic plaque tacked to the front and the windows were circa 1970 aluminum, so probably the condition of the house couldn't be explained away by age. We rang the bell and a frazzled woman in her late thirties answered the door. She had short, curly brown hair that had gone to frizz. She was medium height, plump but not obese, dressed in jeans and a too-big shirt. She had a baby in one of those baby slings attached to the front of her, a toddler hanging on to her pants leg, and two more kids who looked to be in the seven-to-eight-year range. It was hard to tell who was a girl and who was a boy. From the toddler on up, they all had pretty much the same chopped-off haircut and were wearing jeans and sneakers and T-shirts, none of which were pink.

"Melody More?" Diesel asked.

"Yuh."

"Mommy," the toddler said. "I gotta poop."

"Not now," Melody said. "Mommy's busy."

"But I gotta!"

"Stu," Melody yelled. *"Stu!"*

A pleasant-looking thirty-something guy ambled into the living room. "Yuh?"

"Kenny has to poop."

"Again?"

Melody turned back to us. "We're not buying anything, and we already found Jesus."

"We're looking for Lenny," Diesel said. "We were told he moved here after the fire."

"I don't let perverts into the house," Melody said. "Are you a couple of perverts?"

"No," I told her. "I'm a pastry chef."

"How about him?" she asked, eyeing Diesel.

"I'm not sure about him," I said.

"And the monkey?"

Diesel and I had forgotten about Carl. He was standing behind us on the front porch. He did his best to smile and do a finger wave.

"Goggy!" the toddler said. He clapped his hands and ran at Carl. "Goggy, goggy!"

Carl stumbled back, but the kid tackled him and hugged him.

"Eep!" Carl said, arms pinned to his sides, nose-to-nose with Melody's toddler.

"Maybe he shouldn't be hugging him

like that," I said to Melody. "He could have fleas or something."

Melody snatched the kid up, and Carl gave me the finger.

Something crashed in another room, and Melody took stock of the kids next to her. "Who's missing?"

"Mary Susan," one of the older kids said. "And Kevin is getting a time-out in the attic."

"Mary Susan?" Melody hollered. "What was that noise I heard?"

No answer.

"Remember when she broke the fish tank?" the older kid said. "And all the fishes were swimming on the rug and then they got dead."

"I have to see what Mary Susan is up to," Melody said to us. "I guess you can come in. Just don't try anything funny with my kids, or I'll cut your hearts out." She turned to her oldest. "Get Uncle Lenny. Tell him he has company."

So far as I could see, there were six kids and three adults living in a cracker box. Melody was like the woman who lived in a shoe and had so many kids she didn't know what to do. Everywhere I looked, there were toys, kids' books, stacks of baby clothes, sippy cups, and chocolate smudges.

Carl picked a Barbie doll off the floor and studied it. He touched the pointy breast with his finger. "Eep?" he asked, looking up at Diesel.

"It's a doll," Diesel said.

Carl poked the breast again.

"Give it a rest," Diesel said to Carl.

Carl dropped the doll on the floor and flipped it the finger.

"I think he has repressed anger," I said to Diesel.

"I'd like to see it even *more* repressed."

Lenny came into the room and pulled up short when he saw us. "You two!"

Diesel was hands in pockets, back on his heels and smiling. Friendly. "How's it goin'?"

"It's goin' okay. No thanks to you. You blew up my house."

"It was an accident," I told him.

"My whole life was in that house."

"Including your paddle collection," Diesel said.

Lenny grinned. "Okay, so I owe you for that. Good to get that monkey off my back."

"Eep?" Carl said.

"Nothing personal," Lenny said to him. "Figure of speech."

Two dogs ran through the room and out the front door.

"There's a lot going on in this house," I said to Lenny.

"Tell me about it," Lenny said. "It needs rubber walls."

"Have you heard from Mark?" Diesel asked him.

"Not in a couple days."

"If he wasn't in his apartment, and he wasn't at work, where would he be?"

"Here, maybe. I don't know where else. I guess he has friends, but I don't know them. We all got kind of weird after Uncle Phil died. Kind of pulled into our own obsessive worlds. Is there a problem with Mark?"

"It's possible he's with Wulf."

"It turns out Wulf is scarier than Uncle Phil," Lenny said. "I was a glutton for punishment, and I gave it up pretty fast."

"Where did he take you?"

"I don't know. He did one of those pressure point things, and I was out like a light. When I came around, I was in a big empty room. All it had was a folding chair, and

Wulf sat in it most of the time while his crazy servant guy described his favorite tortures to me. When he got his tool kit out, I told him what he wanted to hear, and next thing, I was wandering around Pickering Wharf Marina."

"What did the room look like?" Diesel asked him. "High ceiling? Paint color? Cement floor? Traffic noise? Windows?"

Lenny closed his eyes and thought about it. "High ceiling with exposed air-conditioning ducts. So it might have been in an industrial area. Walls were white. Ceiling was black, including all the ductwork. Floor was . . . I'm not sure. Maybe cement or tile. Not wood or carpet. I didn't hear anything. No traffic. A phone rang once, but it was far away in another room. No windows." He opened his eyes and looked down at Carl. "What's with the monkey?"

"He adopted us," I said.

"That was a bust," I said to Diesel when we were back in the SUV.

"It was a long shot."

"You've been following Wulf. Don't you know where he lives?"

"Gwen tells me he's staying in a brownstone in Boston on Beacon Hill. Wulf isn't a small-town kind of guy. Wulf likes luxury and privacy."

"Shouldn't we look there?"

Diesel stopped for a light. "Wulf would never interrogate anyone in his personal space. And he'll probably keep Hatchet locked down somewhere in Salem."

"So how do we find Mark?"

Diesel shrugged. "Don't know. When I first got involved in this, I thought Wulf had a road map to the Stones. Now I'm thinking he only had one small piece of the puzzle. Somehow, Wulf got a line on Uncle Phil and went sniffing after the rest of the More clan. I caught him following Shirley, so I concentrated on her. I thought we were trailing behind Wulf, but after we got the ladybug and the information about the two other inheritances, I'm guessing it was the other way around. Wulf probably snatched Lenny because we were in Lenny's basement."

"And then Lenny spilled the beans about Mark?"

Diesel shrugged. "Or maybe Mark was just the next name on Wulf's list. For that matter, Mark might not be with Wulf at all. Maybe Mark just took off."

Twenty minutes later, we were idling in front of Lenny's house. The black Ferrari was parked at the curb, and Wulf stood on the sidewalk, watching Hatchet kick through house debris.

"They're still here," I said to Diesel.

"Not exactly," Diesel said. "The Ferrari's been moved. It's not in the same spot. Wulf went somewhere and came back."

"I bet if we sit and wait, he'll lead us to Mark."

"It's not that easy. Wulf is a master at slipping away."

"But we could try."

Diesel pulled to the curb and parked behind an Econoline van. "We could try."

The sun dropped to the tops of the buildings, the clouds glowed scarlet, and the sky darkened while we waited. When twilight deepened to nightfall, Wulf whistled to Hatchet. Hatchet stopped his search and made his way through the charred rubble, stirring up clouds of soot with every step. There was a brief exchange between Hatchet and Wulf that involved some kneeling on Hatchet's part, and Hatchet got into the Ferrari.

Wulf turned, walked directly to us, and

bent a little to talk to Diesel through the driver's side window.

"You don't need to waste your time following me," he said. "I won't lead you to him until I'm done with him."

The corners of Diesel's mouth twitched into a small, humorless smile, and he looked ahead to Hatchet sitting in the Ferrari. "You're going to have to get your car detailed," he said to Wulf.

Wulf flicked his eyes to his car and back to Diesel. "That's so not funny," Wulf said. He looked over at me, our eyes held for a moment, and he moved from the SUV to his Ferrari. There was a flash of light, smoke swirled in the glare of Diesel's headlights, and the Ferrari was gone.

"I hate when he does that," Diesel said.

There were still no Spook Patrollers standing vigil at my house when we rolled in, but Glo was hunkered down on the front stoop.

"What's up?" I said to her. "I thought you had a date."

"It turns out he's allergic to mushrooms. I met him at the restaurant and everything was going great until he accidentally ate a chunk of portabello in his salad and did projectile vomiting. And then after that, he got all swollen and blotchy and couldn't breathe, so I took him to the walk-in clinic to get a shot, and then he wanted to go home."

"That's horrible."

"Yeah. Go figure. Anyway, I was in Marblehead, so I thought I'd stop in. I thought Diesel might be able to help me with my levitation spell."

"Spells aren't my gig," Diesel said.

"Yes, but you've got special powers."

Diesel opened the front door. "I don't have special powers. I have enhanced abilities."

Cat was sitting in the middle of the living room when we walked in. Carl did the scary smile and gave Cat a finger wave, Cat hissed at him, and Carl shrunk back and farted.

"Chill," Diesel said to Carl.

"I'm hungry," Glo said. "I didn't get a chance to eat, what with the vomiting and swelling and stuff. Maybe we could order out for something."

"I haven't got a lot in the house," I said,

"but I could make you a grilled cheese sand-wich."

Glo's eyes got big. "Grilled cheese would be awesome."

"I could use a grilled cheese," Diesel said.

"Eep!" Carl said. "Eep, eep."

"Three grilled cheeses coming up," I said.

I assembled the bread and butter and cheese, and Glo thumbed through *Ripple's.*

"I found a different spell from the uppity one," Glo said. "I have it marked here. The description says it's helpful for moving difficult objects."

"Have you read it out loud yet?" I asked her.

"No. I thought I'd wait and do it here where Diesel can do damage control. Sometimes my spells don't turn out exactly perfect."

I put my big fry pan on the cooktop. "What object are you going to move?"

"I thought I'd try something small. Like a glass."

"No glass!"

"Bread? Cheese?" Glo asked.

"No. I'm using the bread and the cheese. I don't want enchanted food."

Glo looked around. "How about the toaster?"

"Sure. Do the toaster."

"Light as air, listen well, rise to the command on words spriggam, barflower, my will be done." Glo pointed her finger at the toaster. "Spriggam, barflower, my will be done. I command thee to rise."

We all watched the toaster for a beat and *BANG!* The toaster burst into flames. Diesel pulled the plug and dumped it into the sink.

"I think it rose a little before it caught fire," Glo said.

"It jumped when it exploded," Diesel told her.

Glo threw her arms up in exasperation. "I don't get it. I know I read it correctly."

"You didn't need powdered octopus suckers or anything, did you?" I asked her.

"No. It's all right here in black and white." Glo read the spell out loud again, following along with her finger. "Spriggam, barflower, my will be done."

A shout went up from the street.

"Oh no," Glo said. "Now what?"

We ran to the door and looked out at Mel Mensher. He was standing on my sidewalk, watching three other members of the Spook Patrol chase after the Spook Patrol van.

"It just took off," Mensher said. "We parked it, and we all got out and started checking our equipment, and next thing, the van's going down the street all by itself."

The van jumped the curb at the curve in the road, bumped over Mrs. Dugan's front yard, and crashed into her oak tree. The three Spook Patrol guys pulled up and stood hands on hips, looking at the van.

"Honest to gosh, it was an accident," Glo said.

I pushed Glo back into the house and closed and locked the door. "The driver obviously forgot to put his parking brake on," I said. "That's our story, and we're sticking with it."

Diesel was frying grilled cheese when we got back to the kitchen. "And?" he asked.

"The Spook Patrol van took off down the street all by its lonesome," I told him.

"Nice," Diesel said.

He flipped a sandwich onto a plate, handed it to Glo, and put a second sandwich into the fry pan.

"You can cook," I said to him.

"No," Diesel said. "I can't cook. I can

make a sandwich if no one else is going to make it for me."

"I bet I could find a cooking spell," Glo said.

Diesel and I answered in unison. *"No!"*

Diesel gave the second grilled cheese to Carl, and I took over the fry pan.

"It really ticks me off that Wulf is going to get Mark's charm," I said to Diesel. "We should have been more aggressive with Mark. We let him slip through our fingers."

"Roughing up Normals is frowned upon by the BUM," Diesel said. "Especially if the Normals haven't done anything wrong."

"What about Wulf? Wulf kidnaps people and does who-the-heck-knows-what to them."

"Wulf doesn't work for the BUM. He has his own set of rules."

"He killed a man. Why aren't you ordered to capture him or something? Why are you only authorized to stop him from getting the Stones?"

"Wulf has friends in very high places. Beyond that, I can only assume there are circumstances that justify my orders."

"You don't look like a guy who would be

good at taking orders," I said, plating his sandwich.

Diesel fixed his brown eyes on me. "It's a struggle."

"Maybe I need to go to wizard school," Glo said. "Someplace where I could take a course in spell recitation. Do you suppose there's a wizard school? Maybe an online course?"

"Wizards aren't real," I said to Glo. "There are no wizards. And wizard school would be a big scam."

"Criminy," Glo said. "Just let me know how you feel." She looked at Diesel. "What do you think?"

"I don't know any wizards personally."

"But do you think there could be wizards?"

Diesel finished his sandwich and put his dish in the dishwasher. "*Could be* covers a lot of ground."

"Well, I think there could be wizards," Glo told him. "I bet Ripple was a wizard. And I bet the book is magical."

Diesel got a bottle of water from the refrigerator. "Have you ever let Lizzy hold it?"

"No!" Glo scooped the book off the

counter and handed it to me. "Do you feel anything?"

"It might be a little warm."

"Is it glowing?"

"No, but it has a faint green aura."

"What does that mean?" Glo asked.

I shrugged. "I don't know. I'm new to all this."

We looked at Diesel.

"No clue," Diesel said. "Not my area of expertise, but the grilled cheese was excellent."

"So maybe someone put a whammy on my book, and that's why the spells don't work right," Glo said. "Maybe there was some rival wizard, and he jinxed Ripple's book." She took her book back and shoved it into her tote bag. "I'm going to talk to Nina from the Exotica Shoppe tomorrow. I'll get to the bottom of this."

CHAPTER TWENTY

I walked Glo to the door, and we looked down the hill to Mrs. Dugan's yard, where a tow truck and police car were parked, lights flashing. Mel Mensher had joined the rest of his crew at the crash scene, and all was quiet at my house.

"Shoot," Glo said.

"Faulty parking brake," I reminded her.

Glo grimaced, got into her car, and drove away.

"I like her," Diesel said, standing behind me. "She has imagination." He slid an arm around my waist and rested his chin on the top of my head. "I like you a lot more. No logical reason for it."

I thought it was great that he liked me, but it would be better if he knew why.

"I know why," he said, reading my mind, his lips brushing against my ear, "but I'd jeopardize my standing as a macho jerk if I gave you a big gooey list of reasons. And if I was honest, it would lean heavy to smooth skin and soft breasts."

"Unh."

"Is that a good grunt or a bad grunt?"

"I thought you were reading my mind."

"Sometimes your mind is a mess."

"I was thinking your standing as a jerk is intact."

His arm tightened slightly around me, and he kissed me just below my ear. "That's a huge relief."

The kiss sent a rush of pleasure humming through me, and I unconsciously murmured, *"Mmmmmm."*

Good grief, I thought. Did I just make that utterly rapturous sound? Did I actually *moan* out loud? Over a kiss, no less. And it wasn't even a *hot* kiss. The kiss had been almost *friendly*!

"I made that sound because I was thinking about cupcakes," I told him.

"Sweetheart, you *wish* a cupcake could make you feel that good."

I was speechless. I felt my mouth drop open and my eyes go wide.

Diesel grinned down at me. "On a scale of one to ten, how offensive was that remark I just made?"

"Seven."

"I'm off my game. I can be much more offensive than that."

Something to look forward to.

He turned his attention to the Spook Patrol at the bottom of the hill. "I think we owe them a favor," he said, pushing me out of the house, locking my front door behind us.

"What kind of favor?" I asked. "I thought we didn't like them."

He took my hand and tugged me down the sidewalk. "They're okay. They're just doing their job."

We walked past the cop car to Mel Mensher, and Diesel expressed his sympathy. "Too bad about your van," Diesel said to Mensher. "How are you guys going to hunt spooks without it?"

"The tow truck guy said the damage was minimal," Mensher told him. "And in the meantime, Richie went to get his wife's minivan."

"I have some information you might find interesting," Diesel said. "Can I borrow your notepad and pen?"

Mensher pulled his pad and pen from his jacket pocket. "What kind of information is this?"

Diesel wrote something in Mensher's book and handed it back to him. "See for yourself."

Mrs. Dugan was standing on the other side of Mensher. She had her arms folded in front of her, watching the van get towed off her tree. She was in her seventies, with short white hair and a fireplug body. Her husband had passed on, and she lived alone with an obese beagle named Morty. Mrs. Dugan and Morty walked by my house twice a day taking their constitutional.

"Will your tree be okay?" I asked her.

"It's got some bark peeled away, but I think it'll be fine," she said. "I couldn't help but notice Ophelia's cat came back. I saw him sitting in your window earlier today. Isn't that nice. I was worried about him. It's not like he's a normal cat. What with his eye and all."

"Do you know how he lost his eye?"

"No. Ophelia would never talk about it. She was very sensitive when it came to that cat."

"Do you know his name?"

She thought a moment. "I don't believe I do."

I said good-bye to Mrs. Dugan, and Diesel and I made our way up the hill to my house.

"I thought Cat 7143 came from the shelter," Diesel said.

"It did. But it turns out it was my Great Aunt Ophelia's cat."

"Makes you wonder, doesn't it," Diesel said.

"Compared to the rest of my life these days . . . it's not even a four on the one-to-ten wonder scale. What information did you give to Mensher?"

"I gave him Wulf's Boston address," Diesel said.

That got a smile out of me. "Does Wulf have a sense of humor?"

"He won't have one about this."

"Not at all?"

"The first time Mensher clicks off a picture, Wulf's sphincter will get so tight his eyes will cross."

We were almost at my house when Richie motored past us in a green minivan. He stopped next to the tow truck, and in the glare of headlights, Mensher and his crew off-loaded equipment from the broken van to the new minivan. There was a short discussion between Mensher and the tow truck operator, Mensher and his crew piled into the minivan, and the minivan drove away and disappeared around the corner.

"Off to Beacon Hill," Diesel said.

"You threw them under the bus."

"Yep."

"What if Wulf does the burning claw thing on them?"

"They'd probably get a reality show out of it."

"The last guy to get the burning claw also got dead," I told him.

"Wulf won't kill these guys. Unless he's in a really bad mood. And even then, he'll probably just maim one or two of them."

"Oh great. Now you're making me an accessory to maiming."

"It's not like it's major maiming," Diesel said. "It's only a handprint."

"That's horrible."

"You're such a girl," he said, smiling at me, like I was dumb but redeemingly cute. He pulled me the short distance to the Cayenne, opened the door, and motioned me in.

"Where are we going?" I asked him.

"We're going to stop a potential maiming."

Beacon Hill is a quiet, historic neighborhood in the heart of Boston. Streets are narrow and tree-shaded. Sidewalks are bumpy. Houses are pricey, ranging from shabby chic to totally renovated and opulent. Parking is impossible.

The Spook Patrol had somehow managed to snag the last legal parking place on the hill, and Diesel settled for a space that wasn't so legal. He parked blocking a driveway one house down and across from the green minivan.

Months ago, when I first came to town, I took a walking tour of the area, so I knew we were on one of the more desirable streets. The houses were mostly Federalist style. Some were single-family and some had been converted to expensive multitenant condos and apartments.

Wulf lived in the middle of the block in a single-family, perfectly maintained example of a Greek Revival brownstone. The small, manicured front yard was bordered by a fancy black wrought-iron fence. Curtains were drawn, but a bar of light was visible in a second-floor window. The Spook Patrol was parked smack in front of the house.

"I don't see Wulf's car," I said to Diesel.

"He has parking in the rear."

"Do you think he's home?"

"I know he's home," Diesel said. "Do you have an ass cramp?"

"Big-time."

Beacon Hill streets are lit by gas lamps. Not as efficient as halogens, but bright enough to watch the Spook Patrol guys organizing themselves. There were five of them, including Mel Mensher. There was Richie, a chubby guy I'd heard called Gorp, a Pakistani named Milton, and a skinny little guy no one ever talked to. Richie was on his cell phone. Mensher, Milton, and Gorp shuffled back and forth on the sidewalk, looking at the house through binoculars, taking readings with their ghost-o-meters. The skinny little guy hauled a camp chair out of the minivan, set it up on the sidewalk, and settled in with his computer.

Diesel and I were snug in the Cayenne, in a dark spot on the street between gas lamps and under the shade of an oak tree. After ten minutes of watching the Spook Patrol, Diesel slid an arm around me and nuzzled my neck.

"What are you doing?" I asked him.

"Isn't it obvious?"

"Yes! Stop it."

"The girls never said that when I was in high school."

"This isn't high school. We're supposed to be stopping a maiming. And besides, the monkey is watching."

Diesel stared out the window. "There's no maiming going on." He flicked a glance at the backseat. "And the monkey is sleeping. So what's the problem?"

I sucked in some air. "You make me nervous."

"I noticed."

"I go into a panic when you get close."

"Does that happen with all men or am I special?"

"It's you."

Diesel smiled, his teeth white against his usual two-day beard. "I like it."

"It's uncomfortable!"

"I could make you even more uncomfortable," Diesel said, "but you're off-limits to me. Unmentionables can't join with other Unmentionables. There are consequences." He ran his finger along the nape of my neck. "That's not to say we can't fool around."

My heart jumped to my throat at his touch. "What sort of consequences?"

"One of us would lose all Unmentionable power," Diesel said.

"Are you serious?"

"Unfortunately, yes."

Isn't this typical. Every time I meet a great guy who actually has two eyebrows, he's either gay or married. And now I can add Unmentionable to the list of unavailable men.

"No problem," I said. "Just because you throw me into a panic doesn't mean I would fling myself into your arms at the first opportunity. I'm perfectly in control of the situation."

"Lizzy, you have no idea. My Unmentionable skills aren't limited to opening locked doors."

"Jeez Louse."

"Yeah," Diesel said. "I could make us fit together like a Chinese puzzle. Unfortunately, we have a job to do that requires both of us keep our skills." A smile twitched at the corners of his mouth. "And it would be a shame if you were the loser and you started making lousy cupcakes."

A light flashed on over Wulf's front door, and we both turned our attention to the house. Mel and Gorp were standing on the small cement porch, instruments in hand.

"Guess they got tired of waiting," Diesel said. "Looks like showtime."

The door opened and Wulf appeared. He was in his usual black. Black shirt, black slacks. He looked at Mensher, and then his eyes moved left and locked onto Diesel's Cayenne.

"Uh-oh," I said. "Can he see us?"

"Yes."

"So he knows we set him up."

"Yes."

Mensher said something to Wulf, and Wulf didn't respond. Wulf looked like he was sending death rays in our direction. Mensher pointed to the ghost-o-meter in Gorp's hand, but Wulf paid no attention. Mensher took a step back, raised his camera, there was a flash when Mensher snapped a picture, and Wulf snatched Mensher by the neck with one hand and lifted him off the ground. Wulf had reached out so fast, it was like the flick of a lizard tongue snagging a bug from a tree limb.

"Yow!" I said, jumping in my seat, leaning forward. "Do something. He's going to kill him."

Diesel stayed relaxed behind the wheel, watching Wulf with an expression that was somewhere between mildly annoyed and mildly amused.

"He won't kill him in front of me," Diesel said. "Even if I wasn't here, I doubt he'd kill him. Wulf has a code of ethics."

Wulf released Mensher, and Mensher fell back on his ass with his hands to this throat. I was guessing Mensher would wake up tomorrow with a unique burn scar on his neck. Wulf swept past Mensher and Gorp, down the short sidewalk to the van. He walked behind the van, momentarily disappearing from sight. He circled the van, stepped back, and gestured toward it. A circle of fire raced around the van and the van exploded. Tires flew into space, a black cloud rose to the sky, and the van turned into a fireball.

Carl popped up in the backseat and looked out the window. "Eeep!"

"No big deal," Diesel said to Carl. "Just a lot of flash."

"Effective flash," I said to Diesel. "It's going to get rid of Mensher."

"For the moment," Diesel said. "Don't underestimate Mensher. He's like a dog with a bone. He might not know exactly how to categorize Wulf, but he knows for sure he's not normal."

Wulf calmly walked up the sidewalk and disappeared inside his house. Mensher and his team huddled together in front of the burning van. Fire trucks screamed from blocks away.

"We can go home now," Diesel said, cranking the engine over. "The Wulf Show is done for the night."

Twenty minutes later, Diesel pulled into a strip mall in Swampscott and parked in front of an all-night supermarket.

"We need food," he said. "You cleaned

us out when you were on your eating rampage."

We slid out, locked the Cayenne, walked a few feet, and . . . *beep, beep, beep*.

"Tell me again why we have this monkey," Diesel said.

"No one else would take him."

"And?"

"That's it."

"Why can't we put him in a basket and leave him on the Humane Society doorstep? Or even better, pack him up in a box and FedEx him to India. They love monkeys in India."

"I thought you were friends."

"I knew him in a previous life," Diesel said.

Beep, beep, beep, beep.

Diesel jogged back to the SUV, opened the door, and Carl bounded out.

"Do they let monkeys in the supermarket?" I asked Diesel.

"Put him in a shopping cart and make him sit on his tail, and people will think he's a hairy kid. If anyone makes a remark, tell them you have rights and threaten them with a lawsuit."

CHAPTER
TWENTY-ONE

We got as far as the produce aisle with Carl in the cart, and a guy stacking grapefruits stopped me.

"Is that a monkey?"

"Are you making fun of my child?" I asked him.

"No, ma'am, but he's kinda hairy."

"He gets that from his father."

The produce guy looked at Diesel.

"Not my bad," Diesel said.

"Well, you gotta have clothes on your kid," the guy said. "We don't let naked kids in here, no matter how much hair they got."

There was a small display of kids' clothes

by the checkout. Mostly T-shirts with *Massachusetts* written on them and a couple toddler-size shirts with pink elephants. I slipped an elephant shirt over Carl's head, bought a package of Pampers, and taped Carl into one.

"What do you think?" I asked Carl.

Carl looked at the elephant and gave it the finger.

"It's the best I could do," I told him. "They don't sell Armani here. Anyway, it's cute."

"It's pink," Diesel said.

"And?"

"Just saying."

We made our way through produce and into prepared foods. Carl was slouched in the cart, arms folded across his chest, lower lip stuck out in a pout, not happy with the pink elephant. He perked up when we got to the cereal aisle.

"Would you like some cereal?" I asked him.

Carl jumped to his feet, snatched a box of Froot Loops off the shelf, ripped it open, and stuck his face in the box.

"Hey!" I said to him.

He took his face out of the box and looked at me.

"Manners."

He threw the box over his shoulder, into the basket, and focused on the display of Frosted Flakes. "Eeee?"

"Okay," I told him, tossing Frosted Flakes into the basket beside the Froot Loops, "but this is the last of the cereal."

"Look at us," Diesel said. "We're the all-American family."

We rounded the end of the cereal aisle and quickly walked past women's personal products and men's sexual necessities. I paused at dental care.

"Does he brush his teeth?" I asked Diesel.

"I don't know, but he should," Diesel said. "I'm not looking forward to waking up to monkey breath."

"Do you brush your teeth?" I asked Carl, showing him a toothbrush.

Carl looked at the toothbrush and shrugged. He didn't know toothbrush. I tossed the toothbrush and some toothpaste into the cart. We rounded the end of the aisle and pushed into cookies and crackers.

Carl was instantly standing again. Carl liked cookies. "Eep!" he said, pointing to

Fig Newtons, Oreos, Nutter Butters. "Eep. Eeeep." Carl was in a frenzy, jumping up and down, wanting everything. He grabbed at the Mint Milanos.

"Wait," I said. "I don't know if monkeys can eat chocolate." I looked at Diesel. "Can monkeys eat chocolate?"

"Lizzy, I can open locks, sniff out evil, and I can give you the best time of your life, but I don't know a whole lot about monkeys."

"Let's stick to peanut butter and gingerbread," I said to Carl. "When I get home, I'll Google chocolate."

We added a couple bags of cookies to the cart and moved on to dairy. I needed butter, eggs, and milk.

Carl spied rice pudding and frantically pointed to it. "Woo, woo, woo!" he said.

"Sure," I said, handing him a tub of rice pudding.

Carl opened the tub and looked inside. He swiped some up on his finger and tasted it.

"You're not supposed to eat it now," I told him. "You have to wait until we get home."

Carl looked at me and then looked at Diesel.

"I don't think he understands," Diesel said.

"Later," I told Carl. "Not now."

Carl stuck his face into the tub and slurped up rice pudding.

"Listen, mister," I said to him. "That's unacceptable behavior." I cut my eyes to Diesel. "You need to do something with your monkey."

"*My* monkey? Sweetie Pie, he is not *my* monkey."

"Okay, maybe he's *our* monkey."

Diesel took the tub of rice pudding from Carl. "I'm only admitting to joint possession of the monkey if I get joint possession of the bed."

"You have that anyway. I can't get you out of it."

"Yes, but you have to like it."

"No way. You can't make me like it."

"I could if I had half a chance," Diesel said.

Carl tried to grab the rice pudding from Diesel, but Diesel moved it out of his reach and put the lid on it.

"Eeeee!" Carl shrieked. *"Eeeeeeee."*

"Do something!" I said to Diesel.

"I don't carry a gun, but I could choke him until his eyes pop out," Diesel said.

"You need to go outside and take a time-out," I said to Carl.

"Eee?"

"Yes, you."

Carl thought about it a beat and gave me the finger.

"That's it," I told him. "You're grounded for life. No television. No dessert. And forget about the Froot Loops."

Carl reached for the Froot Loops.

"No!" I said.

Carl gave the Froot Loops the finger, climbed out of the cart, and stood next to Diesel, shoulders slumped, knuckles dragging on the ground.

A skinny teen with spiky purple hair and multiple studs and rings stuck in his face stopped to look at Carl.

"Whoa, lady," he said. "That's an ugly kid you got here. He looks like a monkey."

Carl shrugged.

I guess from a monkey's point of view, it was difficult to tell if that was a compliment or an insult. From my point of view, it was clearly an insult, and I experienced a bizarre rush of maternal outrage.

"I don't like you trash-talking my monkey," I said to the spike-faced guy. "And your face looks ridiculous."

"Not as ridiculous as your hairy mutant in that shirt," he said.

Carl snapped to attention. "Eep?"

"It's a girlie baby shirt," the kid said.

Carl threw his arms in the air in an *I-told-you-so-and-I-knew-this-shirt-was-stupid* gesture. He ripped the shirt off, turned around, pulled his diaper down, and mooned me.

"That's my boy," Diesel said.

Carl pulled his diaper up, grabbed an egg from my carton, and threw it at the spike-faced guy. It missed the guy, smashed against the dairy display case, and slimed down the glass. Carl reached for a second egg and Diesel scooped him up and held him at arm's length.

"We're going to have to work on your throw," Diesel said to Carl.

"Get him out of here *now*," I said to Diesel. "I'll finish shopping and meet you at the car."

Diesel tucked Carl under his arm and

sauntered off. I looked at the spike-faced jerk, and it was like grade school all over again and I was back to being Buzzard Beak. I marched up to him, smashed an egg on his forehead, and dumped the remaining rice pudding on his purple hair.

"Moron," I said to him.

And then I turned on my heel and wheeled my cart past him, down the bread aisle. Last I looked, he was tasting the pudding that was slopping into his ears and glopping down the back of his neck. I wasn't nearly so calm. I'd never smashed an egg on someone or given anyone a pudding shampoo. I was simultaneously horrified and exhilarated. I did deep breathing through English muffins, and by the time I got to the hot dog rolls, I was able to relax my grip on the cart. No one from security was stalking me. Spike-Face wasn't running after me with retaliatory eggs. And no one was going to tell my mother. I was golden.

CHAPTER
TWENTY-TWO

I love my little historic house. I love that it has a history, that people have celebrated holidays and conceived children and grown old in the house. I love parking in front of it and looking at the door and the onion lamps and knowing its mine, and that I'm now part of the continuum. And I know this is a scary thought, but I like walking into my dark living room from outside, turning the light on to make everything happy and cozy, and having Diesel at my side. How hideous is that?

Cat 7143 uncurled himself on the couch,

stretched, gave Carl the once-over, and re-curled.

"Maybe I should work on a recipe," I said to Diesel.

"Would it involve a steak?"

"It could. It happens that I bought a couple steaks at the store. If I make you a steak, will you sleep on the couch?"

"Yes."

"For real?"

"No," Diesel said. "Will you make me a steak anyway?"

I followed him into the kitchen and watched him dump the bags on the counter. "You could make your own steak."

"I'll make you a deal. I'll give you a back rub if you make me a steak."

I put the milk, butter, cheese, and lunch meat in the refrigerator. "Thanks, but the deal is I'll make you a steak if you promise *not* to give me a back rub."

"Afraid to let me get my hands on you?"

"Absolutely."

I pulled the steak out of the bag, and Diesel's phone rang. Diesel asked for a location, said he was on his way, and disconnected.

"What was that about?" I asked him.

"It was Mark. He's on Pickering Wharf, and he needs a ride."

"Not good," I said to Diesel. "I expect this means Wulf has the charm."

"Probably. We'll find out in a few minutes."

"I'm going to sit this one out. You don't need me to handle anything, and I need cooking time."

Diesel took a banana off the counter. He peeled it, gave half to Carl, and ate the other half. "Keep the doors locked and don't let anyone in. Call me immediately if you sense something weird."

"Okeydokey."

Diesel went to the door, and Carl trailed after him. Male bonding. Go figure. As for me, I was about to tackle pound cake. I had a perfectly good recipe, but it wasn't my own, so I had to build a better pound cake. I assembled sour cream, butter, flour, and vanilla. I could go citrus with a key lime cake. Or I could go exotic with rum. Definitely rum, I decided. I mixed the ingredients, poured the batter into a tube pan, and slid the pan into the oven. I took the big bowl to the sink, ran hot water into it, and the back door crashed open.

It was Hatchet in full Halloween regalia. Green tights, white tunic, chain-link armor jacket, and silver metal helmet that was a cross between Sir Lancelot and Hell's Angels. The one authentic-looking piece of equipment was his sword. It was a genuine, heavy-duty, freaking sharp saber-type weapon with a fancy hand-forged handle.

"Greetings, wench," he said.

"I'm not a wench," I told him. "And what the heck do you think you're doing? You broke the lock on my door, and you're going to have to pay for it."

"Nay, wench. I'm here at my master's bidding to retrieve what is rightly his."

I raised an eyebrow at him. "Your master sent you?"

Hatchet fidgeted with his sword handle. "Not exactly. But it mattereth not. He'll be pleased when I return with the sacred treasure."

"You're not returning with anything. The sacred treasure isn't here."

Hatchet lunged in my direction with his sword drawn. "You lie."

"Yipes," I said, jumping back. "Watch what you're doing with the sword."

"Tell me the treasure location, or I'll cut

you up into tiny pieces. I'll slash you to rib-
bons. I'll rip open your stomach, and all
your guts will fall out."

"That's disgusting."

Hatchet lunged at me again. "It's delicious. My liege lord would be proud.
Perhaps I'll bring him your guts."

So now he was starting to freak me out.
At first sight, it's hard to take Hatchet seriously. I mean, he's a pot-bellied geek in
stupid clothes. Even with a big knife, he's
not especially threatening looking. Talking
about my guts falling out of my body was
making me reconsider my assessment of
him. Plus, his eyes were getting glittery and
crazy looking and the rest of his face was
way too happy. Gleeful, actually.

Help! I thought to Diesel. *Are you listening? Can you hear me?* Probably not.
Probably, he was too far away.

"Here's the thing," I said to Hatchet, putting the work island between us, taking my
cell phone in hand. "Diesel is the one with
the treasure. How about if I call him and
tell him to bring it home?"

"I think not. My superpower tells me the
treasure is near. I can smell it. I can feel
the evil vibration."

"You're a nut," I said to him.

"I'm not a nut," he said. "I'm not, I'm not, I'm not."

He chopped at me with enough force for the blade to split me in two. Fortunately, it was a foot short, and it sliced the air and bit into my butcher-block cutting board. I had my phone in my hand, but I couldn't take my eyes off Hatchet long enough to dial. He yanked the saber blade out of the cutting board, and we danced around the island.

Hatchet's eyes were compressed into black pinpoints, his face was white with rage, and spit flew out of his mouth. "I hate when people say I'm a nut. I hate it. I hate it."

He lunged across the island, tagging me on the arm with the tip of the saber. My phone flew out of my hand, into the sink, and a bright red line of blood oozed from my elbow to my wrist. I grabbed my arm, stumbled back, and Hatchet continued to come at me, crawling over the island. He raised the saber to strike again, and a blur of striped cat flew through the air in front of me and latched onto Hatchet's face. It was Cat 7143 holding tight to

Hatchet, growling low in his throat, his tail bushed out like a bottlebrush.

Hatchet dropped the saber and batted at Cat. "Get him off!" Hatchet shrieked, his words muffled by fur.

I was dumbstruck. I'd love to say I rose to the occasion, grabbed the saber, and so filled Hatchet with fear that he went to his knees. Truth is, I stood with my mouth open and my feet glued to the floor. Probably, it was only for a moment, but it felt like a lifetime.

Cat climbed to the top of Hatchet's head, leaving a series of bloody dots where his claws had dug into the sides of Hatchet's face. Hatchet swatted Cat off his head and ran out the back door into the night.

Cat leaped onto the butcher block and watched Hatchet leave, and when the sound of a car engine catching came through the open back door, Cat relaxed back on his haunches, curled his half-tail around himself, and went into his grooming ritual as if nothing had happened. I closed the door and propped a kitchen chair against it to keep it closed.

"Thanks," I said to Cat. "That was really brave of you." I stroked his glossy back and realized he was on my cutting board. "Probably, you shouldn't be sitting on the board," I told him.

Cat stopped grooming and looked at me.

"You're right," I said. "You can sit wherever you want."

I wrapped half a roll of paper towels around my arm to keep from bleeding on everything and secured the towels with Scotch tape. I plucked my cell phone out of the soapy sink water and tried to dial Diesel. No luck. The phone was dead. I could call him on my kitchen phone, but I didn't know his number. It was locked up in the dead cell phone. Blood was beginning to ooze through the toweling on my arm, so I grabbed my purse and went to the front door. I cautiously looked out and measured the distance to my car. I had keys in hand. I stepped out, quickly closed and locked the door, ran to my car, and drove to the hospital in Salem.

The whole hospital procedure had taken just a little under an hour. I'd been fortunate to get injured in the lull between rush-hour fender benders and late-night bar brawls. I'd also been fortunate that most of the cut hadn't required stitches, and I was already up to date on my tetanus shot. I drove the short distance back to my house and found Diesel and Carl standing at the open front door. Carl was looking curious, as always. Diesel was uncharacteristically grim.

"Have you been home long?" I asked Diesel, dragging myself out of my car, suddenly exhausted.

"Only long enough to see the broken door, the blood on the kitchen floor, and the saber. I was about to have Gwen start calling hospitals."

"I'd explain it all to you, but I'm so tired I can barely stand."

"My heart stopped beating for a full five minutes when I walked into the kitchen," he said. "The instant I saw the saber and the broken door, I knew it was Hatchet. If I'd found him before I found you, he'd be dust."

"I tried to call you, but my phone got dumped in the sink during the scuffle and died."

"As long as it was just the phone that died," Diesel said, following me into the house, looking at my arm bandaged from wrist to elbow. "How bad is it?"

"I caught the tip of the saber. It didn't slice especially deep, with the exception of a small part in the middle. It only required seven stitches."

"And Hatchet?"

"Cat attacked him and scared him away."

Diesel smiled. "Are you serious?"

"Yes. Cat was awesome."

"I'll never begrudge him another muffin." He looked over at the door. "Since your door got kicked in, I assume Hatchet was acting without Wulf."

"Hatchet was having delusions of greatness. He had a fantasy of presenting Wulf with the charms."

"I have a fantasy," Diesel said. "Would you like to hear about it?"

"I already know about fantasies number seven and eight. How does this one stack up?"

"This one is much better."

"Maybe you want to save it for when I'm not doped up on painkillers."

"Yeah, we don't want to waste this one. You look like you're done for the day."

I took the burnt cake out of the oven, trudged upstairs, brushed my teeth, changed into pajamas, and crawled into bed. I turned the light off, and ten minutes later, Diesel slipped under the covers next to me. One minute after that, Carl climbed under the covers and inserted himself between us.

Diesel flipped the light on.

"Out," he said to Carl.

"Eep?"

"Where do monkeys usually sleep?" I asked Diesel.

"Trees, cages, Dumpsters. The last time I had to live with this one, he slept on the couch."

"So get him settled on the couch. There's an extra pillow and quilt in the hall closet."

Diesel slid out of bed and pulled Carl out from under the covers.

"Jeez Louise," I said to Diesel. "Could you put something on?"

"Don't look if you don't like it."

That was the problem. I liked it a lot. And there was no way I wasn't going to look.

"It's easier protecting you if I'm next to you," Diesel said. "And this is the way I sleep. Just deal with it."

I woke up minutes before the alarm was set to go off. Diesel was asleep beside me, and Cat was sitting at the foot of the bed, watching me in the dark. I shut the alarm off, grabbed some clothes, and went into the bathroom to get dressed. Cat was waiting for me when I came out. He followed me down the stairs and into the kitchen. I poured crunchies into his bowl, gave him fresh water, and started coffee brewing.

Carl came in from the living room, dragging his knuckles, fur sticking every which way, eyes bleary.

"You didn't have to get up this early," I said to him.

Carl shrugged, took the box of Froot Loops off the counter, shoved his hand in, and ate a fistful. I did the same with the Frosted Flakes. Ordinarily, I'd take my coffee out to the back porch, but this morning I hesitated. The back porch didn't feel safe anymore. My door was broken and my arm throbbed where it had been sutured. Diesel had cleaned the blood off the floor and the saber was gone. The kitchen looked normal, but it would take a while before I felt completely comfortable.

I was pacing with my coffee, muttering to myself, angry that my life was disrupted, angry that I'd become afraid of the dark, when Diesel ambled in. He was barefoot, and from the way his jeans rode low on his hips, showing nothing but skin, I suspected he was wearing just the jeans. He poured himself a mug of coffee and drank it black, lounging against the counter.

"How do you feel about carrying a gun?" he asked me.

"I'm scared, but not *that* scared. I wouldn't know what to do with a gun."

"I could teach you."

"I'd rather not," I said.

"A gun would protect you against Hatchet."

"What about Wulf?"

"I'm the only thing that can protect you against Wulf."

I closed the box of Frosted Flakes and put it away in the cupboard. "Do you think Hatchet will come after me again?"

"I don't know. He's a loose cannon. Hard to say what he'll do."

"I was so tired last night I forgot to ask you about Mark."

Cat was on the counter by Diesel, and Diesel instinctively scratched him behind the ear while he drank his coffee. "Mark was waiting for me at the wharf. He had five fingerprints on his neck from Wulf, but not an entire handprint. Between the mess we made in Mark's apartment, the fire, and Wulf kidnapping him and burning him, Mark was rattled to the point where he barely had a coherent thought."

"What about the charm?"

"You were right about the charm. Mark had it on him the whole time. He carried it in his pocket. It was a dragonfly. The charm's in Wulf's pocket now."

"So it's two for the good guys and one for the bad guy. Does this mean our work is done?"

"No," Diesel said. "It means I don't know how to complete the job."

"All the gluttony pieces have been found. What's left to do?"

"The legend is that there were seven Stones representing the seven sins. Nothing is said about a Stone being fragmented. I always thought if the three charms were combined, they might somehow become one Stone, or else lead us to the real Stone."

"So you're thinking there's a chance the actual Stone is out there somewhere, still undiscovered. And if that's the case, Wulf has a chance of finding it."

Diesel finished his coffee, rinsed his mug, and set it on the counter next to the sink. "It's not a good chance, but it's possible. Give me a minute to get dressed, and I'll drive you to the bakery. I don't want you on the road alone."

Fridays are always busy. People entertain on Friday night and businesses have lunchtime celebrations that range from baby showers to retirement ceremonies. And all those things need meat pies, breadbaskets, and cupcakes. By eleven A.M., the corporate lunch orders were out the door, and the shop was empty of customers. Clara was in clean-up mode, and I was icing cupcakes for afternoon pickup.

Glo stuck her head into the kitchen. "Have you got a minute?"

"Why?" Clara asked, looking like she might not want to know the answer.

Glo scooted through the kitchen to the

back door. "There isn't anyone in the shop right now, and I want to show you something."

"It better not be another monkey," I said to her. "Or another cat or rhinocerous or iguana or abandoned bear cub."

"It's none of those things," Glo said, disappearing into the parking lot and reappearing holding four brooms. "I got to thinking about the broom thing. I mean, there are all kinds of brooms, and maybe it makes a difference, right? So I got a bunch of them." She leaned the brooms against the counter and opened Ripple's book to the soaring spell. "I don't really need *Ripple's*. I know the spell by heart, but I thought it wouldn't hurt for someone to follow along just to make sure I have it perfect."

Clara pulled the plugs on the big mixer, the blender, and the coffeemaker. "Just in case," she said.

I thought it was no wonder there were rumors of Clara's magical powers. She had electric hair that defied rubber bands, hairspray, hairclips, and style. Her eyes were almond-shaped, slightly tilted, fringed by dark lashes. Her lips were thin but seemed right for her face. She wore big hoop earrings and a delicate silver cross on a chain around her neck. And she walked fast with a forward tilt, her chef coat flapping behind her, making it easy to imagine her on a broom.

Glo was a more difficult vision, looking like she'd be more at home at the mall than standing behind a witch's cauldron. Yet here she was with her array of possibly enchanted brooms.

"I got this one at the hardware store next door," Glo said, selecting a wooden-handled, straw sweeper number. "That hardware store is as old as Dazzle's. I thought there was a good chance they'd have a wizard broom."

She straddled the broom, took a deep breath, and concentrated. "Uppity uppity rise thyself," she said. "Wings of magic, heart of believer, eyes open, spirit soar. Uppity uppity rise thyself."

Nothing. Glo repeated the spell. Still nothing.

"Did I say the spell right?" she asked me.

"Yep," I told her. "It was perfect."

She set the broom aside and threw her leg over a disposable dust mop. "This is a long shot, but no stone unturned, right?"

"And if the spell doesn't work, you can clean the shop floor with it," Clara said.

"Uppity uppity rise thyself," Glo chanted. "Wings of magic, heart of believer, eyes open, spirit soar. Uppity uppity rise thyself."

She opened her eyes and looked over at me. "Well?"

"Sorry."

"No biggie. I've got two more." She grabbed a broom with a blue plastic handle and a yellow plastic brush cut at an angle. She stuck the broom between her legs, closed her eyes, and said the spell. She opened her eyes and blew out a sigh. "I'm not feeling it. I know this one isn't the right broom."

We all looked at the remaining broom. It had a high-gloss mahogany wood handle and a nicely tied-together natural straw sweeper end.

"I saved the best for last," Glo said. "I got this broom from Nina at the Exotica Shoppe. She said it was her best performing broom."

"Did she say it would fly?" Clara asked.

"She said it had real potential in the right hands."

First off, I couldn't relate to the whole flying thing. I got a sick stomach at the thought of clipping along with nothing under me but a broomstick and air. I suppose I'm a big, boring chicken, but I had no desire to hang glide, ride in a hot-air balloon, or parachute out of a plane. I hated roller coasters and Ferris wheels, and I threw up on the teacups at Disney World.

Second, I was still having a hard time with the whole enhanced ability stuff. Some of it, I could buy into. Like I could see where someone might be able to sense certain kinds of energy. I could understand that some people were stronger than others. And it seemed reasonable that I might have an instinctive sense regarding cupcake ingredients. I had a harder time understanding Diesel's ability to open doors. I was completely freaked that Wulf could burn flesh with the touch of a fingertip. And flying on a broom was way out of my believability comfort zone.

Nonetheless, Glo wanted to fly, so I was going to make an effort at being supportive. I gave Glo two thumbs up. "Go for it," I said, plastering a smile onto my face.

"Thanks," she said, climbing onto the broom. "I think this might be it." She squinched her eyes tightly closed, gripped the handle, and repeated the spell. "Uppity uppity rise thyself. Wings of magic, heart of believer, eyes open, spirit soar. Uppity uppity rise thyself."

She opened her eyes and looked over at me. "Did you see it move? Did my feet come off the ground? It felt like I got a little lift."

"Maybe a little," I said. "It was hard to see from here."

Glo looked at Clara. "Did you see it?"

"Not exactly, but I wasn't watching your feet."

Glo focused on the broom handle. "Here goes again. I have a feeling I'm just going to zoom away this time."

She ran through the spell and waited a beat. We all held our breath, but nothing happened. No uppity. No rising. No soaring.

"Crap," Glo said. "Damn and double damn and phooey."

She dropped the broom to the floor and kicked it across the room. The broom ricocheted off the wall, flipped end over end, bounced off the work island, and crashed through the back window.

No one moved for a full minute. We were eyes wide, mouths open, frozen in place.

"I didn't see that," I finally said. "I swear I didn't see anything."

Clara picked her way through the pieces of glass on the floor and looked out the window. "Uh-oh."

"What *uh-oh*?" I asked her. "I hate *uh-oh*."

"I don't see the broom."

We went outside and looked around. No broom.

"A dog must have carried it off," I said.

Glo squinted up into the sky. "Come back, broom," she yelled. "I'm sorry I kicked you."

We all looked up to see if the broom would return.

"I feel like an idiot," Clara said. "I'm standing here expecting to see a flying broom."

We trooped into the kitchen and closed the door.

"I didn't want to say anything when we were outside," Glo said, "but I think that broom was really mean-spirited."

"You should get your money back," Clara said. "I wouldn't pay for a broom with an attitude."

I picked up where I'd left off with the cupcake icing. "It was just a freak accident," I said more to myself than to anyone else.

Clara used one of Glo's brooms to sweep up the window glass. "I'll go along with the *freak* part."

Diesel sauntered in through the entrance from the shop. "How's it going?" he asked.

No one said anything. We were all contemplating the question, not sure of the answer.

His attention moved to the broken window. "What happened there?"

"Angry broom," Glo said on a sigh.

Diesel cut his eyes to me.

"Glo kicked it to the wall, and then it sort of did a cartwheel and flipped itself through the window," I told him.

"Hard to get sympathetic about a broom and a broken window when I've got a monkey sitting in my backseat," Diesel said.

"I know. I'm sorry," Glo said. "It turns out it's surprisingly difficult to place a monkey."

Clara scooped the glass up in a dustpan and dumped the pieces into the trash. "At least we're neighbors to a hardware store. I'm going to run next door and find someone to fix my window."

Diesel looked at his watch and then at me. "How much longer until you're done?"

"I have to decorate this last batch of red velvet and do a little clean-up. Maybe ten minutes."

CHAPTER
TWENTY-THREE

By the time I had my workstation clean and I was ready to leave, Clara had returned and was measuring the broken window with George Henley from Henley's Hardware.

"See you tomorrow," I said to Clara. "Have a nice day, George."

"Back at ya," George said. "Make sure you're on your game tomorrow. I'm getting paid in cupcakes. I got a whole week coming to me."

I put together a box of meat pies and cupcakes, grabbed my purse and sweatshirt, and walked through the shop. Glo was behind the counter, reading *Ripple's,* periodically glancing up to make sure no customers had sneaked in on her.

"See you tomorrow," I said to Glo. "I hope your broom comes back."

"Fat chance of that," she said. "It hates me."

Diesel was parked at the curb, looking bored behind the wheel. Carl was in the backseat, sitting in a booster chair, strapped in, watching a movie on a small DVD player. He had a box of Froot Loops and a sport bottle of water on the seat next to him.

"You're spoiling him," I said to Diesel, sliding onto the passenger-side seat.

"I'm in survival mode. Since we can't seem to get rid of him, I'm doing whatever it takes to neutralize him."

Carl looked up from his movie and gave Diesel the finger.

"What's he watching?" I asked Diesel.

"*Madagascar.* He likes the monkeys."

I handed out meat pies and put the cupcake box on the floor between my feet. "We're going home, right?"

"Wrong," Diesel said, pulling into traffic. "Mark was fried last night. I got the high points out of him, but I want to see if he remembers more now that he's calmed down. I called him a couple minutes ago. He's at Melody's house."

"Mark gave up the charm. What else can he tell you?"

"I don't know, but it feels like there's more."

Diesel went through three meat pies and two cupcakes en route to Melody's house. He parked at the curb, behind Lenny's Camry, and we got out and stood on the sidewalk, looking at Carl in the backseat.

"He should be okay," Diesel said, locking the Cayenne. "He's got about forty minutes more on the movie."

Melody's front door banged open and a kid stuck his head out.

"Are you visitors?" he yelled.

"Yes," I said.

"I can't let you in," he yelled back.

And he slammed the door shut.

Diesel walked to the door and rang the bell.

"What?" the kid yelled from inside.

"I want to talk to your Uncle Mark," Diesel said.

"No."

Diesel opened the door and stepped into the house.

"Help!" the kid yelled. "HELP! Burglar!"

Three more kids ran in. One wrapped his arms around Diesel's leg. Another bit Diesel in the ankle, and a third kid kicked Diesel in the back of the leg. Diesel picked the ankle biter up by the back of his shirt and focused on the kid who'd kicked him.

"You do that again, and I'll turn you into a toad," Diesel said to the kicker.

"Can you do that?" I asked Diesel.

Diesel looked over at me, the ankle biter still dangling in the air. "Do you really want to know the answer to that question?"

"No," I said. "And don't do it in front of me."

Mark walked into the living room. He held a clear plastic bag filled with bite-size candy bars. He shook the bag and the kids snapped to attention, all eyes on the candy bag.

"What's going on?" he asked the door-keeper kid.

"He's a burglar. He's gonna take our telebisions."

"This is Diesel," Mark said. "He isn't a burglar. He came to talk to me."

"Mom said don't let anyone in when she isn't home."

"It's okay. I'm here."

"But Mom said . . ."

Mark threw the candy bag into the dining room. "Fetch."

The kid took off after the candy, and the other kids followed. All but the kid hanging at the end of Diesel's arm. His legs were running, but he wasn't going anywhere. Diesel put the ankle biter down, and he went off like a shot after his siblings.

"Do you have kids?" Mark asked Diesel.

"No," Diesel said. "I have a monkey."

Mark nodded. "How's that working for you?"

"Not all that good," Diesel said.

"Sorry about the charm," Mark said, his hand unconsciously going to the burn marks on his neck. "I have a feeling I gave it to the bad guy."

"Where did Wulf take you?"

"I don't know. He walked up to me, and it was lights out, and then I was in a room that looked like it might have been a warehouse or a factory. Sort of a loft that had been cleaned up. The ceiling was painted black, with exposed air ducts, whitewashed walls. It had a cement floor. No windows. One door. I wasn't there very long. He explained what he wanted. I said no. He burned my neck, and I gave him Uncle Phil's bug. Next thing I know, I'm on the wharf."

"You didn't tell him anything else?"

"Nothing else to tell," Mark said.

"When your uncle was alive, did he ever talk about the charms?"

"No."

"SALIGIA Stones?"

"Nope."

"How about gluttony?" Diesel asked.

"No. Uncle Phil was a scary old coot, but he didn't have any obsessions like Lenny and me. Uncle Phil preached everything in moderation."

"Do you know where he kept the objects he distributed as inheritances?"

"No. The estate lawyer had a locked fireproof metal chest on his desk when we filed in. He unlocked the chest and took out the will and the inheritances. Each inheritance was in its own little box, tied up with a gold ribbon. We were told not to open the box until we were alone, at home. My box contained the dragonfly charm and a slip of paper with the bad luck warning."

"Do you still have the slip of paper?"

"No. Instructions were to destroy it and never speak of it. And there was a short video that came out of the chest. The lawyer played it in his office. It was Uncle Phil, looking like he'd risen from the dead, repeating the bad luck warning. It scared the crap out of all of us, including the lawyer."

"Have you had any other dealings with the lawyer?" Diesel asked.

"No. He died a few months after Uncle Phil. Secretly, I was half afraid it was because he talked about the inheritances. I know that's stupid, but the whole thing was creepy. What's this all about anyway?"

"Your dragonfly was part of a larger treasure," Diesel told him. "It probably doesn't have a lot of monetary value, but it's a collectible."

"Must be a heck of a collectible," Mark said. "That Wolf guy isn't normal."

He'd got that one right. Not normal was an understatement. Of course, if you wanted to get technical, it turns out I might not be entirely normal, either.

"Uncle Mark," one of the kids called. "Kenny pooped in his pants again."

"Trust me," Mark said to Diesel. "You're better off with the monkey."

"Hard to believe," Diesel said. "Is there anything else you can tell us about the inheritance?"

Mark shook his head. "Uncle Phil took his secrets to the grave."

"And that would be where?" Diesel asked.

"His grave? There's a family plot in the old cemetery next to the Presbyterian church on Oyster Hill Road."

A kid waddled to the edge of the living room. "I made poo," he announced.

I wasn't crazy about cemeteries, but Phil's grave held more appeal than Melody's living room. I'd like to think I had maternal instincts locked away in me somewhere, but the truth is, at the moment, they for sure didn't reach out to a kid who made poo.

"Good idea," I said to Diesel. "Let's talk to Phil."

Diesel grinned down at me. "Abandoning Mark's sinking ship?"

"Absolutely."

"Call me if you think of anything new," Diesel said to Mark.

"That was my last bag of candy," Mark said. "I'm a dead man."

Carl was still watching the movie when we reached the Cayenne. The cupcake box was empty on my seat, and Carl had icing stuck in his fur.

Diesel angled behind the wheel and rolled the engine over. "I was looking forward to those cupcakes."

"Take me home, and I'll make more."

"I thought you were all hot to visit Uncle Phil."

"Well, yeah, who wouldn't want to go to the cemetery and talk to a dead guy? It's just that I thought you really wanted cupcakes, and I wouldn't mind if you talked to Uncle Phil without me. That way, I could stay home and bake, and you could do your communing-with-the-departed thing."

Diesel drove out of Melody's neighborhood and went south to Oyster Hill Road. "You aren't afraid of cemeteries, are you?"

"Of course not. I might not like them as much as a shopping center, but I'm not *afraid* of them. That would be dumb. I mean, it's not as if zombies live there."

Oyster Hill Road runs up Oyster Hill and heads west. The cemetery and church are at the crest of the hill. The surrounding land is rocky, not lending itself to development. The small, white, steepled church is two hundred years old. The cemetery is much older. Witches were forbidden from resting in hallowed ground, but legend has it several were secretly buried in Oyster Hill Cemetery in the dark of night by grief-stricken relatives. I figured chances were good one of them was in the More family plot.

Diesel wound his way up the hill and parked in the small lot next to the church. We were the only car parked. The church looked locked up tight. It was the middle of the day, but the sky was overcast, threatening rain.

Carl glanced up from his movie and saw the boneyard. "Eep!"

The cemetery was to the rear of the church. It covered a couple acres and was a jumble of centuries-old, weathered headstones hodgepodged in with new. The grass was trimmed. Not nearly golf course quality but not hardscrabble, either. A footpath led to an elaborate wrought-iron gate and continued on to the center of the cemetery. The gate was open, welcoming all who might enter. There was no fence attached to the gate. Just the gate. The three of us got out of the car and walked to the edge of the cemetery.

"How are we going to find Uncle Phil?" I asked Diesel.

"We're going to wander around and look for him."

"Oh joy."

He tugged at my ponytail and took my hand. "Stick close to me, and I'll keep the zombies away."

His hand was warm over mine, and the heat radiated up my arm and spread to my chest and headed south.

"Jeez," I whispered.

Diesel looked down at me. "Are you feeling the heat?"

"Yes."

"Do you like it?"

"I don't know. Maybe."

"Let me know when you decide," Diesel said.

He led me through the gate and along the path, with Carl following close on our heels. We walked past the Hagard family first. Some of their stones were too old to read, the carving worn away by rain and time. Emily Hagard was missed by her sons. She died in 1817. Lily Hagard had an angel carved into her headstone. Lily was stillborn. The Ramsey family was farther up the hill. Again, some of the stones were rounded and worn smooth. Bernard Ramsey and his wife, Catherine, had an elaborate eight-foot-tall angel carved into granite looking out for them. Across the footpath, Elijah Beemer was also protected by a large winged angel.

"Lots of angels here," I said. "I like the concept of angels, but I have a hard time with the wings. Can you imagine growing something like that out of your back? You'd have to sleep standing up."

The More family plot was about twenty feet past Elijah Beemer's angel, almost at the top of the hill, almost dead center of the cemetery. There were a lot of Mores crammed into the small space. Christian More, Marion More, Andrew More, Ana More, Harry More, and more Mores. Philip James More had the newest headstone. *Cave Cave Deus Videt* was carved into the granite.

"Do you know what the inscription means?" I asked Diesel.

"It's Latin. Beware, Beware, God Sees. It's from the Hieronymus Bosch painting *The Seven Deadly Sins and the Four Last Things.* Bosch completed the paint-on-wood panels in 1485."

"What are the four last things?"

"Death, Last Judgment, Heaven, and Hell."

A chill ran through me. *Cave Cave Deus Videt* was a grim departing message. "Phil took his role as guardian of the sins seriously."

"Yes. And obviously there was no one next in line he felt he could trust with the power."

"Why didn't he turn it over to your Marshalls?"

Diesel shrugged. "He might not have known about the BUM. For that matter, I'm not sure he was an Unmentionable. The More family could have been guarding the Stone since the Middle Ages or before."

I looked around. "So some of the other people buried here might have been guardians."

"It's possible," Diesel said, reading the inscriptions on nearby gravestones, pausing at a stone that resembled Phil's. "Harry More died in 1965, and he has the Latin warning on his stone. He could have been the one to pass the Stone to Phil."

"Here's another," I said. "Alicia More Riddley died in 1901. The warning is on her marker. Plus, there's a very old stone next to hers that looks like it has the warning. The date of death was 1603 or 1608. The inscription is only partially visible."

"Interesting stuff, but it doesn't help me," Diesel said. "I was hoping Phil would talk to us." He nudged me forward. "Stand on his grave and see if you get anything."

"No way! That's creepy and irreverent and sacrilegious."

"It's grass and dirt and none of the above."

"Then why do you want me to stand on it if it's only grass?"

"I want to know if something empowered was buried with Phil."

"There's five feet of dirt between him and me. I'm not going to feel anything."

Diesel picked me up and set me down in front of Phil's headstone. "Give it a shot."

I sunk my teeth into my lower lip, stopped breathing, and concentrated.

"Well?" Diesel asked.

"This is icky."

"Do you notice anything unusual about Phil's grave?" Diesel asked.

I looked around. "No."

"Look more closely. The sod has been cut. And some of the grass surrounding the grave has soil on top of it. Phil was buried seven years ago. This ground should be settled, but it has some give to it."

"Which means?"

"I think Phil might have very recently gone for a walk."

"Get out!"

There was the sound of a car turning into the parking lot. The engine cut off, and a door slammed. A moment later, a second door slammed shut. After a few seconds, a figure appeared at the edge of the cemetery. It was Shirley, and she was carrying a large cardboard box. She soldiered up the hill, head down, laboring. She raised her head when she was halfway up the hill and gave an audible gasp when she spied us at graveside. Her eyes narrowed, and she forged ahead.

Diesel draped an arm around me. "She doesn't look happy to see us."

"Gee, big surprise."

Shirley stopped just short of Phil's grave and pressed her lips together, her arms wrapped around the box.

"Hey," I said.

"How's it goin'?" Diesel asked Shirley.

"Gobble," Shirley said. "Gobble, *gobble*."

It was hard to believe Glo could quote a bunch of words from *Ripple's* and turn Shirley into a turkey. My first instinct was to yell at Shirley and tell her to stop fooling around. My second instinct was to look for cover in case she started shooting.

"What's in the box?" Diesel asked.

Shirley stepped forward, turned the carton upside down, and dumped a load of packaged food onto Phil's grave. Opened boxes of cereal, Oreos, Wheat Thins, macaroni, saltines, taco shells. Bags of M&M's, chips, popcorn, raisin bread, peanut butter cups, pretzel nuggets, jelly beans. Jars of spaghetti sauce, pickles, mayo, peanut butter, and grape jelly.

"Gobble!" Shirley said to Phil's headstone. She stuck her tongue out at it and made a face. "Gobble, gobble, gobble,

gobble," she said, her voice rising to a pitch that could break glass. *"Gobble, gobble, gobble, gobble!"* She jumped up and down on the boxes of crackers and bags of candy. Her face turned red, and she worked up a sweat. *"GOBBLE, GOBBLE, GOBBLE, GOBBLE, GOBBLE!"* She stopped to catch her breath, and she looked at the mess of smashed food and boxes. "Hmph," she said. She tipped her nose up, spun around on her heel, and without giving us so much as a glance, she swished off down the hill.

"Hey," I called after her. "You can't just leave this stuff here. It's littering."

"Gobble gob," Shirley said, and kept going.

"At least she's venting," I said to Diesel. "That's healthy, right?"

Carl wandered onto the grave site and picked through the massacred junk, testing out peanut butter cups, jelly beans, and pretzel nuggets. He stuffed an unscathed box of Pop-Tarts under his arm, and he latched onto a can of Easy Cheese.

"I need to talk to Shirley," Diesel said, heading for the lot.

"Good luck with that." Unless he spoke *gobble*, he was going to have a problem.

Shirley was at her car when Diesel and I caught up.

"I need to talk to you," he said. "It's important. Is there anything else you can tell us about your uncle or the inheritance?"

Shirley looked at him like he was from Mars.

"Okay, so you can only gobble," Diesel said. "We can communicate in writing."

Shirley took a pad and pen from the glovebox, scribbled something, tore the paper off, and handed it to Diesel.

"What does it say?" I asked Diesel.

Diesel read from the paper. "Gobble. Gobble. Gobble."

"Are you kidding?" I asked Shirley.

Shirley sucked in air, her mouth compressed, and her eyes shrunk to the size of little ball bearings. "Gobble," she growled. And then she launched herself at me, wrapped her hands around my neck, and took me down to the ground, where we rolled around slapping and shrieking.

Diesel stepped in and separated us, dragging me to my feet, keeping Shirley at arm's length. "If you're not going to do this in Jell-O, it's not worth watching," he said to me.

"Crikey," I said to Shirley. "You need to get a grip on yourself."

Shirley wrenched away from Diesel and dusted herself off. "Grmmph," she said. And then she deflated like a balloon with a leak. And a tear slid down her cheek.

"I guess this has been a hard week," I said to her.

Shirley took a tissue out of her pocket and dabbed at her eyes and blew her nose.

"We'll figure it out," I said. "We just have to find the right spell."

Shirley nodded, still looking deflated. She slumped into her car, cranked the engine over, and drove away.

"I was trying to be positive," I said to Diesel, "but honestly, I'm not sure we can un-gobble Shirley."

Diesel watched her leave the lot. "I'm not sure we want to. I don't want to hear what she has to say if she ever goes normal again."

A light rain was sifting down on us, and the cloud cover was the color and texture of wet cement. Not ideal weather for a cemetery visit. Not ideal weather for *anything*. Diesel and I climbed into the SUV, and Carl scampered in after us. Carl's movie had run its course, but he had a cache of food to occupy him.

"Did you feel anything at all when you were on Phil's grave?" Diesel asked.

"No."

"Feeling something would tell us a lot. Feeling nothing tells us nothing."

"Do you really think Phil might not be there?"

"The grave has been disturbed, and grave robbing isn't beyond Wulf."

"Why would Wulf want Phil?"

"Don't know."

"And where would he put him?"

"Don't know that, either."

"You don't know much, do you?"

"I know you're going to be my downfall," Diesel said.

"And yet you persist in hanging around."

"I have no control over it," Diesel said. "It's my destiny."

"You're the moth, and I'm the flame?"

"Yeah. It's damn pathetic."

I didn't feel like a flame. I felt like an idiot. I had grass stuck to my shirt and dirt smudges on my jeans from rolling around with Shirley. I'd been so panicked, I could barely remember anything, except that I'd done a lot of ineffective slapping and screaming. If Diesel hadn't stepped in, I'd be just another body rotting in the cemetery.

Diesel stopped for a light and grinned over at me. "You were holding your own."

"I was terrified. That was the first time I've been in a fight. I've never even *seen* a fight in real life. I was just trying to keep her away from me."

"Next time open your eyes."

"First off, there isn't going to be a next time. And second, I didn't want to see her hit me in the face."

"It's been my experience that women don't hit. They claw and kick and gouge. And the really nasty ones bite."

"I didn't want to see any of that, either. Do you have a history of duking it out with women?"

"No, but this wasn't the first time I've had to wade into a catfight."

CHAPTER
TWENTY-FOUR

The wind picked up and the light drizzle turned to a steady rain that slashed across the windshield. Diesel was moving south from the cemetery, following a side street through the center of Salem. A lone figure stood on the sidewalk half a block away. She was drenched to the skin, looking up into a tree.

"It's Glo," I said to Diesel. "Pull over."

Diesel rolled to a stop beside Glo, and I lowered my window.

"What's going on?" I yelled.

"It's my broom. It's stuck in the tree."

I looked at the tree, but I couldn't see a broom. "Are you sure?"

"Yes. I saw it blow past the shop, so I ran out and followed it down the street. And now it's stuck in the tree."

Glo was wearing a short denim jacket, a short black skirt, black tights, and black motorcycle boots. Her red hair was plastered to her head, and water dripped from the hem of her skirt. She shielded her eyes from the rain with her hand and pointed to mid-level on the tree. "It's a little more than halfway up," she said.

"I have to see this," Diesel said, cutting the engine, unbuckling his seat belt. "I know it's pouring rain, but I'll always wonder if I don't see for myself."

We both got out and stood in the rain, next to Glo. We followed her line of sight, and sure enough, there was a broom stuck in the tree.

"If you could boost me up, I could get the broom," Glo said to Diesel.

Diesel lifted Glo to the first branch, and Glo scrambled the rest of the way. She reached the broom, wrapped her hands around it, and tugged.

"Shoot," she said.

"What's wrong?" I called up to her.

"It's really stuck. It got rammed between two branches."

"I'd go up and help her, but the branch she's on wouldn't support me," Diesel said.

Glo did some grunting and swearing. "Ugh," she said. "Double ugh!" She put her foot to the tree truck, leaned back, and pulled, but the broom didn't budge. "I think it's afraid to let go," Glo said.

"Maybe it doesn't *want* to let go," Diesel said.

"What*ever*. I'm done. I've had it with this broom." She turned around and climbed down the tree. "Honest to goodness," Glo yelled, stomping back and forth in the rain, flapping her arms. "It is *so* annoying. This broom has been nothing but trouble. The heck with it. I don't even want it anymore. It can stay in the stupid tree forever."

Tree leaves rustled in the wind and rain, a branch creaked, and the broom fell out of the tree and hit Glo on the head. Glo staggered forward a little and stared down at the broom.

"I guess I loosened it," she said. "And the wind did the rest."

Diesel picked the broom up. "Do you want it?" he asked Glo.

"I suppose so," Glo said, taking the broom. "I mean, I paid for it and all."

"Where's your car?" I asked her.

"It's at the bakery. I saw the broom go by like a tumbleweed, and I took off after it."

I opened the back door and scooped up Carl's crumpled wrappers and rogue Froot Loops. "The bakery is almost a mile away. Get in and we'll give you a ride."

"I'm all wet," Glo said. "I'll make a mess."

"I'm living with a monkey," Diesel told her. "You couldn't come close on your best day."

Glo slid onto the backseat and set the broom next to the window. She slicked her hair back from her face and looked at Carl. "Wow, look at all the cool food," she said. "You're a lucky monkey."

Carl gathered his food close to him and inched away from Glo. He leaned over and looked at the broom. "Eep," he said.

I was watching over my shoulder, and I swear the broom twitched.

"Maybe you don't want to let Carl get too close to the broom," I said to Glo.

"It's just a dumb broom," Glo said. "Carl can't hurt it."

"Yes, but I'm not sure the broom likes him."

Diesel glanced over at me. "Are you okay?"

"It twitched," I whispered to him.

Diesel looked in the rearview mirror at Carl and then at the broom. "I don't see any twitching," he said to me. "Maybe you just have low blood sugar. We'll get you a cupcake when we drop Glo off."

"Thanks," I said, "but I don't want a cupcake."

"I *always* want a cupcake," Diesel said.

He turned a corner, and the broom slid across Glo and whacked Carl before Glo had a chance to grab it and set it back in place.

"Eeep!" Carl said. And he shot goo from the Easy Cheese can at the broom. The cheese hit the broom mid-stick and stuck like snot. Carl shot some more, and it missed the broom and hit the window.

"Knock it off," Diesel said to Carl.

Carl gave Diesel the finger and shot goo onto the back of his head and onto the dashboard. Goo was flying everywhere.

Carl was in an Easy Cheese frenzy. I had goo in my hair and goo on my soaking-wet bandage.

Diesel pulled to the curb, got out of the SUV, yanked Carl out of his booster chair, set him on the roof rack, and got back behind the wheel.

"Omigosh," I said. "You can't leave him up there. He'll blow away."

"I'll drive slow," Diesel said. "I won't go over fifty."

Two blocks later, we were at the bakery. We all jumped out and looked up at Carl. He was soaking wet, gripping the roof-rack rail with his hands and tail. He sat up and gave Diesel the finger.

"It's a good thing I'm not a violent person," Diesel said, looking at Carl. "We're going into the bakery," he said to him. "Are you coming?"

Carl gave him the finger and stayed on the SUV roof, and the rest of us went inside. Clara was behind the counter, her face frozen into a grimace at the sight of three people and a broom dripping on her floor.

"I rescued the broom," Glo said to Clara, setting it in the corner.

"Maybe you should put it in your car,"

Clara told her. "I just fixed my window. In fact, maybe you should drive the broom back to the Exotica lady and trade it in."

Glo got a box and filled it with cupcakes for Diesel. Water ran off her sleeve and puddled in the display case and at her feet. "I know this makes no sense at all, but I kind of like the broom. And I think it might be starting to like me."

"No charge for the cupcakes if you promise to leave immediately," Clara said. "I don't want to have to explain the monkey on your car to my customers."

We took our cupcakes and squished out of the bakery. It was raining hard, and Carl was hunched on the SUV roof looking half-drowned and cranky.

"Would you like to ride inside?" Diesel asked Carl.

Carl shrugged.

"I'm going to take that as a *yes*," Diesel said, lifting Carl off the roof and stuffing him into the backseat.

I buckled myself in with the cupcake box on my lap and crossed my arms to keep warm. The wet was getting to me. "I'm done," I said. "I'm soaked, and I'm cold, and I'm not having any fun."

"Understood," Diesel said. "We're going home."

Two blocks from the bakery, Diesel rolled the window down and squinted against the rain blowing in.

"I can't stand it," he said. "The car smells like wet monkey."

Zzzzt. Easy Cheese shot past Diesel's ear and stuck to the windshield. I turned and glared at Carl. He was pressing the Easy Cheese nozzle, but nothing was happening. He was out of Easy Cheese.

"I told you not to put him on the roof rack," I said to Diesel.

"My mistake wasn't putting him on the roof rack," Diesel said. "It was letting him back inside."

We parked at the curb and walked around the house to the kitchen door. By the time we were inside, we were drenched again and dripping water by the bucketful. Cat came to welcome us, sniffed at Carl, and growled low in his throat. I couldn't blame him. Carl smelled really bad. It turns out wet monkey isn't a great aroma.

"We need to do something with Carl," I said to Diesel. "He's got Easy Cheese and

Froot Loops stuck in his fur, and he smells like a sick water buffalo."

Diesel filled the kitchen sink with warm water, dunked Carl in it, and soaped him up with dish detergent. He rinsed him off, I wrapped him in a towel and rubbed him dry. When I turned him loose, he was lemon fresh and weirdly fluffy.

"Maybe we should have used a conditioner on him," I said to Diesel.

Carl smelled his arm and picked at his fur. "Eeee."

I was no longer dripping, but I was still wet to the bone. I kicked my shoes into a corner and peeled my socks off. "I'm taking a shower. I'm going to stand under the hot water until I'm as red as a lobster."

Diesel selected a cupcake from the box. "I'm right behind you."

"You don't mean that literally, do you? I mean, you aren't planning on sharing a shower with me, are you?"

Diesel glanced over at me. "Is that a possibility?"

"No."

"Your loss," Diesel said.

"What about the forbidden Unmentionable joining thing?"

"Doesn't mean we can't get naked and ogle each other."

"Wouldn't that be frustrating?"

"Honey, every moment I spend with you is frustrating."

I wasn't sure if that was hot frustrating or annoying frustrating, and I didn't want to ask.

"Both," Diesel said. "And you need to get out of those wet clothes. You're starting to look pruney."

I ran upstairs, grabbed dry clothes, and jumped into the shower. I was halfway through shampooing my hair and the water turned cold.

"Damn!"

Ten minutes later, my hair was dry, I was dressed in sweats and shearling boots, and I'd replaced the soaked gauze with a couple giant Band-Aids. I stomped down the stairs and into the kitchen, where Cat, Carl, and Diesel were working their way through the box of cupcakes.

"You used all the hot water," I said to Diesel.

"Wrong," Diesel said. "I didn't have any hot water."

"Well then what happened to all the hot water?"

Diesel turned the tap on and waited for it to get warm. "How old is your water heater?" he asked.

"It came with the house. It looks pretty old."

We went down to the cellar and looked at the water heater. It was completely rusted out and leaking water.

"I'm no plumber," Diesel said, "but I know a dead water heater when I see one."

He turned the water off, and I mopped the floor with some old towels.

"I can't afford a new water heater," I said. "It's not in my budget."

Diesel looked at the sagging overhead beams and the crumbling foundation. "You have bigger problems than a water heater."

"I know. I need the money from the cookbook. It's my only hope of fixing the house."

"How close are you to finishing your book?"

"I'm almost done, but that's not my problem. My problem is selling the darn thing."

Diesel followed me back to the kitchen. "I can get you a water heater, but I can't solve your more serious issues. Unlike Wulf, I don't have unlimited funds at my disposal. I don't draw a salary on this job."

"You work for free?"

Diesel got a soda from the fridge. "I have everything I need." His eyes held mine for a beat. "Almost everything."

Carl jumped from the counter to the floor and farted. So much for the sexy moment, I thought. Saved by monkey gas.

"Dude," Diesel said to Carl. "You need to lay off the cheese."

The phone rang. Diesel answered and passed it to me. "It's your mother."

Terrific. The one time in the history of the world Diesel answers my phone, and it has to be my mother.

"Who was that man?" my mother asked. "I thought I had the wrong number."

"He's just a friend."

"Oh?"

"Not that kind of friend," I told her.

"I have a wonderful surprise," she said. "Your father was selected to attend a seminar on public transportation customer relations in Boston tomorrow, and he's on his way. Lou Dribbet was supposed to go, but he passed a kidney stone last night and wasn't up to flying. It was all very sudden."

"Dad's flying?"

"Actually, he's landed. I tried calling your cell phone all day, but you weren't picking up."

"My cell phone died, and I haven't gotten a new one yet."

"Well, he's on his way. He should be at your house any minute now. He's so excited. He's going to spend the night with you and go to the seminar hotel tomorrow."

"What? No! Not a good idea."

"Why not? You have a guest bedroom."

"I haven't got a bed in it."

"He can sleep on the couch then. Goodness knows it won't be the first time he's had to sleep on the couch. Sometimes I can't take the snoring. That man could wake the dead."

The doorbell chimed, and I felt my heart constrict to the size of a raisin.

"I think Dad's here," I said to my mom. "I'll talk to you later."

I hung up and focused on Diesel. "You have to go."

"No."

"YES!" I grabbed him by the front of his

shirt and got into his face. "My father is at the door. He's spending the night here, and he's not going to like that you sleep in my bed."

"Tell him we're engaged."

"We're *not* engaged. And even if we were, it wouldn't be good enough."

"So tell him we're married."

"That's insane!" I said. "And besides, I don't have a ring."

"Tell him you lost it. Tell him it slipped off into the mixing bowl when you were making sticky buns and someone took it home and ate it."

The bell rang a second time, and I hurried to get the door before my father was completely drenched. "I'm begging you," I yelled to Diesel as I ran. "Sneak out the back way."

My father is a big man. Six foot tall and chunky. The family joke is that if he wasn't driving a bus, he could be pulling one. He's as strong as an ox, but he's the family softy, crying over sad movie endings, a sucker for puppies and kittens, buying mushy Valentine's Day cards for my mom. He's completely not the disciplinarian in my family, but he wouldn't put up with a man in my bed if there wasn't a ring on my finger.

I found him hunched on my front stoop, holding a small yellow umbrella in one hand and a suitcase in the other. His rental car was parked at the curb.

"For a minute there, I was afraid you weren't home," he said, leaving the umbrella outside, stepping in with his suitcase.

"I was in the kitchen, talking to mom."

He looked around my living room. "This is nice. You've made a real home here. I only was in this house once, and it was over twenty years ago. I remember it as being fussy, with stuff crammed everywhere. Seems like it's a little more lopsided now, but that's how it is with these old houses, I guess."

Cat strolled into the room and gave my father the once-over.

"I didn't know you had a cat," my father said. "What's his name?"

"Cat 7143. Cat, for short."

My father squinted at Cat. "He's only got half a tail. And there's something weird with his eye."

"It's glass."

My father went blank-faced for a moment. "Is that Ophelia's cat?"

"I don't know. He came from the shelter."

"If it's Ophelia's, he must be the oldest cat on the planet. Ophelia was telling us she had a one-eyed cat when we visited her, but no one ever saw it. We always figured she was making it up. And in the years before she died, she'd tell your grandmother crazy things about the cat. How the cat could read her mind. And that he was actually a ninja."

Oh great, I thought. Just what I need . . . another mind reader in the house. I looked over at Cat, and I swear he looked back at me and winked. Okay, so I guess he could have just blinked his one good eye, but it seemed like a wink.

"You know what we should do?" I said to my dad. "We should go out for dinner. I know this bar that makes unbelievable wings."

"No way. I sent you to cooking school. I want to see what you can do."

"I haven't got a lot in the house," I told him.

"Do you have beer?"

"Yes."

"Then I'm a happy man. You can make me a sandwich, and we don't have to go out in the rain. And there's a game on tonight. I see you have a television."

"Right."

And I might have a big, strange guy in my kitchen. I hadn't heard the back door open or close.

"There's something I should tell you," I said. "I don't exactly live here alone."

"I know," he said, moving past me toward the kitchen. "You have a one-eyed cat."

"Yeah, but there's more."

"More?" He stepped into the kitchen and stopped dead in his tracks. "Does your mother know about this?"

I sunk my teeth into my lower lip and followed behind him. "I can explain."

"Your mother would have a heart attack if she knew you had a monkey in your kitchen."

"That's all? A monkey?" I peeked in and did a fast scan of the room. One monkey. No Diesel.

"That's Carl," I said to my father. "I'm taking care of him while the rescue organization finds him a real home."

"What kind of monkey is he?" my father wanted to know. "His fur is all fluffy. He looks silly."

Carl gave my father the finger, and my father's eyebrows went all the way up to his hairline.

"He's sensitive about his fur," I said.

My father looked like he was working at squelching a grimace. "You're sort of living in a loony bin."

Yeah, I thought. And this is just the tip of the iceberg.

CHAPTER TWENTY-FIVE

An hour after my dad arrived, I had dinner on the dining room table. Steak, mashed potatoes, and green beans. And vanilla pudding for dessert.

"This is great," my father said, taking his seat, shaking out his napkin. "I'm starved."

Carl had followed us in and was standing on tiptoe, peeking over the edge of the table, surveying the food.

"He looks hungry," my father said.

"He's always hungry. He just ate enough junk food to feed half of China."

"Maybe he needs green beans after all that junk food."

Carl bobbed his head up and down. Yes, he needed green beans. He scurried into the kitchen and returned with a plate and silverware. He plunked the plate and silverware down on the table, climbed onto a chair, and sat erect on his haunches. He could barely see over the table. He jumped down, ran into the living room, and came back with a throw pillow. He carefully placed the throw pillow on his chair and climbed on board. Now he was just right for the table.

"Eep," Carl said, hands folded in front of him.

"I wouldn't believe it if I hadn't just seen it," my father said.

I spooned potatoes and beans onto Carl's plate, and I gave him two small pieces of steak. Carl picked a green bean up with his fingers, smelled it, and ate it. When he was done with his beans, he popped a piece of steak into his mouth and chewed. His lips curled back, his mouth opened, and the half-chewed piece of steak fell out.

"Guess he doesn't like steak," my father said.

Carl looked at his mashed potatoes, and he looked over at me. "Eeee?"

"Mashed potatoes," I told him. "Do you like mashed potatoes?"

Carl shrugged.

I ate a forkful of potatoes. "Mmmm," I said. "Good." I handed him his fork. "You try it."

Carl vigorously shook his head no.

"It's easy," I said to Carl. "You just stick the fork in and scoop up potatoes."

Carl looked from the potatoes, to me, to my father. He looked at the fork and tested a prong with his finger. "Eeh."

"If you can work a DVD player, you surely can manage a fork," I said to him.

Carl sucked his lips in and squirmed in his seat.

"Be a man," my father said to him. "Eat your potatoes!"

Carl squared his shoulders, forked up a glob of potatoes, and concentrated. He got the potatoes almost to his mouth, the fork twisted ever so slightly, and the potatoes fell off onto the floor. "Eeep!" Carl narrowed his eyes and dug into the potatoes again with the same result. *"Buh!"* He flipped my father the bird, threw the fork across the room, grabbed a handful of potato, and shoved it into his mouth.

My father dug into his food. "This is like eating with your brother."

After dinner, my dad and Carl settled onto the couch and tuned in to the ball game while I cleaned the kitchen with Cat keeping me company.

"This is a real pain without hot water," I said to Cat. "First thing tomorrow, I'll call a plumber and get an estimate on a new water heater."

Cat fixed his good eye on me and didn't say anything.

"I love my house, but I didn't have this problem when I was renting," I said to him. "I paid my rent, and that was it. I guess you wouldn't know about that if you've always lived here with Ophelia. I suppose you've had your own problems, what with your eye and tail and all, but at least you've never had to find money for a plumber." I put a pot of hot water on the stove to heat. "And by the way, I never thanked you for saving me from Hatchet. I really do appreciate it. That was very brave of you."

Cat sat statue still.

"Are you really a ninja?" I asked him.

No answer.

"I guess I didn't expect you to tell me," I said to Cat. "It's all pretty far-fetched anyway."

I finished the kitchen and went to the living room with a clean quilt and pillow for my father. I looked out the window and checked the street. No Spook Patrol. No Hatchet. No Diesel. I told myself it should feel good to be free of Diesel, but truth is, I missed him. Thank goodness he wasn't around to hear me think it.

"How's the game?" I asked my dad.

"Tie, but Baltimore's gonna win."

Carl gave my father the finger. Carl obviously wasn't an Orioles fan.

"Maybe you shouldn't tell Mom about Carl," I said to my dad.

"Too late. I already sent her a picture. I got a new cell phone, and it's got a picture function. It's magic. It's your brother who's gonna be upset. You just replaced him as family goofball."

"He worked for years to keep that title."

"Yep," my father said. "And you just kicked him to the curb. All his tattoos and loud motorcycles and bad table manners can't compete with your monkey."

"I was afraid you might not understand."

"What's not to understand? You have a monkey who gives people the finger."

"He's only temporary," I said.

"Your brother will be relieved."

Carl burped and scratched his butt.

"It's like he's human," my father said.

"If it's okay with you, I'm going to skip the game. I have work to do on the computer."

"Don't stay up late. I know you go to the bakery early. And don't worry about me. I'll be fine here on the couch."

"One more thing. My water heater conked out today. I'm getting a new one tomorrow, but in the meantime there's no hot water."

Rain drummed on the roof and ticked against the window over my desk. I'd put in a solid hour of work, and I'd finished the final edit on the part of the cookbook dedicated to entrees. I'd answered some e-mails from friends in New York, and I'd read through two news sites. Cat was curled in the worn-out easy chair alongside my desk. He looked relaxed and asleep, but his ears were pricked forward in listening mode.

"Bedtime," I said to Cat.

His eyes opened, and he stood and

arched his back in a stretch. He followed me out of my office and into my bedroom. The television was still on downstairs, so I closed my door to muffle the noise. A sticky note had been left on my pillow.

Be extra careful. I'm not there to protect you.

The mystery wasn't who wrote the note, but how the heck Diesel got it onto my pillow and then left the house without being seen. I looked in my closet, under the bed, and in the bathroom, checking behind the shower curtain, just to make sure he wasn't lurking somewhere.

Ten minutes later, I was in bed, and Cat was sitting on my chest.

"I suppose you're protecting me ninja-style," I said to Cat. "Or maybe you're just trying to keep warm. Either way, I can't breathe. You have to get off my chest."

He didn't move, so I lifted him off and set him next to me. When I woke up the next morning, he was back on my chest.

"You're killing me," I said to Cat. "I'm lucky I didn't die in my sleep. Maybe I should cut back on the cat food. You weigh a ton."

Cat stood and did the back arch thing

again. He stepped off my chest and sat at the bottom of the bed. He didn't look like he was worried about his weight. And either he knew an idle threat when he heard one, or else he didn't understand a word I was saying. If he was a ninja, maybe he only spoke Japanese.

I skipped my morning shower, opting to wear a ball cap rather than attempt to wash my hair in frigid water. I dressed in my usual jeans, T-shirt, and sweatshirt, and I quietly walked down the stairs and sneaked into the kitchen. I poured out some kibble for Cat and gave him fresh water. I could hear my dad snoring on the couch, and I assumed Carl was with him. I started making coffee and then thought better of it.

"I don't want to wake my dad," I whispered to Cat. "I'm going to eat breakfast at the bakery."

Cat was hunkered down in front of the back door. I approached the door, and Cat growled at me.

"I fed you," I said. "And you can't go out."

Cat didn't move.

I reached out to move him, and he slashed at me.

"Bad cat!"

I shoved him with my foot and squeezed past him, out the door. The last thing I saw was his face in the window, and the last thing I heard was Hatchet calling me a stupid wench. And then everything went black.

The room was cool and quiet. Lights were dim. The walls were taupe. Across the room was floor-to-ceiling black glass. Some of the mind fog lifted, and I realized I was on my back. Not hurt, but disoriented. There was nothing between my kitchen and this room. I had no idea how I'd got here. No memory of capture, but I knew I'd been physically moved to an unfamiliar place. I had a rush of panic and then a flash of insight. Wulf. I couldn't see him, but I had a sense of him. This wasn't the warehouse that Lenny and Mark More had described. This place felt serene and was fully furnished.

I was on a couch in a living room, I thought. I swung my legs over the side and sat. Furniture was all clean lines, ivory and cocoa. Expensive art on the walls. The black glass was a window. The street was at least twenty floors below. I moved my eyes left, and spotted him. He was motionless in a chair across the room, his dark eyes fixed on me. His face was almost as pale as the ivory chair. His glossy black hair was loose, swept back, falling to his shoulders in waves.

"My apologies," he said, his voice soft. "Steven acted without my direction. Although, it has turned out well, because here you are . . . unprotected by my annoying cousin."

"Where are we?"

"You're in my home."

"It doesn't look like the brownstone."

"This is a new address," Wulf said. "A necessary inconvenience."

I looked around the room. "Does Hatchet live here, too?"

"No."

"How did Hatchet get me here?"

"Stun gun and then a mild anesthesia. He was a paramedic in the military."

"He's insane."

"Yes, but sometimes in an amusing way. His obsessive brain is currently mired in the Middle Ages, but he's actually quite brilliant. He's an authority on paralytic toxins and Inquisition torture techniques. And as you know, he's one of only two people living who can identify an empowered object."

I walked to the window and looked out. We were in Boston. The sun was rising, tinting the black sky red at the horizon. A few car lights slid along the streets. I could see the Common below me. Behind me, the far end of the room opened to a marble-floored foyer and elevator. Wulf was occupying a penthouse. If Diesel were living here, there would be shoes left lying around and a sweatshirt draped over a chair back. Wulf's home was pristine.

"Is there a Mrs. Wulf?" I asked him.

"No. I live alone."

He crossed the room to stand behind me. When he moved, there were no sounds of footsteps, just the barest rustle of cloth. He made no attempt to touch me, but I could feel his energy field edging against mine.

I stepped away from him into a more benign space. "I'm supposed to be at work."

"You have something I want. After you give it to me, you can leave and go to your work."

"What do you want?"

"Information."

"That's it?"

"Eventually, I'll require more from you," Wulf said. "When I possess all of the SALIGIA, I'll need to take your gift away. Unless, of course, my much too normal cousin loses control and risks his power before I have the pleasure of your company."

"Aren't you afraid of the risk?"

"If I have the SALIGIA, there will be no risk."

"You're assuming I would cooperate in this."

"I'll have no trouble persuading you to cooperate."

That was a chilling thought.

"How many charms do you have?" he asked me.

"*I* don't have any. Diesel has one from Shirley More. And you have the charm from Mark More."

"And Lenny's charm?"

"Lenny's charm got exploded."

"Yes, but not destroyed," Wulf said. "The empowered object can shift forms, but it can't be destroyed."

"It doesn't seem to me that Lenny's charm matters. We're at a deadlock. The hunt for the SALIGIA is done. You and Diesel each possess a charm, so the charms will never be combined."

Wulf's eyes dilated totally black. "One way or another, the charms *will* be combined, and the first of the SALIGIA Stones will be found."

Yipes. For a nano-second I thought I saw tiny flames flicker deep in Wulf's eyes. Probably, it was a reflection from the candles on the sideboard. The other explanation was that he was the devil. Either way, he was wigging me out with the SALIGIA stuff.

"Four members of the More family were given identical boxes when the estate was settled," Wulf said. "Sadly, the estate executor died shortly after the will was read and property was distributed. So I can't encourage him to share his information. There's no record of the four recipients, but we've managed to find three of them. I don't suppose you know who the fourth is?"

"I thought there were only three."

"Three were at the reading of the will. The fourth didn't attend and was privately given the box. Neither Mark nor Lenny knows the identity of the fourth More. And you've effectively silenced Shirley."

"Why are you sharing this with me?"

"There are far too many Mores in the Salem area, and searching for the correct one will be tedious. I'm going to let you find the last More for me."

"I'm working with Diesel."

"In the end, it will come down to a deal and a roll of the dice. It doesn't matter who finds the last charm. Possession of the Stone is all that matters."

"Why do you want the Stone?"

Wulf thought about it for a moment, his eyes still intense and fixed on me, his energy prickling against my skin. "I suppose I enjoy the hunt," he said. "And the power of the SALIGIA fascinates me."

"Diesel will turn the SALIGIA over to the BUM for safekeeping, so it won't be used for evil purposes."

"Admirable," Wulf said. "And predictably boring."

"Would you use it for evil purposes?" I asked him.

"Evil is relative."

"That's a convenient attitude taken by people who do bad things."

Wulf smiled at that, but the smile was small and didn't extend beyond his mouth. "Perhaps." He picked a slim cell phone up from an end table and tapped a number in. "I'm done with her . . . for now," he said into the phone. "She'll be on a park bench on Boylston, in front of the swan boats." He disconnected and turned his attention back to me. "Face the window and close your eyes," he said, moving behind me, placing his hand on the back of my neck.

His grip was firm, and his hand was warm. A wave of panic slid through my stomach, and my heart tap-danced in my chest. "Who did you call?" I asked.

"I called your ride."

And then an electric charge buzzed down my spine and hummed in my head. My legs gave way, my vision blurred, and the last thing I remember was Wulf wrapping his arms around me.

CHAPTER TWENTY-SIX

I shook my head in a reflex action to clear the confusion. I was sitting on a bench at the edge of the park, and Diesel was squatting in front of me, holding my hands. The line of his mouth was tight with anger, his eyes showed concern.

"Are you okay?" he asked.

"I don't know." The truth is, I felt okay, but Diesel looked worried and a little shaken, and his anxiety was infectious.

"Do you know your name?"

"Lizzy."

"Do you know how you got here?"

"No."

"You were with Wulf," Diesel said.

"Oh yeah. Now I remember." I looked down at my hands. "Am I burned? Do I have blisters anywhere?"

"The parts of you I can see look okay. I'd rather wait and examine the rest of you at home so I can take my time. Right now, we need to get moving. I'm illegally parked."

"You're supposed to be a powerful Unmentionable. Can't you cloak your car in an invisibility shield? Can't you make the sign disappear from the handicap parking space?"

Diesel tugged me down the path to the sidewalk. "No, but I can make you wish you were nicer to me."

I looked up and down Boylston Street, but I didn't see Diesel's SUV. "Where's your car?"

"I swapped it out. I was getting a migraine from the monkey smell."

The only car illegally parked was a black Porsche turbo. "You swapped it out for a turbo?"

Diesel opened the passenger-side door for me. "Gwen takes whatever is available and fits me." He angled himself behind the wheel and pulled into traffic.

"Where do the cars come from?"

"I don't know. I never get an answer when I ask, so I've stopped asking."

"Wulf is living in one of the high-rise condos bordering the park. He had his own elevator, so I'm guessing it's a penthouse."

"That sounds like Wulf."

"It was nice. Beautiful art on the walls and elegant furniture. And Wulf wasn't terrible. He was very quiet and civil, but there's something about him that frightens me."

"Maybe it's because he burned you, and he kills people." Diesel took the road through the park and turned toward Storrow Drive. "How did it go with your dad last night?"

"It was good except for the mashed potatoes."

Diesel cut his eyes to me.

"Carl wanted to sit at the table and eat with us," I told him. "So I fixed him a plate of steak and green beans and mashed potatoes."

"You didn't try to get him to eat mashed potatoes with a fork, did you?"

"Yeah."

"Been there, done that," Diesel said.

"Anyway, everything else was nice, and it was great to see my dad. I miss my family, and I wouldn't mind living closer, but I don't miss northern Virginia."

Diesel hit the entrance to Storrow and went from zero to seventy in about three seconds. Traffic was all coming into the city, and we were leaving the city.

"I was waiting for you in front of your house," Diesel said. "I didn't expect you to come out the back door."

"I didn't want to wake my dad."

Diesel's brows knit together. "I usually sense Wulf. I don't know how I missed him this morning."

"It wasn't Wulf. It was Hatchet. He stungunned me and brought me to Wulf's penthouse. Why didn't you just read my mind?"

Diesel grinned. "You don't actually think I can read your mind, do you?"

"No. Of course not. That would be ridiculous." I gave up a sigh. "How do you always know what I'm thinking if you can't read my mind?"

Diesel slowed for traffic, changing lanes for the Tobin Bridge. "Lucky guess?"

I wasn't sure what I hated more . . . thinking Diesel could read my mind, or knowing I was so transparent he always knew what was in my head.

"Anything happen in Wulf's condo that I should know about?" Diesel asked.

"It turns out there are *four* charms. Wulf wants me to find the fourth one. I said I was working with you, and he said it didn't matter. He said it'll come down to a deal and a roll of the dice."

"Why doesn't Wulf have Hatchet find the fourth charm?"

"I don't know. Maybe he thinks it'll go faster with two people looking. At any rate, you apparently need all four charms to find the real Stone, and Wulf's determined to find the Stone."

"Do you have any idea who that fourth charm holder might be?" Diesel asked.

"Yes. Do you?"

He nodded. "Yep. I'm guessing it's serial mom."

That was my guess, too. She wasn't at the reading of the will, but she was in the photo with the other charm holders. And she started having children at the right time.

"I need to get to the bakery," I told Diesel. "I'll be done around noon, and we can go talk to Melody. I imagine mornings are chaos in her house anyway."

It was precisely seven o'clock when Diesel dropped me off at Dazzle's. Clara was up to her elbows in bread dough, looking like she needed a vacation. Her hair was more eccentric than usual and shot with flour. Her expression was somewhere between a death in the family and royally pissed off.

"Where the heck have you been?" Clara half shrieked.

"I was kidnapped."

"That's no excuse," she said. "You could at least call."

I hung my sweatshirt on a hook by the door and buttoned myself into a clean chef coat. "I don't have a cell phone. And anyway, I was unconscious a lot of the time."

Clara pushed her hair back with her hand, and a glob of bread dough stuck in the hair just above her ear. "I was really worried. Ten more minutes, and I was going to start calling hospitals. How could you get kidnapped? Where was Diesel? I thought he was supposed to be protecting you."

"My father unexpectedly showed up last night, and there was no way I could explain Diesel without creating a family crisis. So I kicked Diesel out. I guess it was a dumb thing to do, because Steven Hatchet was waiting for me when I opened the door to come to work this morning."

"Who's Steven Hatchet?"

"He's the guy who sliced my arm."

"You said it was a freak accident with your carving knife."

I measured out the flour, sugar, salt, and baking powder for the first batch of cupcakes. "I fibbed."

Clara stopped working and looked at me. "I'm starting to get a bad feeling."

"Steven Hatchet supposedly is an Unmentionable. And supposedly, we're the only two people on the planet who have the ability to find certain empowered objects."

"The SALIGIA Stones."

"Yes. Unfortunately, Hatchet is a complete psycho nutcase who thinks he's living in the Middle Ages. And now, his whole life is centered around impressing Wulf. He calls him his liege lord. And it gets even better, because Hatchet is an authority on toxins and torture."

"Cripes," Clara said.

I dumped butter, milk, the flour mixture, and vanilla into the big mixer and turned it on. "Anyway, Hatchet snatched me and brought me to Wulf's condo."

Clara had both hands flat on the island, leaning toward me, eyes wide. "You were in his condo? Omigosh, what was it like?"

"It was in a high-rise on the park in Boston. Beautifully decorated. Old Masters type art on the walls. They looked authentic, but what do I know."

"What about his bedroom and his kitchen? Does he cook?"

"I only saw the living room." Thank goodness.

I whipped up egg whites, added them to the rest of the batter, and filled the cupcake tins. I shoved the tins into the oven and started another batch of cupcakes.

A half hour later, I pulled the cupcakes out of the oven and set them on a rack at my workstation. Clara came over and looked at them with me.

"What are they?" Clara wanted to know.

"Cupcakes."

"They don't look like cupcakes. They're all flat and lumpy."

"I don't get it. My cupcakes are always perfect. I've been making cupcakes for as long as I can remember, and I've never had this happen."

"Maybe there's something wrong with the oven. Maybe you forgot the baking powder."

"I have a second batch baking in the lower oven."

We went to the oven and looked in. Disaster. My chocolate cupcakes were oozing over their wrappers and dripping onto the oven floor.

"This is horrible," I said. "How could this be happening?"

Clara's face went pale. "You've lost it."

"Lost what?"

"Your ability to make Unmentionably superior cupcakes."

"That's ridiculous. It was the flour or something."

"It happened to me," Clara said. "I never talk about it, but I'm going to tell you because you have to know. I used to be an Unmentionable. I come from a long line of Unmentionables."

"Get out!"

"There was this guy I was dating after my first divorce," Clara said. "He was really nice, and one thing led to another, and next thing, we spent the night together. And when I woke up in the morning, I was a Normal."

"Are you serious? What was your ability?"

"Cookies. I still make cookies, and they're okay, but I used to make cookies that were perfect. And my cookies made people happy."

"They still make people happy."

"It's not the same. Everyone who bit into one of my Unmentionable cookies smiled. And then there was the other thing," she said.

"There was more?"

"If I really concentrated, I could bend a spoon just by looking at it."

"Jeez."

"I know it's a parlor trick, but I really enjoyed it. The cookies I can manage, because I can still make decent cookies, but I feel bad about losing the spoon bending." Some of the color returned to Clara's cheeks. "It was great at a dinner party. All of a sudden, someone's spoon would curl up, and everyone would freak out."

"No one knew it was you?"

"Some might have suspected. It was known that the Dazzles weren't all normal. Mostly, there were all sorts of wrong rumors about our abilities. Like flying and casting spells. The truth is, most Unmentionable abilities are pretty mundane."

I plucked one of the misshapen cupcakes out of the pan. "I never knew I had help making cupcakes. I just always figured I was really good at it. A natural ability."

"You were right about the natural ability," Clara said.

"So how did I lose it?"

"I suppose you lost it the same way I did. You had sex with another Unmentionable. Did you sleep with Diesel last night?"

"No. I haven't slept with Diesel at all. At least, not that way."

Clara bit into her lower lip. "Wulf?" she whispered.

"Not that I remember."

"That's not a definite *no*."

I put my hand to the island to steady myself. "I was unconscious for some of the time."

Clara fanned me with a kitchen towel. "You don't look good."

I slid down the side of the island and sat hard on the floor, legs out. "I don't *feel* good."

"Is there any other possibility?"

"Hatchet."

I leaned forward, head between my knees, took a bunch of deep breaths, and tried to wrap my mind around the horrible possibilities. "The thing is, I can't imagine either of them doing it."

"You don't think they're capable?"

"I think they're both capable . . . just not under these circumstances. Hatchet is impulsive, but I can't see him messing with a woman he thought belonged to his liege. And Wulf wants me to find the fourth charm."

Clara pulled me to my feet, and we looked at the cupcakes.

"Cupcakes don't lie," Clara said.

My emotions were mixed. The thought that I might have been violated while I was unconscious made my stomach sick. The possibility that I might have lost my Unmentionableness (if in fact I ever possessed it) wasn't completely disappointing. The scary people would leave me alone, and I could return to a normal life of mortgage payments and cupcake making. Okay, so maybe my cupcakes wouldn't be spectacular, but I could learn to make them perfectly enjoyable. I mean, anyone can learn to make a cupcake, right?

"Are there any telltale signs of . . . you know?" Clara asked. "Is your underwear on backwards?"

I checked around. Everything seemed to be where it was supposed to be.

"I'm going to make another batch of cupcakes," I told her. "And I'm going to follow the recipe and concentrate."

Diesel strolled into the shop at noon and stood in front of the pastry case.

"You must have had a run on cupcakes," he said. "There are no cupcakes here."

"I don't want to talk about it," I said. "I want a double cheeseburger, fries, and a chocolate milkshake."

I traded my chef coat for my sweatshirt, hung my purse on my shoulder, and avoided looking at the trash bag that held a little over two hundred cupcakes not fit for sale.

"You're either pissed off or celebrating," Diesel said. "I can't tell which."

I swished past him, out the door to the turbo. "Exactly."

Carl was crammed into the miniature backseat. He peeked out at me and gave me a finger wave.

"Your dad rolled out around ten," Diesel said. "Cat was looking like he needed some alone time, so I brought Carl with me."

"He just fits in the backseat."

"Yeah. It's monkey-size. You want to tell me about your day so far? I'm not getting a clear signal."

"I can't make cupcakes."

"And?"

"No matter what recipe I use, the cupcakes are awful."

"Honey, it's not the end of civilization."

"I thought you would be upset."

"Guess I'm not in a cupcake mood. I thought the cheeseburger sounded like a good idea."

"Cheee," Carl said from the backseat.

"What about my Unmentionableness? You said I made Unmentionable cupcakes."

Diesel rolled the engine over. "I don't know how to break this to you, but not everything I say is true." He glanced over at me, his expression unreadable. "Is there anything *more* you want to tell me about you and Wulf?"

"I was unconscious for some of the time, and when my cupcakes flopped, I got worried that Wulf might have used the opportunity to unempower me."

"Wulf won't unempower you until he's in possession of the SALIGIA Stones. If Hatchet gets run over by a truck, you're the only one who can identify the Stones. And until Wulf has the Stones, he won't chance being reduced to a Normal." Diesel grinned at me. "Anyway, you can count on me to save you from Wulf. The minute I think you're really in danger of getting unempowered, I'll make the sacrifice and do the unempowering myself."

"Gee, thanks."

A half mile later, Diesel swung into a drive-through and ordered burgers and fries.

"This is a new car," I said to Carl, handing him his bag of food. "Be careful. I don't want to see any crumbs or ketchup stains back there."

"Eee," Carl said, taking the bag.

I ate my double cheeseburger and sucked up some milkshake. I checked Carl out in the rearview mirror and saw that he was eating his fries one at a time, working at being neat. I nibbled at a single fry from my own bag and inadvertently sighed.

"There's something going on in your head," Diesel said. "I can feel anxiety leaking out of your ears."

"I can't stop thinking about the cupcakes. What if you're wrong, and they really were part of my Unmentionableness? What if something *did* happen when I was unconscious?"

"You'd still be the same person," Diesel said. "Being Normal or Unmentionable doesn't change who you are."

"It isn't that. I don't care that I might not be an Unmentionable anymore. I never wanted to be one in the first place. It's the way I might have lost it. There's another possibility besides Wulf." I squinched my eyes closed. "It's so awful I can't even say it out loud."

"Hatchet?" Diesel asked.

I nodded my head yes.

Carl tapped me on the shoulder. I turned to look at him, and he burped in my face.

"Yuk," I said to Carl. "That was gross."

"Eep."

"He's drooling," I said to Diesel. "Have you ever known him to drool?"

"Gorp," Carl said. And he threw up burgers and fries and chocolate shake all over the backseat.

Diesel grimaced and rolled his window down. "I totally screwed up my karma. I don't know what I did, but it must have been bad, because now I have this monkey."

"You made him carsick. It's your driving in this car. You rocket around corners, and zoom off from stop lights, and then you stop short."

"Yeah. It's fun."

CHAPTER
TWENTY-SEVEN

Diesel turned a corner and parked at the curb in front of Melody's house. He got out of the car and called Gwen.

"I need a new car," he said. "Immediately. And whoever picks this one up needs a hazmat suit."

One of the kids was already looking at us from the front door. *"Help!"* the kid yelled.

"What's with these kids?" I said to Diesel. "It's like they've watched too many *Home Alone* movies. And I don't know Kevin from Melvin."

"I can go you one better. I don't know Kevin from Mary Susan."

There was another car parked in front of the house. It was a P.O.S. junker, patched with Bondo. It had no recognizable color, a broken side mirror, and it was missing part of the right front fender.

"It looks like Melody has company," I said to Diesel.

Diesel glanced into the car. "It's Hatchet."

"How do you know?"

"I'm a superior Unmentionable. I know these things. And there's a shield with *Sir Hatchelot* written on it in the backseat."

"Mom," the door kid yelled. "It's that man again."

The kid was yanked back, the door slammed shut, and I could hear the bolt thrown.

Diesel put his hand to the lock, slipped the bolt, and opened the door. Melody was on the couch, holding the baby tight to her chest with one hand, cradling the toddler with the other. Two older kids stood beside her. Hatchet was in the middle of the room, dressed in his medieval regalia of green tights, white tunic, and cheesy chain-link armor. He was holding a sword that appeared identical to the one in my kitchen.

"Halt, rude and lowly beast," Hatchet said to Diesel. "How dare thee enter without my permission. I have laid claim to this household for my liege lord, Gerwulf Grimoire. Leave before I smite thee with my sword."

I took one look at Hatchet, and my blood pressure shot into the stroke zone. He'd broken into my house, slashed my arm, kidnapped me, drugged me, and maybe done worse. I heard a very scary sound, like a killer growl from some feral animal, and I realized it was coming from me.

Diesel's hand curled into the back of my shirt, and he dragged me up tight against him. "Let me take care of this," he said.

"As soon as I gouge his eyes out and shove his privates so far up in his body he chokes on them. And then I'm going to rip his head off and kick it down the street."

"It would be good if we didn't gouge eyes in front of the kids," Diesel said.

I was so angry I was vibrating, but I saw his point about the kids. I tried to focus and redirected my venom. "Does Wulf know you're here?" I asked Hatchet.

"He sent me."

"I don't believe you," I said. "I think this is another one of your stupid attempts to impress him with your pathetic devotion."

"It's not!" Hatchet fumbled in his tunic and produced a folded piece of paper. "I have a list," he said. "He gave me a list, and this is number three, and the first two people weren't home. And it's not pathetic devotion. I've taken an oath of fealty. I live by honor and the sword."

"Great," Diesel said. "Honor is good, but you need to sheath the sword."

Hatchet stiffened his spine and pointed his sword at Diesel. "Never will I sheath my sword in your presence. And you will rue my wrath if you don't leave my domain. You will feel the sting of my sword."

"Hatchelot," Diesel said, "give up on the rueing and wrathing and smiting stuff. You sound like a crazy nutcase."

Even in my enraged state, I knew this was a bad thing to say. It was one thing to tell Hatchet you were going to rip his head off. It was an entirely different deal to suggest he was crazy.

"I'm not crazy!" Hatchet screamed, face turning red, going on purple, neck grotesquely corded.

He lunged at Diesel and ripped a hole in the hem of Diesel's loose-hanging T-shirt.

"This doesn't make me happy," Diesel said, looking at the hole. "I liked this shirt."

"Infidel!" Hatchet screeched. "Prepare to die."

Hatchet slashed at Diesel, and Diesel stepped away.

"This is getting old," Diesel said.

Diesel reached out, snatched the sword out of Hatchet's hand, rammed the blade two inches into the wood floor, leaned on it, and bent it to a forty-five-degree angle.

"Fiend!" Hatchet said, his mouth contorted into a snarl. "I'll kill you with my bare hands."

Diesel grabbed Hatchet by his faux armor and lifted him a foot off the ground. "Here's the deal," Diesel said. "I could pull the plug on your power, but the BUM wouldn't like it, and it would put Lizzy at risk. Ditto killing or crippling you. So I'm going to send you on your way, but I'm sending you with a warning. If you touch Lizzy or cause her a single moment of grief, I'll find you, and it won't be good for you."

Diesel opened the front door, with Hatchet still dangling off the ground, and he pitched him out. Hatchet flew twenty feet and face-planted, and Diesel closed the front door and turned to Melody.

"We need to talk," Diesel said.

Melody's eyes were wide and her mouth was open. "Unh," she said.

"Four people inherited a charm from Uncle Phil," Diesel said. "Were you one of them?"

Melody chewed on her lower lip.

"I know a warning went with the inheritance," Diesel told her, "but the danger to you and your children is greater if you keep the charm."

Melody was wearing a honeybee charm on a slim gold chain, and she fidgeted with the necklace while she debated her dilemma.

"It's the bee, isn't it?" I said to her. "That's what you inherited from Uncle Phil."

"The note said I'd have bad luck."

"Everyone makes their own luck," Diesel said.

I put my hand out. "Can I hold it?"

Melody unclasped the chain and placed the necklace in my hand. I felt the warmth radiate from my open palm and up my arm.

The bee glowed gold, orange, and finally bright red.

I nodded to Diesel. "This is it."

"I know this is special to you," Diesel said to Melody, "but it's very old and should be returned to the rest of the collection."

One of the toddlers spotted Carl hanging back by the door. "Goggy!"

"Eep!" Carl said, turning tail and scurrying out of the house. Two dogs raced through the living room and ran out after him. There was a lot of monkey chatter and barking from the front yard, and the toddler screwed up its face and started crying.

"About the necklace," Diesel said.

"Take it," Melody said. "I appreciate the help with Sir Hatchelot, but honestly, I could do without this additional drama. Close the door on the way out, and don't forget your monkey."

I thanked Melody, pocketed the charm, and peeked outside to see if Hatchet was still looking like roadkill on the front lawn. Fortunately, Hatchet and his wreck of a car were nowhere to be seen.

Diesel closed the door on Melody and

her brood, and we crossed into the neighbor's yard, where the dogs had Carl treed.

"It'd be so easy to leave him here," Diesel said, looking up at Carl.

"Would you really do that?"

"No."

Diesel whistled to Carl, and Carl dropped onto Diesel's shoulder.

"You're such a softy," I said to Diesel.

"Yeah. I'm a pushover for monkeys."

We walked back to the sidewalk and found that the monkey-barf car had disappeared, and in its place sat a king-size white sedan.

"What is it?" I asked Diesel.

"It's a Lincoln Town Car. An old one."

"It's really long."

"Yeah. And really white," Diesel said.

He opened the back door, and Carl jumped in and bounced around on the big bench seat.

"Chee, chee, chee," Carl said.

I slid onto the front passenger seat and ran my hand over the white upholstery. "I feel like I should be in a wedding or going to a prom," I said to Diesel.

"I hate to disappoint you, but they're not on the schedule."

It was almost two o'clock when Diesel parked the Lincoln in front of my house. It was a balmy seventy degrees, and the sun was bright in a blue sky. General Eisenhower was on his stoop, taking in the day. Aside from the general, the street was deserted. Two blocks away, at the foot of the hill, locals were buying flats of pansies at the little flower shop, sitting on city benches with their coffee and chai, and heading for Crocker Park with their golden retrievers and baby carriages.

"This is a nice family neighborhood," I said to Diesel. "Doesn't it make you want to have a baby?"

"No," Diesel said. "Not at the moment."

I rolled out of the Lincoln and checked my mailbox. Two pieces of junk mail, my credit card bill, and a letter from an agent. I tore the agent letter open and read it. Short and sweet. No thanks.

"Damn, damn, damn!" I said. "I've had it. I'm done. What the heck do you have to do to get published anyway? I bet this guy didn't even read my proposal. I hate him. I don't even know him, and I hate him. I hate the whole publishing industry. And I hate this money-pit, broken-down house. I should never have left New York."

I tore the letter into tiny pieces, threw them on the ground, and jumped up and down on them and kicked them around. I stopped jumping, closed my eyes, and counted to ten.

"Unh!" I said.

I opened my eyes and looked at Diesel. He was smiling.

"Feel better?" he asked me.

"I guess."

"Did you mean anything you said?"

"No."

Cat was sitting in the front window, watching us, and he dropped to the floor when we walked in. His tail wasn't bushy and his single good eye looked intense but not insane, so I thought it was a good bet the house was secure.

"As you can see, I'm fine," I said to Cat, bending to scratch him behind the ear. "Next time, I'll pay attention to you."

"What's that about?" Diesel asked, heading for the kitchen.

"Cat knew Hatchet was waiting for me, and I ignored his warning."

Diesel went to the fridge and got a bottle

of water. "Hatchet must have been really motivated to get up and out that early in the morning."

"He's an odd guy. He's stuck in this Middle Ages time warp, swearing fealty to Wulf, but underneath it all, I don't think he has a subservient personality."

"Underneath it all, he's probably criminally insane." Diesel turned the tap on and watched it run hot. "Gwen had a new water heater installed. No charge. She said it was a necessary business expense. She said she remembers what I looked like after chasing down a yak herder who'd gone to the dark side in Tibet, and it wasn't pretty."

"How long were you in Tibet?"

"Weeks. It was impossible to find that guy. All yak herders look and smell the same."

It was hard to imagine Diesel not looking good. The scruffier he got, the sexier he looked.

Diesel gestured to the counter. "I got you a new cell phone. Your number hasn't changed."

"Thanks." I slipped the phone into my pocket and looked Diesel over. "You ever have your sperm count checked out?"

His eyebrows raised a quarter of an inch. "Excuse me?"

"Just wondering. Not everyone's got good swimmers, you know."

"I imagine my swimmers are okay."

"Nice to know, because considering your superior genes, you'd be a terrific baby maker."

Diesel grinned over at me. "Is that an idle compliment or are you going somewhere with it?"

"I'm thinking it might be a good idea for us to have a baby. In fact, if it works out, we could have lots of babies. Okay, I know we're supposed to save the world from evil, but I don't see why we can't make babies *and* save the world."

Diesel stuck his hand out. "Give it to me."

"What?"

"Melody's charm."

"Do you think it's affecting me?"

The grin turned into a full-on smile. "Yeah."

I pulled the necklace out of my pocket and gave it to Diesel. "I guess this means you don't want to make a baby."

"Rain check," Diesel said.

I heard the television turn on in the living room, and I stuck my head in to see what was going on. Carl and Cat were on the couch, and Carl was scrolling through the guide.

"Is he a Normal monkey?" I asked Diesel.

Diesel chugged half a bottle of water. "I don't know. What's he watching? Lifetime? Disney? Fox?"

"He's trying to buy porn."

"Good for him," Diesel said.

"Don't encourage him. Maybe you're not father material after all. Maybe I need to go out and find someone else." I looked at my watch. "It's too early to troll the bars. I guess I could try my luck at the mall or a supermarket."

Diesel finished his water and pitched it into the recycle bin. "You're not serious."

"Of course I'm serious. I'm not getting any younger. If I don't hurry up, all my good eggs will be gone, and I'll be left with only second-rate eggs."

"This is even more bizarre than the food obsession and the hanky panky spanky," Diesel said. "I need to get some distance between you and the charm. I can't let you see my safe place, because it would put you at risk with Wulf. You're going to have to stay here. I'll only be gone a half hour. You have to promise not to go out alone."

"Sure," I said. "But then you have to help me with the baby making."

"Deal."

Diesel locked the door on his way out, and I joined Carl and Cat on the couch. Carl had given up on adult movies and settled on a ball game. I think baseball on television is like watching grass grow. I was moments away from falling off the couch in a stupor when Glo called.

"I've got it. I know this is it," Glo said. "I found a reverse spell for Shirley."

"And?"

"And I need you to come take a look at it. Clara isn't here. She went to the bank. And anyway, I don't know if she's a good judge of spells. You're an Unmentionable. You must sense some of these things."

"Actually, no."

"Well, you're all I've got."

"Can you read it over the phone?"

"No! What if there's something wrong with it. I could blow a fuse and shut down the entire Northeast grid."

I hung up and wrote a letter to Diesel explaining the emergency. I taped the letter to the door and told Carl to make sure Diesel saw it. I grabbed my purse, went to the front door, and hesitated. I'd promised Diesel I wouldn't go off on my own.

"Only one thing to do," I said to Cat. "You have to come with me."

Twenty minutes later, we were at the bakery. Glo was waiting with Ripple's book lying open on the glass case, and her broom was propped against the wall behind her. She was dressed all in black, and she had a shiny gold star stuck to her forehead.

"It's Cat 7143!" she said. "What a cool surprise."

Cat jumped onto the glass case and sat back on his haunches so Glo could scratch his neck.

"What's with the star on your forehead?" I asked her.

"I got the idea when I was at Office Depot yesterday. Clara asked me to stop and get paper for the printer, and I saw these stars. You know, it's all about accessorizing."

"That's so true."

"And you can't go wrong with gold."

"Hardly ever."

"And I thought they might be magical. You never know about these things." Glo turned the book so I could see the spell. "This is it," she said. "Take a look at it, but don't read it out loud."

I glanced at the spell and slid the book back to Glo. "It looks okay to me," I said, "but honestly, I'm not an expert. I didn't pick up anything wrong with the gobble spell until Shirley turned into a turkey."

"Here goes," Glo said. "I'm going to do this long-distance by visualizing Shirley."

"Do you think that will work?"

"I've been reading up on it, and this spell should be a good traveler. Anyway, I'm afraid Shirley will shoot me on sight if I go to her apartment."

"Good point."

Glo took a deep breath and followed word for word with her finger. "Magic come, magic go." She took a small plastic bag half filled with white powder from her pocket and threw a pinch of the powder into the air. "Wizard, witch, pickle pie in your eye." She threw another pinch into the air. "Cast out all spells on Shirley More." Glo turned around three times and clapped her hands.

Cat sneezed and shook his head.

"Should there be a sign that it worked?" I asked Glo. "Like a flash of light or a bell ringing?"

"*Ripple's* didn't say anything about that."

"What was the powder?"

"I don't know exactly. I got it from the Exotica store. It's supposed to be a spell enhancer."

We stood for a couple beats, waiting for a sign, but no sign was forthcoming.

"I hope it worked," Glo said.

"Me, too."

"It's a little scary, since in the past some of my spells haven't turned out perfect."

That was a gross understatement. I searched my brain for a change of subject and settled on her broom.

"How's the broom doing?" I asked her.

"It's a process," Glo said.

The door opened and Clara rushed in. "I just saw Shirley. She's three blocks away, and my guess is she's headed for the bakery, and she's going at it like Godzilla storming Tokyo."

"Oh no!" Glo said. "Lock the door. Does she have a gun?"

"Not that I could see," Clara said. "You didn't do any more reading from *Ripple's,* did you?"

"It was just a teensy spell," Glo said. "And it was a do-good spell, I swear."

Clara looked around. "Were there any explosions? Fire? Did anyone get shingles?"

"Yipes! There she is!" Glo said, spotting Shirley through the window.

Shirley threw the door open, and Glo ducked down behind the counter.

"Ta da," Shirley sang, making an expansive gesture. "I'm not gobbling anymore."

Glo peeked over the counter.

"I owe you all an apology," Shirley said. "The whole gobbledegook thing wasn't your fault at all. I went to the doctor yesterday after I visited the cemetery, and he decided to take me off the blood pressure medication. He said it was possible that I was talking funny from the medication, plus the power of suggestion. And he was right. It just kicked in. I was walking down the street, coming to the bakery to buy bread, and I felt something go *ding* in my head, and it was like this week never happened."

"Gee, that's great," I said to Shirley. I looked over at Glo. "Isn't that great, Glo?"

"Yeah," Glo said. "That's great."

Clara moved behind the counter. "What kind of bread do you want?" she asked Shirley.

"Rye without the seeds."

Clara bagged a rye bread and handed it to Shirley. "It's on the house."

The back door opened and closed, and Diesel and Carl moseyed in.

"Shirley can talk," I told him. "It just happened."

"Congratulations," Diesel said.

"Sorry I went goofy at the cemetery," Shirley said. "What was it you wanted to ask me?"

"I wanted to know about Phil's funeral."

"It was just an ordinary funeral," Shirley said. "A short ceremony at the funeral home chapel and then a few words at graveside. I didn't know any of the people."

"Was anything buried with Phil? A keepsake or a photo?"

"Not that I know, but it was a closed casket. The viewing was closed casket, too. I guess he left really specific instructions about all that. I barely got here in time. He died, and the next day I was on a plane. The lawyer sent me a ticket. And then Phil had an evening viewing, and he was buried the next morning."

"Do you remember the funeral home?"

"It was Chippers, but they're not here anymore. Old Mr. Chippers died last year, and his kids sold the business."

"Anything else?"

Shirley took a moment. "That's all. Except he had a special casket. I guess he picked it out himself and had it waiting. I think that's kind of gruesome, but it seems Uncle Phil had his quirks."

"Can you describe the casket?"

"Dark wood. Like mahogany. And lots of carvings. Vines, flowers, bugs. Very ornate. And a big eye on the top of it."

Shirley left with her bread, and Clara, Glo, and I exchanged looks that said *What the heck am I supposed to think now?*

"I suppose it could have been the blood pressure medicine," Glo finally said.

"You never know how people are going to react to medicine," I said.

"Anything's possible," Clara said.

Diesel put his hand to my neck and squeezed a little. Not hard enough to leave a bruise, but hard enough to get my attention. "You weren't supposed to go out of the house without me."

"No. That's not entirely accurate," I said. "You told me not to go out alone. And I'm not alone. I brought Cat."

"Cat doesn't count," Diesel said.

Cat jumped to his feet, arched his back, and hissed at Diesel, showing dagger-sharp fangs.

"I stand corrected," Diesel said.

CHAPTER
TWENTY-EIGHT

It was seven o'clock, and Cat and Carl were back in front of the television. Diesel was on a stool in the kitchen, one leg extended, one leg bent, arms crossed over his chest, watching me work.

I was rearranging my pantry, checking expiration dates, lining up cereal boxes and jars of jelly. It was a lame attempt to convince myself I had some control over my life. Okay, so I might not be able to get rid of Diesel and his save-the-world deal, but dammit, I could set my pantry in order. And when I was done with the pantry, I was heading upstairs to the sock drawer.

"I'm surprised you're hanging out," I said to Diesel. "Shouldn't you be thumb wrestling Wulf for the last charm?"

"Yes, but it's more fun watching you decide if the jelly should be color coordinated or alphabetized. And when you reach for stuff on the top shelf, I get to see skin between your shirt and your jeans."

"I didn't know you were interested in fun."

"Honey, I'm all about fun."

"It looks to me like you're all about responsibility."

Diesel stood and took his cell phone out of his pocket. "It's a phase. And you're right about Wulf. I should be thumb wrestling with him." He tapped a number into his phone and waited while the connection was made. "We need to talk," Diesel said into the phone. He listened for a long moment and stared down at his shoe. "Understood," he said. And he hung up.

"Is he going to give you the last charm?" I asked.

"I've never understood the function of the charms, only that they would either lead us to the Stone or that in some magical way they would *become* the Stone. Apparently, that's Wulf's ace in the hole. Wulf figured out that the charms were keys. And he knew what the keys opened. And unfortunately, he has that object in his possession."

I had a horrifying flash of insight. "Uncle Phil's casket."

"Yes."

It took Diesel twenty minutes to collect the three charms. Just enough time for me to finish straightening my sock drawer. I'd tried my best to stay calm by keeping busy, but my stomach was churning. Carl and Cat had refused to stay behind, so we had them with us in the Lincoln.

The sun was setting on Salem when we rolled into town with the windows down, the idea being that the rush of air might save me from going gluttonously nutty.

"How are you doing?" Diesel asked me.

"Doughnut," I said.

"Excuse me?"

"I'm fine," I told him. "I've got it under control. Hot dog."

Crap! Did I just say *hot dog*?

"Try to hold it together," Diesel said.

"You know how you get that tickle in the

back of your throat when a killer cold is coming on? I have that tickle everywhere."

The address Wulf gave Diesel was close to Pickering Wharf Marina. It was a two-story, warehouse-type building with a corrugated metal roof and cinder-block sides. FRUG SEAFOOD STORAGE had been painted onto the cinder block. The lettering was weathered and faded. There was a FOR LEASE sign in the small downstairs window beside the front door. Diesel parked in the adjacent lot, and we all trooped into the building.

Hatchet was waiting in the front office. He had a Band-Aid across his nose and a chunk of skin missing from his forehead.

"Who goes there?" Hatchet said.

"Sir Diesel, Sir Monkey, Sir Cat, and Maid Lizzy," Diesel said.

Hatchet motioned to a corridor. "My Lord awaits you."

At the end of the corridor was the large room that Lenny and Mark had described. White walls. No windows. High ceiling that was painted black and had exposed ductwork. A casket rested in the middle of the room, and Wulf stood at the head of the casket.

"If I'd known there was going to be a parade, I'd have brought my elephant," Wulf said, taking in Carl and Cat.

Diesel looked at the casket. "How long's Uncle Phil been sitting out here?"

"Not long," Wulf said. "I've had him in the frozen fish locker."

"Good to know. I thought the dead fish smell was coming from Hatchet," Diesel said.

"Did you bring the charms?" Wulf asked Diesel.

Diesel took the charms from his pocket and held them in his palm so Wulf could see.

"They have an excellent selection of baby carriages at Target," I whispered to Diesel.

"Not now," Diesel said. "Get a grip."

"Was I bad? Do I need to get punished? Maybe I need a good paddling."

Wulf looked like he was thinking about rolling his eyes, and Diesel wrapped an arm around my shoulders and dragged me into him.

"We'll get to that later," Diesel said.

"I'd be happy to paddle the wench if you're too busy," Hatchet said.

Diesel cut his eyes to him, and Hatchet took a step back.

"Just a thought," Hatchet said.

"Why did you dig Phil up?" Diesel asked Wulf.

"Six weeks ago, I happened upon Philip More's diary, and I realized he was a SALIGIA guardian. At one point in the diary, late in his life, he said he would take the Stone to his grave, and that it could only be rescued by all the Humbugs in Salem."

Diesel looked at the charms. "And you think these are humbugs?"

"There are four bugs carved into the lid of the casket. Mark More's dragonfly charm fits into the dragonfly carving."

"But it wasn't enough to open the casket?" Diesel guessed.

"No," Wulf said. "The casket is sealed, and I'm not inclined to open it with force."

There were some strange creaking sounds, and howling, and Michael Jackson singing in my purse.

"What the heck?" I said.

"It's your cell phone," Diesel said. "I used 'Thriller' for your ring tone."

I pulled my phone out and saw it was my dad. We had a two-minute conversation, and I returned my phone to my purse.

"He was just checking in," I told everyone. "He's at a conference."

Wulf and Diesel exchanged glances, and Wulf gave his head an almost imperceptible shake, like he couldn't believe they were saddled with me.

"What do you want from this?" Diesel asked Wulf. "You can't have the Stone. The Stone goes to the BUM."

"That's so tedious," Wulf said.

Diesel shrugged.

"I could force you to give me the Stone," Wulf said.

Diesel did a tight smile. "I don't think so."

"It probably wouldn't end well for either of us," Wulf said.

"Yeah, and Aunt Sophie would be pissed."

Wulf took a beat. "Legend has it that when a guardian dies he's buried with an inscribed tablet. I'll give you the Stone without a fight, but I want the tablet."

"Deal," Diesel said. "My instructions are to get the Stone."

Diesel placed the ladybug on its carving and the bug hummed. "Nice," Diesel said. "Very clever. And it feels like there's a slight magnetic pull, holding the charm secure." He placed the honeybee on the honeybee carving and the bee hummed.

Diesel was about to place the cockroach on the casket, and my purse rocked out with "Thriller" again.

"Excuse me," I said. And I answered my phone.

"I'm beginning to appreciate Hatchet," Wulf said to Diesel.

Diesel smiled. "She has her moments. And she makes cupcakes."

I disconnected and stuffed my phone into my pocket.

"Well?" Diesel asked.

"It was Glo. Her broom ran away again."

"I would appreciate it if we could get on with this without more interruption," Wulf said in his eerily quiet voice, his eyes riveted on mine.

"Lighten up," I said to Wulf. "Glo lost her broom again. This is a big deal for her. And what have we got here anyway . . . a dead guy and a Stone. Do you think they can wait for three minutes longer?"

Diesel gave a bark of laughter, and Wulf looked like he was trying hard not to sigh. Diesel set the cockroach onto the cockroach carving, and we listened to the bug hum.

"Your turn," Diesel said to Wulf.

Wulf laid his dragonfly on the dragonfly carving. All four bugs hummed in unison, locks tumbled, and the casket lid released with a hiss of air.

Carl wrapped his arms around Diesel's leg. "Eep."

Cat's ears pricked forward.

"Open it," Wulf said to Hatchet.

Hatchet's face paled. "Me?"

Wulf glared at Hatchet, and Hatchet tentatively reached out and touched the casket. Nothing happened, so Hatchet stepped a little closer and raised the lid. We all peered inside, and no one said anything for a full minute. Diesel was the first to speak.

"Where's Uncle Phil?" Diesel asked.

"I don't know the answer to that question," Wulf said.

The casket held a small stone and a metal tablet the size of a greeting card. No ashes. No body. No Uncle Phil.

Hatchet was closest to the casket. His

breathing was rapid and shallow, and his skin looked clammy.

"The Stone," Hatchet said. "The SALIGIA Stone. It's beautiful. Can you hear it? It's singing."

I wasn't hearing any singing, and I didn't see all that much beauty in the Stone. I mean, it was a plain ol' rock the size of a duck egg, for crying out loud.

"Fear not, my liege, these thieves shall not have our Stone," Hatchet said. "This Stone belongs to thee and me." Hatchet plunged his arm into the casket and grabbed the Stone. His eyes bugged out of his head as he stared at the Stone in his hand. "I can feel the power," he said, almost reverently. "It's inside me. It's like I'm the Stone. Like I'm a god."

"The God of Gluttony?" Diesel asked.

Hatchet cut his eyes to Diesel. "The God of Everything."

Diesel looked over at Wulf. "Do you want to run with this one, or should I take it?"

Wulf smiled his joyless smile. "It's your Stone."

"Yeah, but it's your minion."

"No longer," Hatchet said, snatching the tablet from the casket, drawing his sword. "I have the power now. And I have the knowledge. And very soon I'll have *all* the Stones."

"What's he talking about?" Diesel asked Wulf.

"The tablets kept the guardians connected. Every guardian carried another guardian's tablet. So whoever possesses the tablet has an opportunity to find the next Stone, providing they can understand the tablet's inscription. The tablets were forged centuries ago and are written in an arcane language, which Steven won't be able to read."

"Don't underestimate me," Hatchet said. "I'll figure it out. I have one Stone, and I won't stop until I possess the rest. I don't need you anymore. Now *I* have the power."

"Give me the tablet," Wulf said.

"The tablet's mine," Hatchet told him. "You lose."

"Close your eyes," Wulf said to me. "I'm going to kill him."

I looked to Diesel. "Is he serious?"

Diesel shrugged. "Probably."

"Don't be crazy," I said to Hatchet. "Give him his tablet."

Hatchet's head snapped around, full

focus on me. "I'm *not crazy,* you idiot wench."

He flicked his arm out, grabbed me to him, and held his sword to my neck, the blade sharp against my skin.

"Don't anyone come near," Hatchet said. "If anyone comes close, I'll kill her. I swear I'll do it."

He was surprisingly strong, considering he was such a lump of dough. He had me tight against him, and I could feel his whole body shaking, could smell the cold sweat of fear and insane obsession. I looked first to Diesel and then to Wulf. Both men were tuned to Hatchet, waiting for the moment to make a move.

Hatchet inched toward the door, dragging me with him, sword still at my neck. I stumbled and felt the blade bite into me.

"She's bleeding," Diesel said to Hatchet. "Ease up on the sword."

I could feel a trickle of blood ooze from the cut on my neck and soak into my shirt, and I was hit with a wave of panic. I didn't want to die. I didn't want my throat cut. And I didn't want to bleed anymore. Tears were pooling behind my eyes and blurring my vision. *Help,* I thought to Diesel. *Can you hear me?*

Hatchet reached to open the door, and I saw Cat 7143 fly through the air and latch onto Hatchet's arm. Carl was a beat behind Cat, sinking his monkey teeth into Hatchet's ankle. Hatchet gave a bloodcurdling scream and tried to shake Cat and Carl loose.

Diesel pushed me aside, grabbed Hatchet, and flung him across the room. Hatchet hit the wall with a thud and a grunt and fell to the floor, where he lay dead still, looking like road-kill. The Stone and the tablet lay at his feet.

A couple tears had leaked out, and my nose was running. I wiped it all on my shirt and pressed my hand to the cut. "How bad is it?"

"Not bad," Diesel said. "It's not deep. It won't need stitches."

"It felt like a lot of blood."

He had his arm around me, supporting me with his body. "It had me worried for a minute, but it's going to be okay. The bleeding has almost stopped."

Wulf retrieved the Stone and the tablet.

"This is yours," he said, handing the Stone to Diesel. "We made a deal."

I looked at Diesel. "Why are you letting Wulf have the tablet? It'll lead him to the next Stone."

Diesel slipped the Stone into his pocket. "Like he said, we made a deal. Besides, the Marshalls will keep the Gluttony Stone safe. Wulf will never have all the Stones, and he needs all the Stones to have ultimate power."

"Perhaps," Wulf said. "Time will tell."

Diesel let that hang for a beat. "Give my love to Aunt Sophie," he told Wulf.

Wulf gave a curt nod to Diesel, and his eyes locked onto mine, sending a shot of adrenaline sizzling through me. He stepped back, there was a flash of light, smoke swirled through the room, and when the smoke cleared, Wulf was gone.

Diesel put the Stone into my hand. "Is this the real deal?"

The power buzzed up my arm and spread through my body. The Stone glowed like the sun, and I suddenly wanted *everything*. Not power, like Hatchet, but babies and cupcakes and kisses and peace everlasting. I wanted perfect breasts and pretty

shoes and Thanksgiving dinner. And I
wanted it all *bad*.

"Whoa," Diesel said. "Your eyes just totally dilated, and you're drooling. Maybe
you should give me the Stone."

"Never," I said.

Diesel pried my fingers open and took
the Stone. "Wulf must not have touched
you. You haven't lost your Unmentionable
ability after all. And if this is what happens
to you with the Gluttony Stone, I can't wait
until we go after Lust."

I glanced at Hatchet, still on the floor
but moving, flopping around a little.

"What about Hatchet?" I asked Diesel.

We all walked over and stared down at
him.

"He's coming around," Diesel said. "He'll
have a headache, but he'll be fine."

"You should do something. Arrest him.
Or unempower him."

"I'm not authorized," Diesel said. "Besides, he'll go back to being only moder-
ately crazy now that he's lost the Stone."

Hatchet opened an eye and looked up
at me. "Wench," he said.

Cat hissed at Hatchet, Carl gave him
the finger, and I accidentally kicked him. I

accidentally kicked him *hard*. Twice. And then we left.

A half hour later, we were back on Weatherby Street. I was trying to keep it together, but I was sweating from the effort. Images of birthday cakes, pot roasts, baby blankets, Hershey bars, Cheez Doodles, cases of wine, new towels, frilly undies, and rooms filled with kittens were clogging my brain. I wanted them all.

Diesel walked me into my living room, along with Carl and Cat.

"I have to take the Stone to the BUM," Diesel said. "Do *not* go out of the house until I return. It's going to take a while for the Stone's effects to wear off."

"But I need strawberry ice cream, a DustBuster, and lots of new socks," I told him. "Isn't there anything you need?"

"Yes," he said. And he pulled me to him and kissed me.